I0819795

THE MAN WHO HAD HIS HAIR CUT SHORT

GREENWOOD PRESS, PUBLISHERS
WESTPORT, CONNECTICUT

translated by S. J. Sackett

a novel by JOHAN DAISNE

THE MAN WHO HAD

HIS HAIR CUT SHORT

This English translation of Johan Daisne's *De Man Die Zijn Haar Kort Liet Knippen* is dedicated to Marjorie

Library of Congress Cataloging in Publication Data

Thiery, Herman, 1912-
The man who had his hair cut short.

Translation of De man die zijn haar kort liet knippen.
Reprint of the ed. published by Horizon Press, New York.
I. Title.
[PZ3.T34725Man6] [PT6458.T35] 839.3'2'364 75-5001

© *English translation copyright 1965 by Horizon Press*

This edition originally published in 1965 by Horizon Press, New York

Reprinted with the permission of Horizon Press

Reprinted in 1975 by Greenwood Press, a division of Williamhouse-Regency Inc.

Library of Congress Catalog Card Number 75-5001

ISBN: 978-0-8371-7426-6

Printed in the United States of America

Dedicated to my honorable friend, Dr. Jur. Gaston Van Loo.

Never a man / was more bald / like a bowl / nor so ran
aconite / that he drinks / in him sinks / burning bright
and the gash / he has slashed / with his knife
is the noise / of God's voice / in our life.

It is self-evident that all personages and situations described in this book are figures and scenes of what is called a novel. Hence it would be wrong to attempt to find actuality in them. Any suspected similarities are thus misapprehensions, and no author can be held responsible for the accidents of chance or for the imaginative power of his reader.

TRANSLATOR'S PREFACE

Sooner or later, as one reads the leading Flemish literary periodicals, one will come across a discussion of "international stature," for Flemish writers are, if not obsessed, at least concerned with the matter of becoming known outside the boundaries of Belgium itself. To the Netherlands they have easy access, for written Flemish is as much like written Dutch as written American English is like written British English; and, indeed, most Flemings, whether writers or not, would if queried say that the language which they speak and write is "Nederlands"; the word "Vlaams" is rarely used in this connection. But access to the Netherlands is at best only partially satisfying; the Dutch-speaking population of Europe is only a few millions. Consequently, Flemish authors must depend on translation if they are to come widely to European, let alone world, attention. And since only writers of a certain level come to the attention of translators, the finest compliment one can pay a Flemish author is to say that he is of "international stature."

So far as the English-speaking world is concerned, unfortunately, no Flemish author has as yet achieved "international stature." Although his vogue has now passed, older readers may recall the name of Émile Verhaeren; but Verhaeren was a Belgian French author and did not write in Dutch, although his characteristic subjects were often Flemish. Recently there has been some interest in Michel de Ghelderode; but he wrote French too. The only Belgian writer who has become widely enough read in English translation for one to say that he achieved any durable "international stature" was Maurice Maeterlinck; but Maeterlinck, like Verhaeren and Ghelderode, wrote in French. The classic names of modern Flemish prose—Cyriel Buysse, Herman Teirlinck, Stijn Streuvels, F. V. Toussaint van Boelaere, Karel van de Woestijne, Willem Elsschot—cannot be said to have "international stature," at least so far as the English-speaking reader is concerned. And, of course, since poetry is less translatable than prose, Flemish poets have fared even worse. Few in England or America have ever heard of the greatest Flemish poet, Guido Gezelle.

These facts are not necessarily indicative of a lack of quality on the part of Flemish writers. Admittedly, if Flemish Belgium had produced an Ibsen, he would have been as well known as Ibsen; the fact that there is no Flemish writer of comparable fame is an indication that there is no Flemish writer of comparable stature. But many an English-speaking reader is familiar with minor writers in his own language who are inferior in quality to the half dozen Flemish prose masters listed above.

The fault with them—except for Van de Woestijne, who is like the Pater of *Marius*—is rather that they are essentially local-colorists, choosing, of all the elements of fiction, to emphasize place and setting. Their appeal, even to the Flemish reader, is often the fidelity of their description of the details of life in the northern provinces of Belgium. This has naturally tended to limit the interest which readers outside their native land feel in them.

Recently, however, a number of younger writers have been concerning themselves less with the Flemish locale than with the universal problems of mankind, and these have been coming to the attention of readers in other languages. One of the leaders in this movement is Johan Daisne, whose novel *The Man Who Had His Hair Cut Short* (*De Man Die Zijn Haar Kort Liet Knippen*) has been translated into French, German, and Spanish and thus has reached some of the most important reading publics of Europe. This book has indeed been considered by some Flemings the first Flemish novel really to have captured the attention of audiences outside Belgium.

Johan Daisne is the pen-name of Dr. Herman Thiery, head librarian of the Gent Public Library. Dr. Thiery was born in Gent on 2 September 1912, the son of two noted Belgian educators. Although his schooling was interrupted by ill health in his teens, he was able to continue academic work in the thirties and completed work for his Ph.D. in economics at the University of Gent. He wrote his doctoral dissertation, "Philosophical Values in the Economy," while fulfilling his obligation for compulsory military service in the heavy artillery.

Dr. Thiery chose his pen-name, D'Aisne or Daisne, as an allusion to the French region of Aisne, where a wealthy ancestor had lived in the seventeenth century. Works signed with that name began to appear in the mid-thirties, chiefly poetry and some reportage. He also translated some poems by Pushkin; in addition to Russian, he knows Czech and Polish fluently. He has visited Russia and written a history of Russian literature.

When World War II broke out, Dr. Thiery was mobilized as a signal corps officer. After the capitulation of Belgium, he was stationed for some time at Carcassonne, in unoccupied France. It was at this time that he turned to fiction and drama, publishing a number of plays and stories and his first novel, *Stairway of Stone and Clouds,* which appeared in 1942.

He attracted serious critical attention when his play, *The Sword of Tristan,* won a national prize in 1946. *The Man Who Had His Hair Cut Short* won the Burnaert Prize of the Royal Flemish Academy in 1951. Two more of his novels were awarded prizes—*Lago Maggiore* the Merghelynck Prize in 1958, and *The Nostrils of the Muse* the Biennial National Prize in 1960. His most recent novels are *Baratzeartea* and *Like Lace on the Horizon,* published in 1962 and 1964 respectively. His work has inspired four book-length critical studies in Belgium.

In addition to a number of other novels, plays, and collections of stories, poems, and aphorisms, Johan Daisne has published several books on the art of the cinema, which is his special field. He is the administrator of the Royal Belgium Film Library and has served three times on the jury of the World Festival of the Film, once as chairman.

Daisne (the name is pronounced as if it were spelled Dane) classifies himself as a "magic realist." This description seems to be intended to mean that he considers himself a realist, but a more romantic realist than most others. Certainly

The Man Who Had His Hair Cut Short is marked by an utterly convincing air of reality: the details are so full and complete that it seems impossible they could be invented, the portrayal of Antfield is so real that the book seems to be actually the document it pretends to be, and moreover the elements of Antfield's obsession sometimes strike the reader as being so like the records of his own secret thoughts that he squirms uneasily. And yet the book's heavy use of symbolism and especially the fact that its viewpoint character is demented mark its realism as being outside the ordinary.

Since there are elements in *The Man Who Had His Hair Cut Short* which will surely make comparison with *Lolita* inevitable, it is well to deal with them openly here. It is true that the story deals with the obsession of an older man for a girl much younger than himself; it is true that the narrative is told as the confessions of the older man; it is true that the young woman proves more corrupt than her would-be corrupter; and it is true also that, like *Lolita,* the novel is written in a pyrotechnic style—and this is the place for the translator's conventional but sincere assertion that translating these pyrotechnics into English is impossible but that he has done what he could. But there are several counts on which the books are dissimilar: among them, Fran's seventeen or eighteen is very different from Dolly's twelve, and Antfield's love for her is never consummated physically. Those seeking to draw lines of influence from Nabokov to Daisne, moreover, should bear in mind that *The Man Who Had His Hair Cut Short* was first published in 1951.

A connection between Nabokov and Daisne exists, however, although it is more complex than appears at first sight. Daisne himself has admitted that the inspiration for *The Man Who Had His Hair Cut Short* derives from a short story, "The Diary of a Madman," by Nikolai Gogol, an author whose biography Nabokov has written. As one compares the two, it is difficult not to feel that Daisne has in every way improved upon his original, with which, indeed, his novel has little in common. Actually, as Fran points out, Antfield is more like one of Dostoyevsky's self-lacerating characters than like Gogol's madman who thinks he is the King of Spain.

The finest quality of the novel is its masterful psychological portrayal. Although Antfield is insane, Daisne is able to track down every thread in the tangled yarn of his thoughts and perceptions. Time and again the reader is struck with the way in which the ramblings of the narrative ring true to the narrator's derangement. Antfield is a man of many strange and contradictory qualities; we find him as inconsistent, and therefore as real, as ourselves. He is by no means wholly admirable, and though he continually attempts to justify himself, even he is not blind to his weaknesses and aberrations. The quality which the reader is likely to find most repellent in Antfield is that he whines too often; it would be easier to pity him if he did not pity himself so much.

While it is through Antfield that we see the other characters, and therefore through his erratic perceptions, one after another they come to life as his flickering light plays on them. Even Corra, whom we but glimpse, becomes so real to us that we can imagine her reactions if she were to read her husband's confession.

The author is also to be praised for the excellent construction of the work, both for the way in which the details are woven together in the fabric and for the construction of the design itself. As for the details, the symbolism is handled especially well; a good illustration is the way in which the word "antic" is repeated in the last few pages of the work until it comes to have a special meaning appropriate only to Antfield and Fran. As for the construction, it is difficult to say whether the novel is more notable for the admirable craftsmanship with which later developments are prepared for or for the very strong suspense which it generates.

Coleridge once said that the three best plots in the world were those of *Oedipus Rex, The Alchemist,* and *Tom Jones.* Without claiming that Daisne's novel makes a fourth, it is possible to claim that it shares with *Tom Jones* the characteristic that it must be read twice for the excellence of its construction to be savored fully. In both novels there are episodes near the beginning which seem quite different retrospectively from what they did on first reading; the authors give us all the details, but we do not appreciate the significance of these details until we can see them in the light of facts which we do not know until later.

This quality partially at least explains why the novel may seem to open slowly to a reader who approaches it for the first time. Another part of the explanation is that in its broad outlines *The Man Who Had His Hair Cut Short* is designed to build gradually, accumulating power that will finally explode in its brilliant, shattering climax; but for reasons of plot Daisne is also committed to the kind of opening he uses. Significant information must be given, but it must be buried in a welter of insignificant detail so that the surprises he will stun the reader with later will not be given away too early. Any cutting to speed the movement of the opening pages would throw the clues into a sharp relief which would spoil the effects he intends to get from them. The reader who continues beyond the first leisurely pages will find his perseverance rewarded.

One of the most remarkable elements in the novel's construction is Daisne's treatment of time, which is seen as wholly relative. The few seconds which Antfield spends in the corridor outside Fran's hotel room take pages to narrate, for they lasted hours; his murder trial is disposed of in a few sentences, for it passed him in a blur. Thus the only clock in the novel is Antfield's own subjective apprehension of time.

The greatest weakness in the construction is the unnecessary coincidence by which the unnamed corpse in the cemetery at D— turns out to be Fran's father. Here the author's desire to make all the pieces of his puzzle fit together carries him to an extreme; consequently here the manipulating hand of the puppeteer shows through and breaks the web of illusion.

Dutch critics say that Flemish writers tend to have a baroque style; Flemish critics say that Daisne's style is baroque even for a Fleming and that its excessive flamboyance has damaged some of his other novels. But the style of *The Man Who Had His Hair Cut Short,* in all its flamboyance and digressiveness, is perfectly suited to the character of its narrator. Early in the novel Antfield says, ". . . I seldom or never have been able to think 'clearly.' As soon as I want to deliberate on something, everything always becomes mixed up; I work myself into regular snarls and must seem deplorably obscure and circuitous to other people and finally even to myself. . . . I have never been able to come to a full stop." Consequently the first thing one notices about the novel is that it is only one paragraph long—one paragraph of 200 pages. Antfield continually drifts off one subject onto another; sometimes he recalls the first one in the midst of the second and jumps back and forth between them; he rambles wherever his stream of consciousness leads him (and Daisne is wonderful at capturing this); he is continually in the midst of conflicting emotions, and this expresses itself in oxymorons; and when he is excited by an emotion, anything less than the rhetorical flamboyance of Daisne's prose would do him an injustice. The fever of Antfield's brain is mirrored in his style.

Tragic and depressing as Antfield's story is, we must not overlook its moments of comedy. Its very tragedy, in fact, is sometimes carried to comic extremes. Antfield's preparations to visit Fran on the fatal night, for instance, are hilarious. Preparing to enter the cold shower, our timorous hero counts to three—and then counts to three "really" before he takes the plunge. And then all the determinations to remain awake, all the actions taken to ensure wakefulness, have for Antfield the inevitable result: he falls asleep. We could not take him so seriously if he were not so absurd.

The Man Who Had His Hair Cut Short raises all the great questions, all the questions which, because they are the great questions, are also the old ones; but it raises them with so much freshness and immediacy that it is difficult to mind that they have been raised before: What is reality? What is man? How can man adjust himself to society? Why does evil exist? How free is man?

The question of what is real and what is illusion is central to Daisne's novel because we see the events only through Antfield's vision of them, and this vision is deranged. Thus, by the end, we are not wholly sure what has happened. Has Antfield killed Fran? We have seen him do it, yet the undated newspaper clipping assuring him she still lives has been verified by the director of the asylum. Antfield accepts this verification joyously, yet he still writes as if she were dead. The reader does not know what to believe; he does not even really know what Antfield believes. Perhaps Fran never actually existed; perhaps she did but Antfield's whole relationship with her was a disordered fantasy.

If we reject these dizzying possibilities and assume the reality of the experiences recounted in the novel, as in a recent article Daisne has assured us we should, we are still faced, but at another level, with the problem of what is real and what is illusion. Antfield is a sentimentalist, a Romantic, an idealist. Whether Fran is real or not, certainly the image of her that he has constructed is a fabrication. Since we have seen her previously only as Antfield presents her, it comes as a shock when she begins to spit out all the accumulated bitterness of her sordid life. Antfield's Eyebright is, we discover, a poisonous herb.

And yet as Fran tells her story, we discover that she too began her life as a sentimentalist, a Romantic, an idealist. The lesson she learned from Brantink—that love is unattainable and human beings are incapable of it—has disillusioned her, and the disillusionment is what has plunged her into frantic depravity and brought her to long for death.

Life, we are shown, is a poorer thing than Antfield and Fran have imagined it, and consequently they are broken by it, as Emma Bovary was. And yet we cannot leave their story, as we cannot leave Emma's, without thinking that the world would be a happier place to live in if it were somewhat more ideal than it is. "No where," Donne tells us, "Lives a woman true, and fair." But wouldn't it be wonderful if there were one somewhere? Wouldn't it be wonderful if Fran had really been

Antfield's Eyebright? Wouldn't it be wonderful if Fran had really found love? Thus the novel criticizes Romanticism for ignoring the realities of life—but also criticizes life for not being ideal enough, for not coming up to our expectations.

We must not forget, however, that if Antfield never finds his Eyebright nor does Fran find her love, both are really looking in the wrong places. What we see of Corra in those brief and fitful glimpses which Antfield gives us of her suggests that she was capable of offering him the support and sympathetic understanding he hoped for from Fran, if ever he could have communicated to her all the stoppered-up perplexities and confusions he poured out to Fran; and Fran might have found love more satisfying if she had been able to grow into it with a man her own age instead of leaping into it prematurely with an aging satyr. Whether these possibilities could have brought either to happiness is beyond our power to say: Antfield cannot turn to Corra—is it because he feels that he must show her a husbandly image of strength and self-sufficiency and thus cannot bring himself to seek her help?—and Fran is too impatiently rebellious for the boy scouts who dance with her; consequently neither can really be said to have given normality a try.

What is man? Man is seen, personified in Antfield, as being torn between his conscious and his unconscious life. The unconscious self is treated in the novel as a robot, who will run our lives for us if we will keep ourselves from interfering with it. It is Antfield's view that all his trouble is caused by his conscious interference with the robot's activities. Yet it would be possible to argue on the other side—that Antfield's obsession arises from the depths of his unconscious, and that his trouble is caused by his inability to put it under his conscious control.

This deeply divided creature, man, must somehow fit himself into a society of other men; while carrying on the internal struggle which he describes for us so vividly, Antfield must wage war on an external front as well. In both, of course, he fails. His own explanation of his failure to adjust to society is that he was attempting to do something for which he was unfitted by nature. He should have been a gardener; instead, he attempted the law, and it was the constant effort to achieve an ambition beyond his grasp which betrayed him. Consequently he counsels a philosophy of accepting the limitations imposed by nature.

Fran's relations with society are equally unsatisfactory, but for other reasons. She deliberately chooses non-conformity; her failure to adjust comes because she rejects society and attempts to live only for herself and her own pleasures. The search for pleasure, however, has brought Fran only unhappiness and dissatisfaction; and for Fran the wages of sin is self-disgust.

Why does evil exist? Antfield's answer to this question is that man's own stupidity continually causes him to intervene in the order of events, and thus he brings evil on himself. And yet he sees man bound by a chain of fate, powerless to act on his own initiative.

The fascinating question of whether man is free or whether his actions are determined by powers beyond his control is one which haunts Antfield throughout the novel. Could he have avoided the tragedy or was it inevitable? He sees himself in the grip of a chain of accidents that brought him together with Fran after their ten-year separation, and it is difficult not to agree with him that chance and happenstance played a considerable role in arranging their meeting. If he had been able to work up enough courage to refuse Professor Mato's invitation, he would never have gone to D—. It was just by chance that the party went on to meet Professor Zijsma instead of returning home. And then Fran was near the end of her concert tour; a day or two later, and they would have missed her. All of us, certainly, can find similar chains of coincidences in our own lives: if we hadn't happened to be in a certain place at a certain time, we would never have met some person who changed the whole course of our future existences. Throughout the novel Daisne shows us through these chains of events how our lives are often greatly affected by what seem to be the most trivial of occurrences. The questions Antfield raises about these coincidences are two: First, are we really free? Would he have been free to refuse to go to D—? Second, are these coincidences evidence of God's plan for us? Are they really chance, or are they purposeful?

But if Antfield sees himself in the grip of God's plan, he also sees himself impelled by his own character, his own nature. Given the sort of person he was, was he under any constraint or obligation not to change that sort? Once a man realizes his nature, once he obeys Socrates' difficult injunction to "know thyself," does he have to accept himself as he is, or should he try to change himself? Should he, for example, seek psychiatric help? If it was God who made him as he was, does he have the right to interfere with God's plan? (And this leads him to another question—the paradox that God is both creator and judge.) Antfield rejects the idea that he should have sought help; life is a school, and in school it doesn't pay to cheat, because then one doesn't learn what he is there to learn.

As we consider all the questions that the novel raises, we must constantly bear in mind that Antfield is insane and that he is trying to justify himself; for both reasons we cannot take his conclusions as our own or even as Daisne's. Indeed, it is difficult to believe that the author is trying to lead us to any particular conclusion; he seems rather to be raising questions without giving them any definitive answers, causing us to think deeply about these great old issues of man's life, his nature, his relations with society, his relations with God, his freedom, and his destiny.

THE MAN WHO HAD HIS HAIR CUT SHORT

Yes, everything considered, there has always been "something." Hence I am here now and am well here, as everyone should be in the place where he really belongs. I can define this something only with great difficulty, but no matter how long I think about it, so long as I can remember it has always existed, although it has altered its appearance. But it must have been always the same. Everyone must have something like this sometime. With that thought I have often consoled myself, and I have judged it unnecessary to inquire into this knowledge or to interfere in what must be. For that matter, I have always been very skeptical, or rather very hesitant, about such interference. Nevertheless, I admire science a great deal. I cherish a boundless admiration for everything that pertains to knowledge and an almost childlike affection for those who investigate it. I feel myself growing clammy from very humility whenever I think of them, of their enormous labors and of their majestic personalities. They are so serene, so lucid, so strong. Even in the smallest of them—I mean the slightest of build, with bald skulls, gray features, and thick spectacles for their myopic eyes—even in one of these I still recognize the giant, one of Phidias's giants of ivory and gold, a revered demigod from the harmonious world of the ancients. There has always been something in me, a child, a child at once dreary and at the same time glowing with enthusiasm, that wants to fall at their feet. Our director is such a noble spirit, with moreover all the distinguishing physical characteristics of his type. If I choose to examine his hands, his smile is charming. When he smiles, almost nothing changes in his countenance; no wrinkles intrude themselves; his face remains gentle and strong, clean-shaven and ruddily handsome. His expression is always clear and placid and kind; his eyes are as transparent as the sky, and whenever he smiles it is as if the sun rose with a golden light. It is beautiful. And yet I prefer his hands. For it is the basic rule of a look that it should be really a look; and, although the eyes are said to be the mirror of the soul, it is not always there that the spirit speaks. But we have read and heard that so often when we were young that we accept it almost as a universal truth. Now let it be asserted also of the hands that they are such mirrors, at least to the elect. But never have I been so fond of hands as I am of the director's. When I sit with him I scarcely dare to look right at him. My admiration, and then the other thing, makes me embarrassed. Therefore I let my gaze rest instead on his hands, which he always allows to repose calmly before him on the glass plate of his desk, gracefully but in a by no means unmanly fashion. In fact, for a long time I have recognized our director entirely by his hands. I no longer look up at him; I see everything in his hands. He never gestures; they hardly move at all, but in the clear space between left thumb and left index finger I hear him speak as if aloud. I see him speak—and when he smiles, oh, then I immediately notice his rings, his wedding ring and his seal ring, the gold of which then shines even sunnier than his eyes, though still very gently. I may not speak here of our director any longer; I do not want him to think, if ever he should read these lines of mine, that it was my purpose to flatter him, perhaps in order to receive even more favors from him than he has already, in his great goodness, permitted. For that matter, I have also admired Professor Mato, and he is still dear to me, notwithstanding the terrible events which he witnessed and by which he must remember me, although probably it gives him pain to do so. When he stood there in the doorway in his white pajamas, his appearance was not in the least ridiculous, not only because of the sad event that had occurred but also because a man as learned as he has something, at all times and in all places, which raises him above any situation, no matter how serious it may be to those who also experience it, and all the more when the situation may appear silly. Therefore impressionable children do not laugh when a Charlie Chaplin, who is also of the race of demigods, does a so-called comic thing, that is to say when something touches both his oversensitive earnestness and the joke of a situation. Professor Mato's nose is a little hooked, and he has sparse black hair through which you can see his skull. Also there is something unhealthy, sallow, in his complexion, probably from much work and the abominable nature of his labors. His upper eyelids are thick and black, as though incurably tired, and without the independence and expressiveness of his eyes his glance would surely appear proud and haughty—but the eyes compensate for everything. Also they are fleckless as an Aegaean sky, still young and even almost roguish, yet naturally without the frivolity of youth—very earnest rogues they are, as though disguised in the vestments of humanity and enormously burdened with a high mission. I will say nothing of his hands, because of the horrible work that they must perform; for that matter, he usually clothes them with gloves, even when he does not execute that work, as though he himself did not wish to be reminded of it. But his white apron, even though it is concerned in that work and is so often soiled by it—that apron is dear to me. It is so white, so clean, that the stains serve only to show how clean it really is, and undoubtedly a divine serenity exudes from the whiteness and from its spaciousness. Well, I shall try not to think of it any more, but now as I think back for the last time, first of all I see the apron, in that corner of the churchyard, on that red-hot Saturday afternoon, when Professor Mato cut off the head of the corpse. . . . The first thing I see is that apron. I don't want to see anything else but that apron, to consider how white and fair it was, how it arrayed Professor Mato like a priestly robe, and, in the gestures of the horrible gloves which delineated them, like the harmony of the ancients. But that "interference" of Professor Mato was and is post mortem, and even our director does not really interfere more than that. He takes care of; that is a far different thing. I have always hesitantly opposed the actual interference of science, at least in human affairs, and I consider an appendicitis not as a human but as an animal affair. For between science, no matter how glorious I consider it, and what I should like to call God, if it is no sacrilege, gapes an abyss that cannot be leaped, I believe, even by giants or demigods: the riddle of the soul. And now I want to acknowledge that, since the soul influences the body, it can also be influenced by the body, and thus an operation on the appendix also interferes with the soul. But actually distinctions are sometimes only differences of degree, and I feel it is so here. Some of Dostoyevsky's heroes are burdened with his epilepsy, others suffer his tuberculosis or his miraculous insanity. For my part, I heartily approve efforts to cure misfortunes, but yet they may be only good tries; and so far as I have grasped Dostoyevsky, he judges the case similarly, notwithstanding his boundless affection for suffering humanity. And certainly that was a matter of soul. For there undoubtedly exists a causal and purposive bond between the soul and the eventual state of the body's health. There must be resolute souls—and they should not be considered inferior because of this, perhaps the contrary—who cannot set forth on their journey otherwise than in an epileptic body, others who would flourish in bodies suffering from tuberculosis. This can have a very beautiful meaning, and it is a sacrilege, as well as fruitless, to want to interfere in these and to disturb higher causes and purposes. On the other hand, I well know that we feel that it is a sacred obligation to mitigate the sorrows of our fellow humans, and from that standpoint it would be criminal to wish to prevent the increase of knowledge or to wish to withhold from someone the balsam which would give him surcease. Life is full of such contradictions, which we may not solve by eliminating one of the terms. We must try to reconcile both, for I cherish a respectful diffidence toward everything that is, even for the absurd. If it is, it is sure to serve its purpose. And I see that reconciliation in what follows. We must try to help as much as possible, but we must not force anything to happen, and especially we must never do certain things which make us feel that they are unnatural interferences. And is the territory thus restricted—not the nerves? The appendix may be a distant dependency of the soul; but on the contrary the nerves are directly tied to the body, they are rooted minutely in the earth, like a cobweb on a cask of wine. Do not spit on the ground, do not dig in it, for no matter how cautiously you do so you will always bruise it and damage it. Thus have I always felt, vaguely but deeply, even when I was only a child. And when I became physically uncomfortable, when my earth became nervous, I have withdrawn without inquiring into science. Each of us has something of the sort, I considered, and it certainly does not deserve more attention, but still I have never been entirely able to turn myself away from it, and perhaps therefore it has become more important for me than for other people; indeed, it has always been more important for me than for others, and I have therefore had to bestow more attention on it. There is an example of that "something" of mine: I always see the truth in duplicate or triplicate and can never come to a singular conclusion. Hence it is that I seldom or never have been able to think "clearly." As soon as I want to deliberate on something, everything always becomes mixed up; I work myself into regular snarls and must seem deplorably obscure and circuitous to other people and finally even to myself. We all live in the reeds, but I have never been able to make beautiful, let alone useful, pipes out of them. I was entangled in yarn; the world always appears to me as to someone who squints and perhaps is even insane with just such a spiritual strabism. The worst, however, or at least it must be considered bad, is that I believe in the tangle. I believe everything, everything. For everything is only if it *is,* and yet it is if it *has* to be. And what is squinting but to look in another way, which certainly cannot be considered possible unless the different ways now and then exist? And what if, squinting, one sees a spiritual sickness, perhaps, on earth and even in heaven? O Lord God, forgive me for the possibly hazy notion which I have of Your Kingdom, if any particle remains to me of my youth, which was on the outside so pure, and spent with books and movies. . . . Perhaps it is depraved, but I swear to You that I consider the shivers which I have received from that Beauty as only madness. And You know, You still know how I, ardent with love, also humbled myself before the bright whiteness of Knowledge. I was a sturdy boy, and I am still big and strong. But there has always been, deep within me, something frail, something almost ridiculously fragile, something that wears out with miserable quickness, but still remains almost continually quivering, though it be at no more than a painful yawn. I could feel equally—and that again is one of my squinting truths—healthy and strong, and yet there was at the same time someone or something in me as helplessly sick as an animal. I have been for many years a stomach and liver patient, but I have never really believed that it was that, and it wasn't. It was "something" else. Even when I played on the street or went walking with my parents Sundays, I have more than once lived through these experiences, little, but to a child unaccustomed and seemingly painful, so that I felt constrained repeatedly, for long minutes, to stand apart from myself, in order to consider myself and what I was doing, with a great exertion not to squint any more but to see properly and clearly and to wind a firm ball of yarn out of the snarls. To establish some rules in my limitless need: this afternoon I shall read, and look at pictures in the morning, and then play in the street—it was necessary, it was absolutely indispensable that everything should be laid out so fixedly, in order to weigh what I should and should not do. And in doing that I always trembled so, in my neck—in my neck, which was like a buzzing telephone pole—and throughout my whole insides, as if they were full of murmuring wires. Therefore, in order somewhat to combat that, to make me bare in rain and wind, I have always had my hair cut shorter and shorter. Perhaps it was even from a kind of animalistic atavism, for I went to the barber with the greatest pleasure, in order to feel him working on me often, and long, and thoroughly, like a dog who looks beatified because he receives a pat on the head. That Saturday afternoon when Fran left school for good, I had sought the barber beforehand. First because I felt myself so quavery again, and then in order to make myself somewhat handsome for the occasion. I asked the barber to use the finest clippers, and I needed to hear and to feel the cool-warm steel of the grumbling machine quivering on my scalp, pressed hard against my head; in this way my own internal turmoil was drowned. Then I had my hair washed, two times, one right after the other, shivering under the cold trickle of the shampoo. The barber massaged me vigorously, for a long time, and formed much luxurious lather, great emerald bubbles, and then, in a gush, threw the silver can of water over my head, which was distended over the basin, in order to rinse it all away under a gloriously tepid flow. I always used lotion, and that time I chose an even stronger scent. And, moreover, then I had him rub oil on my hair and comb it into a part and brush it down flat. When I looked into the mirror, I saw myself much younger, and my hair almost black again—in any case, the gray top which grew on my scalp was all sheared away. It was the end of the school year and bewilderingly warm. While the barber was working, we had talked about one thing and another, as is customary in the barber's chair. The man had expected that I would complain about a headache, and, pleasured by the working of his hands, I certainly didn't want to disappoint him. However, I had no headache—only I was quivering so in my neck and in my spinal column and indeed everywhere. But there on the barber's chair, that was not entirely unpleasant. For that matter, I connected it with the afternoon's festivities which I awaited. That internal, inward noise was especially annoying and painful on ordinary days, because then it was so foolish in contrast with the pale grayness and inasmuch as it cost me so much effort, both spiritually and physically, to overcome it, even partially, for my work. I say partially, for the efforts have never been very fruitful—and the longer I try, the less fruitful they are—so that even the simplest and easiest work finally becomes a torture. I have never been able to come to a full stop. No matter how wretched my work became, I wanted to get it done all the more furiously. Then the barber said that he had something very efficacious against headache and also against stiffness of neck due to colds. And although I saw myself there in the mirror, sitting so youthful and so strong of build, blushing and cheerful as a lad, I gave him permission to try it once on me. Perhaps it could help me against my unknown disease, for it had no touch of "scientific interference." The barber connected the cord that hung from the ceiling and also supplied the current for the clippers. It was an apparatus no longer than some little instrument, with a large, black rubber knob which was rotated by electricity. The barber rubbed my neck with this, over what he called "the big nerve." The rubber ball kneaded the back of my buzzing head like a dull, furious thumb and thundered weak and hard, cold and hot at the same time. The vibrations which he shot through my whole body were of that sort of pain from which one may expect exaltation afterwards. Thus I put up with that unusual sensation; the barber giggled amicably in the mirror, and when he unplugged the cord again and, after a last brushing, took away the white barber's apron and made a little bow, I certainly felt that I had been fixed up: even the awkward tingling in me seemed to have disappeared. It quickly returned, now stronger, then was drowned again and, as if deafened by the events of the whole further festive commencement afternoon, influenced me by intervals, like the barber with his electrical apparatus. The visitors, the students, the hot light, the music —it was all so buzzing and throbbing, it all roared so much, that my nervousness, already greater than ever, was whipped up or overwhelmed by it. So the afternoon even now spins in my memory from darkness into bright light and then again into darkness, like a gigantic farandole under floodlights. The school is a large, modern building with many broad windows through which the sunlight falls in shrill patches, while by contrast, but only in some corridors, it seems darker. In the evening, in the tea room, there were floodlights. It was then that everything became for me a deadly difficult snarl. Moreover, it was no weekday, I did not have to think about my work, I might for once give up some time to the tangle; in fact, I couldn't do anything else. Snarl, tangle, yet something else, perhaps the most, has always shone through and at the same time obscured my ill-fated existence: now a golden and then an ashen haze, a sort of mist, not over everything but *through* everything, a fog which does not so much surround as it irretrievably permeates everything. When I left the barber and walked out of the fresh, somber station, "it" hung over the great round plaza where the streetcars, coming from all directions, describe a wide, graceful circle before going out in those various directions again. It hung there like a blinding reflection of the sun, flashing from the steel of the streetcar tracks, into which bled the peonies of the public gardens. I must have walked there and leaped aboard a streetcar like a kid, but it seemed to me I walked with an intoxicated head and a staggering soul, groping. Is it possible that certain souls are not well anchored to their bodies, that they flap in them, and sometimes almost thump? And is it impossible that astrologers and fortune tellers and other scholars of the black arts perhaps have something similar and even that a certain bond exists between the soul and a heavenly body? The sun, at noon on the earth, has often been one red torture to me; I walked desperately, like a stranger lost in a far and hostile region, with a drunken curse at the sun, and sick with the desire for another land, for the land of my soul's home, which I have sometimes thought to be the evening star. The streetcar sliced through narrow streets full of shadows and with the soul-brightness of night. The mist still hung there also, a separate light silver fog, in the dark doorways of cool cafes. Sometimes a woman's painted head forked out into the black glare of the plate-glass windows, a face white as the moon, with blue eyelids and a mouth red as peonies. But the streetcar whizzed wildly on. How ridiculous seemed those hazy houses, apparently on the corner of some sweet night-planet! And, when I stepped on the blazing steps of the school, how silly seemed the flashing fire which shot out under my ice-covered sports shoes from the white stones of that beloved hall of youth and innocence! A flood of visitors caught me up and carried me with them to the great lower room where the ceremony took place. That hall was already full, and yet new people continually entered it, people in authority, relatives, and curiosity seekers, all looking cheerful and dressed in their Sunday clothes, some a little old-fashioned and bourgeois, others new this summer. A boy scout, no bigger than my little finger, led me through a hedge of potted plants to the row where there was a chair for me. I laughed confusedly and excused myself, for all the chairs up to mine were already occupied, and I had to make everyone else stand up. They did not get any time to sit down again: the National Anthem resounded, played in a rather jerky fashion from a phonograph record. It was odd: at the same moment all the people stood up and the members of the orchestra, though unseen and absent, sat down. It was now quiet inside the room, except for the blaring music, but at the two great folding doors into the hall it remained noisy. I had a place in the second row. Before me, to one side, stood Judge Brantink, his shoes neat, his head leaning even a trace backward. I could even see his immaculate face, which stared at a point on the wall high above us. The noble posture par excellence when the National Anthem was played. I tried to improve my stance somewhat by bringing my feet closer together, as quietly as possible, but I did not dare to rumple the rug. I am, as I said, very large, and if you're large you always make someone standing behind you angry; in any case, you feel terribly conspicuous, and you wish you were only chest high. And this was certainly not the moment to attract attention to my sports suit, which I had bought, it is true, especially for this occasion, with the hope of making myself appear a little younger. But perhaps I ought to have chosen black because of my position. There! The phonograph record came to an end. The needle still skated for a few revolutions in a scratching groove; then another little boy scout shot forward and shut the machine off. We sat down. I ventured just a glance to each side. I thought I had seen the faces of several ladies and gentlemen previously. I seldom forget faces, and names stay with me a long time too; but all too quickly after being introduced, or after I have stopped seeing them every day, the names and faces come unstuck in my memory and take up places hopelessly remote from each other. For this reason I have never been able to tell the twins Fien and Griet Van Wierden apart, although I could still write down by heart the cunning little differences between those two sisters, who really looked amazingly alike. Therefore I usually meet people with "Sir" or "Madam"; if it sounds somewhat stiff, it is at any rate less offensive than a mumbled name. And to those who greet me very heartily, I throw out a happy and surprised "Hi!"—or "Hi, Buddy," if it is a man—after which I quickly ask how things are with them, and "at home," and "with their work." But that does not always bring clarification, and more than once, after conversing with someone during a whole streetcar ride, I have left him without ever having known whom I had met. I think now that perhaps this could also have been a reason why I had so little benefit in my professional career from connections. And yet that confusion of mine about names certainly does not come from any lack of interest in people. I have always been fond of people; I have found all of them, without exception, immediately interesting; even for the least of them I have always cared admiringly. What they all generated in me was always the same, miraculous and above or beneath all individual differences. I could not say that to them; they probably would not have believed that anyone so amorously sought in them their common humanity and for that reason forgot their names, because it is just of their personal uniqueness that most people speak. Yet if God exists, surely He can be nothing else than blissful universality, the dissolution of all those uniquenesses, the loss of the "something" that, more or less consciously, burdens everyone. But *I* now bear it resignedly, Lord, I bear it quietly, in order to try to expiate the crime I have committed. My daily work used to cost me so much exertion; how should I then hope to come up to Your commandments now with a smaller effort? The alderman who meanwhile had climbed to the podium was also talking about work and strife, but in a somewhat different sense. All aldermen are politicians, and the alderman cannot decently make an exception for Education, Art, and Science. I have heard him a few times, and every time his first sentence was like the toot of the trumpet with which an exalted struggle is begun.

In order not to offend any other public convictions, that battle remains almost a mockery: a tournament without opponents, about such high ideas as Right, Freedom, and Love, on which all current opinions can amply agree. The alderman now began to explain solemnly about this occasion, which was a milestone celebrating the task accomplished but which was also the starting place for further battles. On this task the last hand has now been laid. The public should be able to view it immediately in all its details. For this solemn purpose these annual school exhibitions have been organized in various localities. Now the public is invited by the city council to ascertain the results which have been the fruits of a year's untiring efforts by the faculty and students of this distinguished school. The alderman, moreover, insisted that the awarding of the diplomas to the students of this school should take place today. The students had worked to the best of their abilities. Already, in anticipation, he wished to congratulate them publicly. Now they were going out into the world. The real struggle was about to begin. And he would like to direct a few well-intentioned words to them about that. Life would certainly bring them blows, but if they would always hold before their eyes the living ideal of a community of Love, they would always draw comfort and strength from that vision. And what surer path lay open before them to the realization of that ideal than that of Right and Freedom? The alderman began and finished each sentence on his paper with a vigorous, searching look at the public. His address was a strange, although very fashionable, mixture of his own thoughts and an anonymous framework, or the other way around, for it was difficult to tell what came off his paper from what was said extemporaneously. I sat thinking how I had never received from politics, either in the paper or at public gatherings, one word that has helped me in this life. Politics sets its sights on personal fame and also something else, an even more tangible advantage, the good of all. But it always ignores me, who am still one of those all, and the problems which are the problems of my life. It casts never a glance of its Love on that something of mine which has made my work a torture and has caused me to fight so many hopeless battles. Now it's very strange that most people also do not appear to expect expressions of thought and charity from politics, and so much importance is placed today on things which I should solve, with my dizzy soul, thirsting for clarity, perhaps in too simple, too ordinary, and therefore in too fantastic a fashion: I would give everyone the same wages, abolish valets and maids, build common eating and living houses for everyone, etc. The actuality would have to be more complicated; perhaps I couldn't do it and have ungratefully overlooked the many material goods—and with them also the spiritual, for these are not to be separated per saldo—that politics has given me, as to every one of us, and still gives daily. Perhaps I liked the alderman for that and could even have admired him had he belonged ever so little to the clear and serene world of our director and Professor Mato. I envied that man his struggle, his conviction, his obvious sincerity, and I felt a respectful affection for the two elements which comprised his personality: for the ordinary youth he had been, whose rough heartiness he had retained, and for the higher official he had become, very probably in fact through much work and strife, and who tried to be dignified and earnest. And I wondered whether the combination of those two did not display a mollifying weld of shyness somewhere inside. And look—at that moment the alderman himself made a slip of the tongue: he said "pedogagy." He did not begin to blush, if anything he turned paler, and did not even correct his pronunciation, but went on talking vigorously. A few sentences further, however, he came across the word again and said, with almost military emphasis, throwing a piercing look into the room, "pe-da-go-gic." I have never known in what context, for I had already lost the thread of his reasoning some time before. I have often tried to follow a speaker to the end; I have never been able to. The attention required for that is an extremely tormenting intellectual endeavor. Certainly I should never have been able to make it through the university without shorthand. When I came from a lecture, I scarcely knew what the professor had expostulated so eloquently about, although I had taken everything down mechanically and, albeit in an uncomprehending manner, very completely and conscientiously. Later his text, always awkwardly transcribed, was before me. And the robot which is in each man and which does so much, perhaps even everything, for him, without his realizing it—that good, diligent, reliable spirit has helped me for a long time as well as he could, but the whole blame lies on me, who wanted to wake him up. I still well know when he stabbed me for the first time, or rather: when for the first time it became apparent that, by wanting to "inspire" him, I had on the contrary inflicted a death blow upon him. It was the third or fourth time that I had to speak on the radio. I had managed it rather fluently earlier. But it was about just that that I was going to make a fuss, and I asked my friends at the station whether they had never yet felt, when alone but for the presence of that silly litle microphone, a sudden mad impulse rise up in them to scream, just once, or to perform some other indecency. At first they laughed at me, but they could not have meant to find it funny, for when I repeated my question one of them said, almost brutally, that I must shut up. And then at the end of my talk I screamed. Fortunately, one of those friends was watching me and immediately had the engineer break off the transmission. The public must have heard only a bit of it, without even being able to grasp what was going on. Naturally I have never dared set foot again in that estimable building, where I had so deeply shattered the confidence placed in me; for that matter, I have never been invited back, either. And after that there have been still other incidents, little but similar, all irreparable. Like the time when I rode behind a streetcar on my bicycle. While the streetcar moved forward slowly, I had a fast grip on the handle of the rear platform, in order to ride along with it without having to climb aboard. The streetcar was moving rapidly when I suddenly became afraid, afraid of what might happen if I once accidentally let loose of the handle. And then my hand did let loose. Unconscious, I was carried from the street and taken care of in a drugstore. I have always had a scar on my left hand from my injury. But I may not pursue this subject here; I have promised our director not to remember this any more. Where was I? I've lost the thread of my story, just as when I sat listening to the alderman. Oh, yes, the alderman, with his puffy face, white as flour, and his soft belly. His collar and his shirt, a little crumpled, evidenced the burning heat, but he wore a black suit. And I sat there with a sports suit. Again I looked carefully to the left and right of me. My immediate neighbors gazed straight ahead at the alderman, who was still speaking. The movement of my head, however, was noticed farther up and had the effect of turning a few familiar faces toward me with a friendly little nod. I muttered back, "Madame," and "Hi, Buddy!" I did not dare to look around, but apparently only people in authority, officials, and the faculty sat in the first two rows. A few among them were also lightly clothed, yet none of them so youthfully as I. It disturbed me and made me slightly apprehensive about the shortly forthcoming meeting with the principal. Then suddenly all hands began to clap. The alderman was done and returned to his place, between the headmaster and Judge Brantink, in the middle of the first row. The principal stood up, turned to us, and clapped his hands with short little movements very rapidly, bowing in the direction of the alderman, who sat wiping his forehead and neck. The master clapped to the end and then quickly climbed on the stage, stuck his hand under his beard, and began his speech, without notes, almost without pause for breath, but also with very little beauty of style. While he named the nation, the city, the alderman, and a whole long list of people who weren't there, and said thanks, his seaweed-colored little eyes searched through the room in all directions. I sat, also searching. I sat searching the whole time. Where were the students, where were the students hidden? I blew my nose in order to swivel my head around, while I shifted myself a little, but still in a sitting position, on my chair. They weren't at the back of the room, and they weren't in the front! We sat against the lengthwise wall of the room; the headmaster had apparently arranged for all the light from the other lengthwise wall, the large glass doors of which gave onto the playground, to fall on the podium and on the brightly colored paintings which had been collected on both sides of the stage and which hung on the lemon velvet wall drapes. The large folding doors, at the far left and right of the room, still stood open, filled with people who had not been able to find a place to sit down. But in those corridors it was now as still as a leaf. Were the students there? Were they waiting in a classroom? Just something for the master to hold up his sleeve for the passing moment like a magician until he was able to come to the end of his discourse. Yes, the master had probably given a silent signal, pressed on a hidden little bell, or spoken a certain word that had been previously agreed upon as the watchword—immediately the crowd in the large folding door at the left divided itself in two in order to afford passage first to the secretary, and next: to the "seven"! Again there was applause and open laughter. Had the master said something witty? That would have amazed me, for his witticisms were invariably academic and thus would be enjoyed only moderately by his audience, which, however, was certainly satisfied that what it was laughing at was truly amusing. The applause must have been for the "seven," instead; the principal was already standing to greet them with short little bows and stroked himself contentedly under his beard. He was now at the extreme right of the stage, the secretary at the extreme left, and between the two of them, with some more behind them, elbow to elbow, glittered the seven. For a short time everything was quiet and motionless. I could hear myself breathing by gasps, because of the heat and the delight and precisely because I was trying not to breathe so as not to break the spell. The master now stood, like an old-fashioned photograph, as if to show how long he could hold the pose: one, two . . . or rather, because of his childish manner, eeny, meeny . . . to a number well considered beforehand. Yes, the principal undoubtedly possessed all the qualities of a stage manager. The spectacle was unspeakably lovely. I mean, naturally, aside from the master, and also from the secretary, although this is really ungrateful, for the secretary had a lovely soul and in heaven would put even the most beautiful in this life to shame. Under the years-long influence of the master the secretary had become perhaps a little small-minded, but aside from that she had a lovable, generous, and obliging heart, and one that always, after every fluctuation, repaired the balance when she threatened to become confused. Good Miss Klaassen, Klazina Klazinasdaughter Klaassen, K. K. K. as the students called her. Are you still alive? Do you still wear your spotless suits, as honestly shaped as your own life, with the chaste little white collars that you always arranged to wear a little higher than they were intended to be, in order to hide that hairy wart which surely no one, except your parents of blessed memory, knew that you had? And you always had to put up your hair higher—it always escaped, somewhat sluttishly, from its scanty little bun—and around your neck you had to wear a narrow black velvet ribbon. It gave you the charm of another era, where you fit better. How I still see you there, standing tall on the edge of the stage, with your hands clasped under your book, and one eye gazing steadily at the headmaster-stage-manager while the other, with motherly severity but with such kindness, watches the seven. What a pity that they had to go away from your precious care. Oh, I just want to say: you would have protected them from everything, but it was too late, the calamity had already happened. The seven, the seven! Whenever I think of them, the trilling golden cloudstuff goes before my eyes, through my heart, again. I become feverish, my hands tremble, sobs well up in my throat. I still see all their little faces. I remember all their names, and I even believe that I can put the right name to each face, except for those mischievous, inextricable Van Wierden twins. It was in all respects a remarkable class. Just seven students—the strange, magnetic number—and all seven girls, and all wonderful. Three of those seven were actually very pretty—three, the other magic number. Opinions were divided, moreover, and certain lady teachers, who always judge slightly differently in such matters than men do, found that some of the three prettiest belonged to the group of the four others, so that, to make a long story short, almost all were pretty. Here, however, I shall immediately add, before I go further, that to me they were all equally dear, except for one. I was surely susceptible to their beauty and excellence. Especially as they stood there on the stage, they were a treat for the eye. You had to be really sharp to withstand the temptation of the black weekday pinafores, despite the great swan-white collars that went with them. But now they were all dressed in light, colorful little summer frocks, with due consideration, it is true, to the master's prescripts concerning length of skirt and incision of neckline and the prohibition of naked legs. The difference in wealth among them, which even the black pinafores were not able to cover completely—those pinafores, all of different materials and workmanship—now could be seen perhaps still more clearly, but there was something, each of them still had something else, perhaps only in her posture, that made them all equally attractive. An insignificant gesture, and the humblest frock can snatch a grace as charming as that of the most elegant gown. I suspected that the stage manager had foreseen everything and thus arranged the sequence of the students, from left to right, to begin on the master's side—the side of honor—in the order in which the names would be announced. Indeed. Suddenly the quietness of the *tableau-vivant* was broken and the announcement was made of those moments which had been waited for in joyful and fearful silence: the first instructresses, bearing the final diplomas. But from the roguish face of Miss Freken I deduced that they themselves had had to wait in the corridor, slowly counting to the number the master had imposed. The silence of the room—and I do not believe it is only my opinion when I say that the silence was one of delight—now gave way to a light, gay disturbance. The parents now certainly sat in suspense, even the teachers moved forward on their chairs, and my heart, my heart—oh, it thumped so! But there still remained a moment, for the stage manager had arranged the ceremony as artfully as possible. Miss Freken handed Miss Klaassen the diplomas, with a barely discernible nod, which she added surely from the fullness of her own heart. After that, still just as roguishly, she went to take Miss Klaassen's place, for the master had naturally calculated that the symmetry of his composition must of course not be disturbed. With the diplomas before her, out stepped Miss Klaassen, carefully past the podium and to the right, to stand beside and below the master. Then the master bent for a moment, with a beneficent smile, to take the diplomas from her, stroked himself under his beard, brought the topmost diploma close to his eyes (purely as a matter of form), glanced swiftly at a point high in the air and finally to the right, at the first student. Again the room sat holding its breath. "Elizabeth Nieuwhuizen, *summa cum laude,*" his voice rolled out, as impressively deep as possible. Beps stepped from the row, glowing with satisfaction, notwithstanding that she must have known everything days ago, so as not to embarrass the master's crucial *mise en scène*. Pretty Beps, she stood there so happy and at the same time sensible, her form already luxuriant, so strong and hearty, the beautiful lady of the sweet, comradely type, the substantial, sympathetic, always cheerful comforter. How strange, how strange, that it was not *she* that I . . . . Yes, later I thought about that a great deal, but the thought, so tempting in theory, grew more snarled and fruitless than ever. Fran was always there again, and I could never make Fran's memory give way to Beps's—worse yet, I have never been able fully to disentangle the "seven"; I honestly think that my feelings, except those for one of them, were actually brotherly or fatherly, tender, certainly, but comradely. And the most remarkable of all—it makes me so happy, it puts me in a mood to be thankful in spite of everything—is how always, always, even in the midst of those seven, the image of Corra was present in my mind, and not reproachfully, either, but good and loving, although a little sad, like the oldest sister of the seven. There was applause, hard and long, and I even heard a few cheers of

"Bravo, bravo!" But Beps clearly had received careful instructions. She gave no nod and as yet thanked us only with her eyes. Miss Klaassen took the diploma back from the master and paced three steps toward us in order to beckon to the alderman. He at once reached up, with applause, accepted the diploma, and looked uneasily to the left and right. Beps came down off the stage, walked up to the alderman, stood before him, and nodded. For an instant her warm glance rested also on me. She stood not two steps away from me; I saw how she had perspired under her arms, and perhaps it was only my imagination, but I thought I also smelled her, in a draft from the large folding doors, a soft odor of roses on an adorable body. I nodded heartily and clapped my hands again, soundlessly. Her eyes blinked, and then she looked at the alderman again. He was still sitting down, with the large, solemn sheet of paper in his fists. Out of the corner of my eye, I saw his dead white face look strained but resolute. "Congratulations!" he said, as if to a soldier, and extended the piece of paper with both hands. But then he hesitated, and, although Beps's glance, so good and wise, so full of innocence and inviting innocence in return, rested on him, he rose up suddenly, let the diploma drop, held one of his good-natured paws out to the girl, and her fingers grabbed it around the wrist. She immediately stepped closer to him, and now they stood there like two robust young people, shaking hands with each other. The room cheered gaily once more, and I laughed and clapped with them, but at heart I found him and her so moving that the tears blinded my eyes, and I wanted so eagerly, so soulfully, to feel my hand also squeezed in the delicious, life-giving grip of those two hands. Then the alderman let Beps go, nodded a last look, and made ready to sit down again. But Beps gave a silent, very quick glance, probably not noticed by anyone but me, at the forgotten diploma in his other hand, which was hanging at his side. He quickly handed it to her; she gave a little curtsey and then climbed up to the stage, back to her place. Had the alderman regained his strength from the golden eyes of that handsome farmgirl? However that might be, he shook his impressive shoulders, threw a manly look to Judge Brantink, who still sat jauntily beside his empty chair, and then looked out in front of him in a very determined way, without making any move to sit. He reminded me of a sailor, who has his feet firmly on deck and, as he knows from experience, has nothing more to fear from any storm. Oh, rapture—and he might well be grateful to Beps for the undamaging experience which he had from her so easily —for the second, the second in the class was Fran. Fran, Frannie of that far time! How have I been able to remember everything about Beps so clearly?—I, who, from the moment when Fran had appeared in the folding door, had never taken my eyes off her! And how was I able to pay attention to everything, everything pertaining to Fran, then and through the rest of the whole endless afternoon, in spite of the blinding mist that hung over everything, but most of all over her, in spite of that thunder in my neck, in spite of that boiling in my head and that knocking in my eyes and that howling buzz of happiness and sorrow through my whole being? Fran—she stood there on the stage as if sculpted, with her hair of pale gold, her ivory eyelids, for she looked at the floor the whole time, with her silk frock and her mahogany shoes. "Eufrazia Veenman, *magna cum laude,*" the master blared. Applause burst out again, and in it—stifled, unrecognizable—resounded one "Bravo!": mine. Did the master hear it? His quick eyes did not shoot in my direction. And even *she* must not have heard it; now, indeed, she raised her glance, but it was to the alderman. I saw her come closer. Oh, it is not true, it is not true what is said of the power of fixation, of looking at someone so fixedly that he feels it and finally must look at you. I sat twisting the buttons of my coat with restless fingers. I felt little drops of sweat, mingled with the still liquid hair oil, burn my scalp like cinders. Wasn't that hair almost black again, without gray above the shorn temples, and didn't my suit sit on me youthfully, youthfully? How much older did I seem than the seven? And could anyone out there observe my confusion, my dizziness, my pain? But Fran didn't see it. She didn't see anything. She stood now before the alderman, two arms' lengths away from me. I saw, I heard her breathe: a light rising of her little bosom under her silk frock, and a soft whisper of air along her pale nostrils. Oh, that white, white face, and those dark, night-blue eyes, fixed as I saw them so near, fixed and enigmatic and yet so lovely, glorious enough to devour. She wasn't large of stature, Fran wasn't, and her figure was still slender as a child's. She had a small mouth, but her lips were full and of a somewhat sanguinary red that was perhaps proper and yet made a sharp contrast with the surrounding paleness of her complexion. Or were that white and that red the work of a refined make-up, with which she had dared to defy the stringent regulations of the master? In contrast with her eyes, her lips smiled and by doing so formed a dimple in each cheek. When the alderman wished her "Congratulations," with a voice which made a heavy effort to be vigorous and succeeded in sounding like a dull explosion, she opened her mouth and disclosed two rows of very regular teeth, close-fitting and cruelly beautiful. Within the blood red valentine of her lips, those teeth seemed even whiter than her complexion, and behind them, in the depths, I saw for an instant the dark purple curl of her tongue. But tongue, teeth, and smile vanished when, in her turn, the alderman pressed her hands in his beefy clutch. Inside myself I heard her groan. Even the alderman appeared frightened and gave her her diploma without delay. She curtseyed and turned around. She was going away, away so soon, and she had not looked at me. Yet, just the same, she had glanced for a fraction of an instant at Judge Brantink. But me—my imploring white eyeballs, my pupils black as ink, my nervously scowling eyebrows—nothing of this had attracted her attention. She was going away, yet it was as if she still stood there turned toward us. I saw her back, her legs, her sandals, the fringe of her finely plaited gold-red hair floating on her neck, and at the same time I saw her still there, two arms' lengths in front of me, with that little pearl of sweat between her eyebrows, her hand outstretched for her diploma, a hand which was darker than her face, a hand of which all that could be said was that either her nails had been rubbed to shining beauty or that she had cautiously polished them—her hand which seemed strong and yet was instead slender, with a clearly marked knot of vein—oh, that regal, that alarmingly beautiful hand, of flesh and blood and yet so impervious, that touching, mysterious hand, which knew all of her! Fran had retaken her place in line: again I saw her ivory eyelids, she looked at a point before her on the floor, I sat there for nothing, for absolutely nothing, depriving and radiating my soul—she did not see the consuming blaze of my poor powerless eyes, she did not want to see them, and the golden, bloody cloud between us was already growing thicker and stormier. "Francina Vander Zwalm, *magna cum laude,*" "Adolfina Van Wierden, *magna cum laude,*" "Margareta Van Wierden, *cum laude,*" "Eliza De Boer, satisfactory," "Augusta Herikhoven, satisfactory." Thus the sequence ran, I believe. Of the faces I am sure, but the names—already I begin to doubt the names! The master's voice sounded the same for all, just as stately for satisfactory as for *summa*. And the rest of the ceremonial was also identical: the handing down of the document into the hands of Miss Klaassen, the conducting of the diploma to the alderman by Miss Klaassen, and so forth. The pauses between the calling of the names surely must have been exactly the same, thanks to the internal computer in the stage manager. Happy man, who had such a chronometer in his soul, while I have never been able to see even the slightest order, let alone bring any order into it, in the unrolling of time in head or heart. I continued to look at Fran, to see whether she would raise her recalcitrant eyelids one single time in my direction, and yet all the same I saw each of the girls in succession come from the podium and make a curtsey, and smile, and each be satisfied in her way and blush and perspire a little. And now it was a long time that Fran had remained so strangely quiet, and then suddenly another girl stood before the alderman, replacing the preceding one, because Fran had moved her foot a little and had *almost* looked. Gussie, the last, was in front of me—Brantink had once said to me that he shared my opinion—the third most beautiful in the class. Nearly a child, so large and solidly built, however—and that was certainly unusual—without that comradely air of Beps's, compared to which the beautiful carnality of Gus was too womanly, or rather of another sort of womanliness than Beps's: not so warm, but a little coquettish, if I may use such a word for a girl who was really still a child and whom I even loved as a child. Gus had something languorous about her, and she also worked more drowsily than the other girls; hence it was, apparently, that she came last, for she was certainly not the least clever. The least clever was the next-to-last, Lisa, a child whom I liked very much. She was not richly gifted, and at home her people were poor in material things as well. Her mother was dead; she lived with her father, an aunt, and a little brother, and she had to help a great deal. Once I overheard the master speak to her because she had dirt under her fingernails and on the whole appeared somewhat slovenly. Now she also stood there humbly, but beautiful in her humility, in a very ordinary little blouse, embroidered with diamond-shaped panels so ugly that they were touching. She stood there so tremulously, just as I had always known her, with fearful eyes and her poor forehead full of strain and a shy half-smile on her clumsily marked, poorly colored lips, happy that she had passed and for once had not come in last. Strange, how such meager gifts, honestly and bravely borne, could make someone beautiful, beautiful in her soul. So beautiful, indeed, that I nearly preferred Lisa to Francina Vander Zwalm, who was third in the class and was also considered by the instructresses to be the third prettiest in the class. She was indeed pretty, like the girls who years ago were painted on English china, slim and charming and always exceptionally neat without the least little bit of finery. She got that from the better social class to which she belonged. She always looked very simply dressed, but the material of her suits was of the very best and the style was nothing less than a work of art. And she was also like this inside. She could be mischievous, and indeed was in everything she did with her girl friends, but yet she always remained herself and special: the material of her soul was just such an irreproachable tissue of soft distinction. And was not this attribute perhaps influenced by her appearance? She was generally considered very bright; but perhaps she had not paid enough attention to doing well because it would require too strenuous an effort for her taste in the general rush at the end of the school year. The instructresses also considered one of the Van Wierden sisters definitely pretty, and even beautiful. I believe that she was named Adolfina; in any case, she was the one with a *magna*. The master had just spoken her name, and she had stepped forward; either I began to doubt it again, or I had indeed heard properly. And when immediately afterwards the other little sister was announced, let us say Griet, who had *cum laude,* I was just absent-minded: Fran, as I intended to remark, had whispered something quietly to Beps, without raising her glance, but Beps had then inadvertently looked in my direction. The twins, as I have said, looked amazingly like each other, and the girls, or it must have been their parents, appeared to take an excessive and malicious pleasure in doing everything as each other's mirror image: their hair was arranged the same way, they wore frocks exactly alike, stockings alike, shoes alike, brooches alike. And yet there were very slight differences between them, which did not escape me and which I still remember. The one with *magna cum laude,* let us say Adolfina, had somewhat the color of a goldsmith's beetle in her blonde hair, while the nose of the other, Griet, although pretty, displayed a very slight degree of convexity like an eagle's nose, because of which I finally decided that Adolfina was the prettier. Just the same, they were both very lovable children, whom I recall with a very agreeable feeling of quiet, affectionate regard. Now all of them were standing in the back row. The master had really drilled them exemplarily: the symmetry was matchless. They held themselves perfectly the same all the time, feet together, their diplomas in their right hands, pressed against their bodies, between stomach and breast, and the other arms hung straight at their sides. They had rolled up the documents reluctantly. I was looking at them so hard that I could see again the knotted vein in Fran's lightly tanned hand. How gloriously her stiffly set silver bracelets glittered on the golden skin of her wrist. Yet the master had forgotten something; there was something that he had not been able to make subservient to that will of his that planned everything beforehand. The warm glance of Beps, to the alderman, to Brantink, to me; the shy joy of Lisa; the ivory eyelids of Fran, always cast down. The master spoke again. He wished the children happiness and bade them "not farewell but au revoir" —the centuries-old kindness. He spoke, half turned to them, half to the alderman and the public. He spoke zealously, with little eyes that darted like a kite, so fluently that he did not stop for breath, but with small grace of style. I know nothing of what he said. Scholastic things, which followed docilely in the alderman's footsteps. I looked at the ceiling and at the walls. The room in which we sat suddenly seemed to me like a gigantic mouth, yawning. It was as if, under the principal's words, the students there suddenly appeared to be many more students than they had seemed only a few moments ago. Again there were the pinafores, black as ink, and the glimpse of swan-white collars. Their shoulders seemed to become just a little smaller, and their little heads inclined forward and somewhat horizontally. Now almost all of them stood with downcast eyes, modest and sweet. It was touching to see them, and a little sad. Also incomprehensible. Already such big girls, who seemed so innocent, almost childish, although childish in the best sense, but still it pierced my soul strangely. Sexless women, but that negative concept did not seem reassuring: the discrepancy between what now was and what would be later appeared even greater, the terrifying abyss over which they must yet leap in what was called "life." Oh, Frannie, Frannie, how small you still were then, how slender, still almost without breasts, and it was as if even your fair hand had become darker and as if that knotted vein, like something already too adult, a visible token of mysterious turmoils which she might not yet show, was erased and had never existed except in my strained imagination. Fran

—her girl friends called her "Fra," but I called her "Fran." I don't clearly know why I found that the prettier sound. Perhaps only because it was *my* secret nickname for her, or perhaps on account of associations with "fringe," the golden fringe of hair which floated on her neck, and with frou-frou—the French word for the rustling of ladies' underclothes, bewitching underclothes, in which I had never seen her but had often dreamed—frou-frou, which is just the name these peasant children here give to bangs, such as in fact Fran wore, a light fringe of little pale gold ringlets, dazzling and as if blazing on her forehead, to just above her cinnamon-colored, unusually firm, and purely separated eyebrows, which seemed very proper but were perhaps even then already cunningly plucked and skillfully penciled. Beps had stepped out of the row again. God, what matchless stage-management. One step farther forward than the last time, when she had only been announced and had yet to count before she could receive her diploma from the alderman. This time it was to offer thanks, all by herself. The Nation, the City, the Alderman, the Principal, the Student Body—all were remembered. It was merely academic language, prettily said, with an almost mischievous smile, but also with a kind, deep undertone and a warm glance for everyone. And that warmth actively divided itself among us. Suddenly I saw the master, grayed by his ancient sadness—he meant so well, it was not easy for him, and indeed his scholasticism was perhaps a great deal better and safer than so much liberal progressivism. Yes, in that moment, from that moment on, I have judged him more generously. I have even regarded him with affection and indeed have learned to admire him. And, although he did not wish to allow it to be noticeable, he seemed very moved and gratified by Beps's words, spoken out on behalf of the entire class, although he had apparently planned all of it in advance. But the heart is a strange muscle, today clenched like a fist and tomorrow suddenly sobbing. Then abruptly I became aware that Miss Klaassen had disappeared. I noticed it because she came in again through the big folding door on the left, with a remarkable expression and a little package of white tissue paper. With this she went to stand at the far right of the stage, at the master's place, who now found himself in the middle between K. K. K. and Miss Freken. Behind them, like a living hedge, blossomed the row of students' frocks. Even the master seemed surprised. What was going on? But I wasn't paying strict attention. The master was standing so that I could no longer see Fran. It was as if he did it intentionally. I leaned over only slightly, as far as I dared, toward my right-hand neighbor, and actually transgressed the limits of propriety—Fran was still hidden. Did I not notice that Brantink also sat forward very longingly toward the same corner and apparently as vainly as I? Then suddenly I understood: Brantink, naturally; Brantink was leaving and was now to receive his farewell too. The master was already speaking. It sounded so kind, and yet it seemed a little stiff—apparently, I thought, because the master now spoke to a masculine member of the faculty, to someone of good social position, to whom, because of his principal's dignity, it sounded less suitable to speak so jovially. Brantink, Judge Brantink. He was not yet so old but had come to the school very early, surely all of a quarter-century ago, so that he now had reached the time of life at which he might request a pension for the double hours of lessons which he had given here weekly on the elements of our constitutional, municipal, and penal law. A few months ago, between Christmas and New Year's—that always strange and wonderful week!—he had come up behind me suddenly in a corridor in the Palace of Justice and had chatted with me in an especially hearty fashion, although until then I had had only very slight acquaintance with him. He had the reputation of an outstanding jurist, but it was also said that he led rather a wild life. He was not happy at home, and according to some he was to blame, while others considered him the victim of a plague of a wife. In that unreal week, then, which always retains for me the fairy-tale quality of the Christmases of my almost carefree children's years, Brantink proposed that I replace him at the school. He said that he was too busy at the Palace. I had to accept only for a few months, until the end of the school year.

Then if he still had too much work, he would request his pension, and, if I wanted to, I could be appointed regularly. He himself undertook to arrange this for me. It was an easy course, I could use his notes, and if this extra teaching job didn't help me out, well, I wasn't committed to anything by it; he was convinced, however, that I would be able to make favorable connections with the town council by means of this position. The lessons were given only in the final year, and in it there were only seven students, bright and pleasant. I was a little dazed. In fact, it frightened me somewhat. I could not conceive how Brantink had decided on me. Did he then actually have a good opinion of me? Perhaps I accepted most of it, although I have never been able fully to dismiss the suspicion that Brantink had already approached in the same way someone who tossed a coin and chose by heads or tails. That he had walked up and down in his office and then had opened the door, determined to take the first man who appeared in the hallway by the arm and ask him. Fate willed that *I* appear in the hallway, and so I came into your life, little Fran, from that high, chill, vaulted palace of crime and punishment, in which I still walked in a gown, the solemn garb of my age, of my work (already so recalcitrant), in my black gown with the white bands, to you, Fran, who sat there on a school bench, in your black pinafore with the swan-white collar. Swallowed up in cares about my work, I entered that corridor, struggling against my melancholy, wrestling with my convulsions, and that corridor brought me to a school, to the happiest months of my life, to the Seven, to a classroom with snow behind the panes and later with blossoms and a spring sky in the open window—Easter, the birds, the school bell, so much soft, exciting splendor . . . Frannie, Brantink, forgive me, I could not foresee what would come of that; I did hesitate, but it all had to be as it was. Now and then I met Brantink in the Palace; he always asked me, jokingly, how things went at school, but, I don't know why, I told him little or nothing of my happiness. Perhaps I was ashamed of it. And cautiously, with palpitating heart, I inquired of him whether he still had too much work, although even then I knew painfully that the question had no meaning. Yes, he was always very busy, in fact it was clear that he would never return on a regular basis. But there was also someone else who was leaving at the end of that school year, someone whom I, even though I might stay on permanently, was going to lose forever, even after so short a time. Now here was still the parting of Brantink, who had indeed brought it about that I was hired, and from her, whom I should miss so terribly, without whom the school would be empty, as hateful and painful as a gigantic and incurable wound. I came, and she went, with very little delay, just enough that the wound could be inflicted upon me. Thus it has always been, fate has never spared me, it has never offered me an escape that did not later turn out to be a rope's end to flog me with. I came, and she went; she went as though my coming had driven her away, as though she fled before me, before my miserable person, which indeed had always scared fortune away. My whole life I have dreamed regularly of a glass, an ordinary drinking glass, which I try to set down rightside up the whole night through. It always falls over. And in the morning I can never come out of the door without my streetcar being right there in front of my nose. Did the master make a joke again? There was kind laughter and casual glances in my direction. Had I missed hearing my name mentioned? Thus, Brantink's replacement! God, fear gripped me in the throat, which was already so tight. Perhaps I would have to ask what he said, in order to make an appropriate reply, to thank him, to promise that I should manage things thus or so with the lessons. No, that really could not be; I was not now in a position to do it—and could the master, the careful stage manager, wish such an ill-planned digression on his agenda? I did not hear anything more, my ears were roaring so. The master was quiet. Applause. Miss Klaassen stepped up to the principal and placed the packet wrapped in tissue paper in his hand. Then she took one, two, three and a half steps back to her place at the extreme right of the podium. Reckless *mise en scène*. A quarter step more, and the obliging soul would have fallen off the stage. Of how many reluctant rehearsals must that not have been the fruit! Then the master came down from the stage. He walked straight ahead, to a point in front of Brantink, and reached him the packet—one arm's length, precisely. The gift of the school, of the faculty, and of the students. Thus he said then, in fact, without adding "and of myself," which appeared to me then a meritorious victory over himself, for he never otherwise counted himself among the faculty. I still recall the details, yet my attention was, though sidelong, directed past the principal and his package. By coming down from the stage the master had again unblocked my view of Fran. She was looking. But not at me, although almost at me. I sat just obliquely behind Brantink. Yes, she was still clearly looking very fixedly at Brantink, or at least at the little Brantink-master-alderman group. The alderman had just risen again and grasped Brantink's hand in his propellor. I had not seen that the master had also given Brantink his hand. But that was all right; it could hardly be otherwise before the public. The master had already thanked Brantink publicly and wished him farewell. I looked at Fran, at her eyes which were again as fixed and blue as the night, just as when she had received her diploma from the alderman, two arms' lengths away from me, closer than she had ever been to me before, for in class she sat in the fourth row of benches, right by the window, and in fact I had often cherished for a week in advance the intention of standing in front of my desk once when I was lecturing, walking through the aisle between the desks, pretending to look at their notes—but when the chosen day dawned, I never dared to do it. Not one single time between the bells before and after the lesson did I dare to leave my chair with its hard cushion. My glance even avoided the aisle, as if I were afraid to betray to the girls my unseemly longing. Suddenly Fran had disappeared again. The master stood once more in the center of the stage. Once more, though he may not have been in the exact center. Now Brantink stood in front of the podium, turned partly toward us, partly toward the stage. He held the little packet wrapped in tissue paper with both hands in front of his chest. He gave thanks. Half earnest and dutiful, half roguish. He said something in excuse and of the press of duty . . . the Palace of Justice . . . and that he yet hoped that it had not been so bad . . . a teacher in extraordinary service, not an extraordinary teacher! . . . The room laughed. Brantink's glasses glistened. I admired the inherent neatness of that slender little man, who was by no means still young and yet was still not gray. He had ash blond hair, thin and very finely combed, with a part just past the middle, a little English, the respectable part par excellence. When I was young, I also tried that once, but it would not stay on my lumpy head. That sort of part even has social significance. These criteria are merciless. For the sake of simplicity, consider mankind an egg. An egg has two ends, a pointed and a rounded. Well, the men with pointed heads and English parts are the nobility, while we, the commoners, have heads like rumps. O Lord! forgive me, forgive me. You know better. You know me, it is not my nature to mock. But sometimes You have seemed to me like a peddler of figurines, a most charming pitchman, with all of us in Your good arm. You do not consider any one of us to be above the others. You price your wares without distinction. But I, I have always felt that you have cast your eternal models in such a lamentable mold. Why, why did you not immediately destroy that out-of-fashion piece? I have not been very happy, and I have even had to suffer so much. No, I will be quiet again. I know it, the egg must also have its underside, its behind end, and we who have such heads had better have them shaved smooth, like the poor fool in Gogol, who finally had to drip water on his noggin. Not envious, actually, I have never been envious in an ugly way of Judge Brantink. I allowed him his eminence of race and could admire his head with the same deference as the shapeliness of Francina Vander Zwalm's. For that matter, Brantink was always clad like her, very simply, but in impeccable good taste. True, it was said that he himself sometimes had to sew on again the buttons that had come off his coat and ironed his trousers with his own hands when his wife had run amok; that he even had to cook his own soup when he came home from the Palace. But so far as I could see there was nothing, nothing to it. His nose was very large but also exceptionally noble. And I never saw him otherwise than pale; that was because of his extra work and his profession. Or had his irregular way of life caused the difficulty? Oh, how absurd and incomprehensible it all was—he, so sharp, so quiet and strong, yet washed out—and I, with my prosperous and virile appearance, so shabby-souled and crack-brained! This time Brantink did not seem very fluent in his delivery. He tried to be witty, and then to say something appropriate, scholarly, by way of fatherly hints to the students about life. Too, he couldn't see them well from where he stood. The master and the two schoolmistresses obstructed his view of three of them. Brantink had to manage it carefully; the master deprived him as certainly as me of the sight of Fran. And then suddenly Brantink was at the end of what he must have prepared, of what he had planned in cold blood, in his chill and drafty office, in the presence of clerks and other people of the Palace, as ordinary and unimpassioned of spirit as possible. And he had now said that, and suddenly I saw him standing there defenceless. The packet, I thought, the packet now. Yes, he asked whether he might open it. That was fitting; he must satisfy the curiosity of the public and also allow them to see his expression of gratitude. Three, four times he turned the package around in his hand in order to find the knot in the string. In fact, it looked as if he couldn't see clearly through his glasses. And then the knot didn't want to come untied. What a lamentable blunder of the stage manager's, not to have thought of that! Nevertheless, the master seemed by no means excited. He remained standing undisturbed, with a smile from ear to ear, still as a rock, before Fran. After all these years, now I know, I still ask myself whether his stage management actually failed then or whether what seemed unforeseen was really intentional. Miss Freken finally could look on no longer and shot forward, doubtless on her own initiative, to help Brantink. Brantink unwrapped the tissue paper, looked at the present without taking it out, but with an appropriate nod. Then he held it up for us also to admire. He was a great cigar smoker, whose taste was nice. Brantink was still laughing when he tried to say his last pleasantry, something about many years and every time still recalled by each cigar. . . . But suddenly something was trapped in his throat. Still he brought out, "But that wasn't necessary"—then with a sob he walked back to his place. It was over. The ceremony was finished. The public clapped again, standing up. The students had made a quarter turn, and, led by Miss Klaassen, and followed by Miss Freken, like geese, descended the steps from the stage, the principal still bowing by way of farewell, and left the room like a dinghy through the sea of people, out through the large folding door on the left. It was done, and everyone began to mill around and make noise: shuffle of chairs, babble and movement of laughing and smoking men—it was like a burning, a burning of blood beaten to a rosy froth, both outside and inside me, between which the rotten sail of my soul was stretched like an eardrum in pain. It did not detain me longer. My throbbing memory has preserved everything that happened later, whirling around through scorching driftsand. I felt relieved that I had not had to speak, because what did it matter, compared to the incurable pain that was in me now, that this farewell had inflicted a gaping wound in the martyred stuff of my soul? A vanguard of girl scouts had come to the stage and connected the microphone, which had heretofore been unused and which at present seemed indispensable to drown out the uproar. It was announced that the esteemed public was now invited to honor the exhibition with its presence, and after that was again expected in this room, which would serve as a tea-room and where all sorts of splendid performances would be presented by various students. I let myself drift with the tide, so as to come in with it. The master said good afternoon to me and "Gracious, how young you look in that light suit, Mr. Antfield!" Naturally that was a criticism, although covered with salve, but what could it matter to me, what did this friendly and benevolent and even meritorious sting signify compared to the bite from which my heart bled? So I smiled, as I had already smiled all afternoon and would have to keep smiling nearly to the end, a smile that on the outside must have appeared warm and happy, almost as ingenuous perhaps as Beps's, but that inside, for myself, was sad and embarrassed, the little nervous laugh of Lisa DeBoer. I even wanted to grasp Brantink's hand firmly and say something emotional to him, but he drew back, laughing brusquely. "Now, kid, no foolishness!" he mocked, but his voice was still hoarse and his glasses were steamed over. "Kid"—I actually said it aloud, only a "kid," then, but still *young*. "Young," the master had also said it, young, young, easily almost as young as the seven. It did me good, so much good. Oh, what I had, my "something," was perhaps only a children's disease, and thus not at all so hopeless. I also got a handshake from the alderman that cracked my fingers. "Pleased to meet you," he said, half a head taller than I, pale and determined. It was as if his chewing muscles still had a cramp, as if with the last word of Brantink's farewell. Yes, he was certainly a sentimental man, perhaps even now only a grown-up boy who expended much work and struggle of his hefty body and his heavy head and his clammy hands to be an alderman. It was buzzing with people around us. The alderman moved halfway forward, the master buzzing around him, jauntily followed by Brantink and the corps of teachers. I felt as though I walked by them. And the public walked over everything. Order was maintained in the corridor and on the stairs by an improbable legion of scouts, too large a majority of them still shrimps, periwinkles, peanuts, and other little divots of chaps, but all with chests pushed out high and heroically. The older ones, on the other hand, acted seriously, cowed, as if they did not dare stretch their backs for fear that their already short pants would bare their milky knees. We steamed through the corridors and hallways. The alderman continually stopped here and there for a few moments and nodded cordially, good naturedly. The master spun the net of his clever guiding principle hastily over everyone and then some, even when it concerned exponents of other schools. In the gymnasium—the parallel bars and wall pulleys were partitioned off behind the same lemon velvet which also bedecked the reception room—a splendid exhibition had been arranged by the girls' trade school: lorelei-like young ladies of painted wood with sunken eyelids and glorious gowns, whole trousseaus of soft, beautiful linen, flamboyantly widespread curtains, and many other household goods. In a smaller room everything was light blue and pink, little things for the newborn, enameled bathinettes, tables and chairs for tiny tots, baby boxes and baby bottles and layettes. Against the wall hung lovely pictures of glorious young mothers and their adorable darlings. The young lady in charge of this section had a silver coiffure above an onyx face with two coral cheekstains that looked as if they had been drawn with a pair of compasses. Perhaps this was all makeup—the young lady was not under the direction of our master—but to the eye she appeared the ideal mother, securely gray but eternally young, for the children who live in fairy tales. This was the only room with softened light. The curtains for the windows, light blue curtains, were very tightly drawn. I wanted to remain there longer—so blessedly did the childlike colors and reduced dimensions cool my heated head. But the group sailed forth again. Through corridors hot as deserts, in which blew draughts that were sometimes cuttingly cold. I perspired and shivered. In these corridors stood all sorts of shrubs in stands, as also white plaster statues, painted with ochre, between which we had to twist to get through. Statues nearly twice as big as a man. Naked but with modest obliteration of details, which here moreover, being deceptively heavy, would have fallen off. In place of these, however, these statues showed so many muscles, which were so balled and lumpy, that the squashed people wriggled over to look at them. Work of artists, teachers in the academy, the master explained, classically beautiful and the Ideal and similar representations. But to my taste, a nauseous display of lumps of flesh. Surely, from such bestial mountains of labor, I had always thought, should have come more than these dreary pipsqueaks, but that could not be classically ideal, and in any case that must not be, especially not here, to be showpieces—it cannot be beneficial to anyone to go further into this. Sleepwalkers do not make you more awake, and robots which have once examined themselves are lost. The alderman, in spite of his undauntedness, did not stop long before them. On the other hand, he looked with apparent pleasure at some softly colored still-lifes: flowers, and a window curtain in which a light breeze played. In the commercial school the girls sat in front of the misses, also in black pinafores with swan-white collars. There was machine-gunning with typewriters. The men or the children visiting us expected sudden blows when the little lunatics fell on their keyboards when the alderman appeared in the doorway. Surely a stage manager also reigned here. The corps of teachers whispered sociably among each other. The mathematics teacher laughed openly with a loud plop, but smothered this immediately again when the master shot his piercing little eyes at him with an expression of "it is im-pos-sib-le that I should have heard you correctly!" In a corner of that room was an imitation of a modern office. A teacher played the manager and sat at a large writing desk behind a glass wall, very conceited and busy, giving a student stenotypist a letter; he shrieked into an inter-office telephone in his hand to a student telephone girl who had to operate a little exchange with a huge switchboard in another corner. In the boys' trade school the students were binding books, planing wood, filing iron, building a little section of wall. There could also be found an impressive display of all kinds of parts of automobiles and even of airplanes, I believe, which apparently captivated many of the men. Then, on the second floor, where more customary school-things lay spread out on exhibit, a ridiculous little incident occurred to the embarrassment of the faculty. It went off for the most part with mumblings, but the German teacher and the English teacher had each gone the color opposite their respective complexions: crimson for the lady, gray for the gentleman. I intend to communicate that the German teacher, a good-natured schoolmarm, found out the faithlessness of the gentleman, the English teacher, a German, bald, and venomously regarded as a tattle-tale, which was how his position had been reached. *She,* above all, had wanted to give the credit to the students, and their work unrolled like an endless white sea, without the least relief, nothing but writing, essays, and flat things like that, with a minimum of pedagogic material, purely as I remember, one book, one phonograph record. While *he,* shamelessly, had dragged in everything and then some: all of twelve or sixteen brand-new volumes of a dictionary, with deluxe covers, which not even one student had so much as held in his hand, a whole collection of portraits of authors, such as had never been seen in the school but only in the public library, and not one phonograph record but a whole record library, with the school phonograph as well! That especially the German teacher could not with any possibility get down. The phonograph, which she was also in the habit of using, and which now stood on display there, illegally, like a purely English showpiece. How entirely otherwise had *she* reasoned. That there was only one phonograph. That it could not be divided into four parts, because it was also used in Dutch and French. And the French teacher and the Dutch teacher had thought similarly, just as innocently and soundly as she, not to show off that over-complete battery of materials. No, it was not professional of the English teacher, it was unfair, "un-fair," and he must know better than she precisely what that English word meant. The German lady stood matchlessly on the winds, scarlet and chalk-white in turn, while the sweat of her wrath pearled in dancing droplets from under her hat, lively with diverse flowers and a little canary. She had wanted to speak as quietly as possible, and therefore had turned down her volume control, located somewhere between her throat and her bosom, from which this improbable squeaking sounded. The English teacher, with indeed a rather sneaky glistening of his green glasses, and a bass to which he also applied a damper, attempted to explain to her with crookedly tortuous excuses that this was nothing but a misunderstanding, and an extremely painful one, especially for him; that everything had been done with good intentions by everyone and as usual by himself as well. Unexpectedly we had here two different opinions about the nature of the exhibition, but these concepts were absolutely not incompatible, indeed on the contrary they brought a desirable variety to the whole, and the one was surely not better than the other. In the second place, he was willing to admit, however, that here perhaps was something less than the Good, but for which the students bore the blame, as was summarily indicated, for he was not really responsible if they had built too diligently and too sumptuously. The alderman acted as if he had noticed nothing, for that matter the master attempted to distract his attention to other things farther on, and very politically the alderman nodded with equal approbation, as much at the sea of writing as at the display of dictionaries with the noisy phonograph. I left the room quickly, before anyone else. In a side corridor, I knew, could be found the students' cloakroom. There was no one in that silent little corridor, and also there were no longer any clothes on the hooks. I crept near them furtively. Under each hook was a white label with a blue border, on which each student had had to write her name in round letters. Here was the cloakroom of the seven, twelve hooks, seven labels. I knew Fran's place. "Eufrazia Veenman," I read, in her childlike round hand. I stretched out a trembling finger and stroked the label. My heart quivered like a thief's. I had no expectation of betrayal for a time, for I had planned everything on the sly beforehand; the little gummed-on paper was, however, unfortunately stuck fast! The warmth had partially loosened it from the varnished wood. It must be possible to get it all the way loose without tearing. But I was frightened and bent swiftly to one of my shoelaces. Brantink had come out of the room. I looked up again, red and smiling. He looked playful and a little bored, as usual. No, he could not have seen me. The whole group now came through the little corridor. The alderman mopped sweat from his forehead and neck. Also the principal was hot and stroked under his beard as if he wanted to lighten it. I heard the master reassure the alderman: above, on the third story, the work of the lower classes was yet to be seen, but that was all very much the same and the alderman was of course acquainted with it; if he would perhaps rather go downstairs again, it was so unbearably warm and the master had ordered a refreshment before the tea-room was reopened. The alderman nodded, the group descended the stairs again. I made use of the first side corridor finally to lose the faculty. The students, the seven—where were they now? I walked through corridors and rooms, past statues and people, greeting left and right: "Ha, sir! . . . fine!" hastily onward, afraid that they would hold me up, but apparently no one wanted to. I arrived in the other wing, behind the room where the celebration took place, the part that the alderman had not honored with his visit. In the corridor, one of the walls of which was formed against the long wall behind the timbered-up stage in the reception room and at the end of which the two huge folding doors were once more mysteriously closed tight, lay a thick carpet of brick-red mock velvet. I stumbled, for the large folding door at the left was not quite closed; it seemed as if it expected to be opened so as to pull me through with a bow into the room. I almost fell over one of the Van Wierden girls who just came out of a little side room. "Hello, Griet," I said and began to make a laughing excuse, but it was Adolfina, and she also had to laugh. At once she was gone again. Then Lisa came out of the little side room. I apparently must have rushed at her in too friendly a manner, for she looked more anxious than ever: "Congratulations, Lisa," I said, and then she cheered up. I grasped her trembling hand cordially. She had surely been excited again, for she looked rather red. Even her poor lips had a richer color. "Where are the others?" I asked, without finding another disguise for my zealous curiosity. My voice sounded loud and precipitous in the corridor and in myself. "Inside," said Lisa, and pointed toward another little room. I gripped her by the arm and pushed her before me in comradely fashion. "I want to congratulate them also," I said, "one last time." I said that with as much laughter as I could muster. We already stood in front of the door. Lisa and I knocked together. Then Miss Freken appeared in the crack. She stood there archly and also red; could that have been because of me? "No one may come in," said she in the master's voice and shook her head playfully, whereupon she immediately closed the door again and bolted it on the other side. I stood confused. "They are getting dressed for the fashion show," Lisa finally explained, with her hesitating voice and revolving eyes, which inquired whether she was to blame for not having said it earlier. "Oh," I said and giggled as convincingly as possible. "How nice. Then I understand why I can't go in, eh?" Lisa nodded. I let loose of her arm. I felt that she wanted to go away, or must go away. Above another room I saw a little placard written on in gold paint, and through the open door I saw beautiful geometric mountains of little wafers and bars of chocolate and all sorts of paper cornucopias filled with sweets for sale. A smell of candy wafted toward us through the door, a scent which was delicious both as a fragrance and as a memory of the Christmases of my childhood, but it made me almost sick when I thought of eating. "May I buy you a paper cornucopia, Lisa?" I asked. "Would you prefer jelly beans or chocolate drops? That is, as a small remembrance from your teacher of only a few months!" The child did not dare refuse. She stammered something about "Very much, but I have to help with the show." We were already standing in the candy room. I bought a large sack with chocolate drops and bonbons mixed together. She did not find any words with which to thank me. Perhaps I was too awkward and too jolly. I did not let her have any chance to say anything and laughed at her. "Go now, but help quickly," I shot at her, "and tell the others that I'll treat them, too, as soon as they are ready, but before the show, because I have to go back to the room and after that I may leave. I'll wait for them here. Goodbye, Lisa. Goodbye, child. Again, lots of luck. Your parents must be very happy, aren't they? Now you'll see how well it will go with you!" I had never seen her run away so fast and shyly. And yet she was grateful to me, for in the doorway she looked back at me with a thankful look. Goodbye, Lisa; goodbye, dear child; yes, it will certainly go well with you! I wiped off my sweat and thanked the salesgirl who looked so pretty in her bright pinafore and even a little regal with her white hair ribbon. Didn't I want something for myself? Some of these incomparable pastries, or ice cream? I couldn't. I only laughed. I would, though, like a glass of lemonade. I drank it down as slowly as possible. After that I lit a cigarette and decided that I would buy all the baked goods in sight that looked interesting. But I saw nothing. Then I began to appear ridiculous to myself. A young man in such a youthful sports suit who stayed bungling around in the midst of all that culinary art and bought nothing. I must walk on now. But none of the girls I had invited were coming. Surely Lisa had delivered her message? It wasn't just nothing for her to forget the request of a teacher. But still they didn't come. And now I must leave. I went, sauntered again through the corridor; a cub scout guided me down the carpet which led past the large folding door, beautifully smooth and solid around the corners. I might still be a little dizzy; I could not stumble, or if I did I would have fallen very softly. How sweet it would be if I opened my eyes again to see Fran's pale face and golden fringe of hair over me. But what a murderously foolish spectacle I should have made there, sprawled at full length on the brick-red mock-velvet carpet, blooming in my boy's playsuit! The little scouts would make fun of me and execute an Indian war dance around my corpse, and the patrol leaders and cubmasters would look on snickering. I walked into the little room called the School Museum. It was only a few cubic yards of space, an inconceivably narrow habitation, and hot as a greenhouse. There was a statue of a palissander, standing there, a negress, with dark red lips and white eyeballs. Dreadful to look at, something so sultry as that on a dog day! I felt my heart swoon. In a showcase sparkled reddish ore, the green of the malachite was turbid and depraved, and the pictures on the wall all represented Congolese scenes, overheated and quiet, nothing of snow and ice and evening planets. I had already fled from the volcanic tropics. People came incessantly along the corridor, especially school personnel, who apparently all had something to do with the fashion show and the other numbers in the tea room. Suddenly I felt a little as if I were behind the wings in a theater. My head became warmer and warmer and bubblier and bubblier. The wings, with the dressing rooms of the actors! But I would not stay vacillating here any longer. I kept walking and entered another room. It appeared to be the Bookstore. Indeed, the same portraits were here as were in that sly English teacher's exhibit—and for sale! You could also subscribe to magazines there. I bought a map, chose a book, and said that I would come to pick them up after the celebration. Didn't I also wish to obtain portraits of my favorite authors? The girl, who was sweet, did not let up. I bought the heads of all the authors that were there, our own and foreign, famous and unknown. That prosperous girl also sold books. At that moment I cast a glance to one side, for I did not want to lose sight of the door. Beps! Beps was just walking by. Perhaps she was coming to meet me in the candy room. "Beps!" I cried in a smothered voice and galloped after her. Yes, it was very likely that she was looking for me. She turned and came toward me in a friendly manner, with her warm, sympathetic expression. I grasped both her hands. "Hearty, hearty congratulations! You've deserved it, do you hear?" I said. "Thank you, Mr. Antfield," she nodded gratefully. "No," I said, "not Mr. Antfield any more! Now you have graduated, I am just an ordinary fellow. Call me Govert." She blushed, but again as a friend. "Thank you," she said, "very much." The girl in the bookstore was catching up with us, as charming as she could possibly be, with two books which I had expressed interest in. Another visitor wanted to buy them, but the girl had assured him that I enjoyed prior right of choice. I thanked her for the attention and said that of course I would take both books. I did not have the exact change and paid with a bill, upon which the girl expected me to walk back to the bookstore with her so that she could give me my change. But I was afraid that Beps would get tired of waiting and would presently go off without me. "Just keep the money," I said, "for the Community Chest." The girl thanked me with especial cordiality; maybe I had given her a large bill. What did it matter? This was the last day, the very last day. I saw clearly that Beps now wanted to go on again. Naturally, she still had a great deal to do. I must not hold her up. I stuck out one of the books to her; I never knew the title. "As a small memento," I said, "from your teacher for only a few months." "From Govert," she said sweetly and thanked me. Then she wanted to leave. I held her back, laughing, but inwardly entreating. "Did Lisa tell you that I wanted to treat all seven of you?" I asked hastily. Yes, she was very grateful, very sincerely, it was awfully nice of me, she thought, but she was not able to oblige now. I understood, on account of the fashion show, but afterwards, if perhaps I was still here . . . . And then it was out of me before I could reflect. "And Fran?" I asked, in not much less than a shriek, as it seemed even to me. At least Beps's exterior did not alter, or so little that it was unnoticeable. She still looked understanding, even almost affectionate. "Fran can't eat candy, she has to sing yet," she said softly. I wept inside. Fran did not want to, Fran did not want anything from me, no glance, no bonbon, no slightest word. But presently she would sing and smile for others. "Then," I said, "it's not up to her. I understand very well, do you hear? But give her this book from me, as a little remembrance of the teacher she had these few months." I handed Beps the other book that I had bought in the bookstore. I had neither inclination nor time to read the long title. I could only see in passing that it had a colorful binding, on which young people were portrayed, among them a sportive young girl with wavy blond hair at the wheel of a sky-blue car and with a waving scarf. I was still happy, despite all my misery, that I had happened to choose such a book, such a young, young book, for Fran from me. Beps nodded in a sisterly manner and with her smiling wisdom said thanks to me in Fran's name for the time being. Then she was gone, she also. Those were her last words. I have never spoken to her again. Farewell, Beps, farewell, gracious girl comrade! Where did I walk to now? I no longer know. To and fro, everywhere and nowhere. I only remember that I suddenly stood again in front of the dark-red negress with her tropical sneer and went into the hall again post haste. The cub scouts had given me a leaflet, always the same one, a few times. I tried to leave the little booklets unnoticed on a chair near the bookstore entrance. But the charming and prosperous girl was dearly adjusted to an unparalleled watchfulness. I was not two paces farther along the corridor when she said obligingly, "You have forgotten your leaflets, Mr. Antfield," and started after me. Blushing, I thanked her and had to take the boy scout news again into my possession. Just at that moment the music began to play, lively and blaring, this time from the string band. The corridor was now thick with people, but they divided themselves into two groups and stood along the walls, on either side of the brick-red mock-velvet carpet. I was lost. The performance was now going to commence. I could not get into the celebration room without being frightfully noticeable. The master would doubtlessly look severely wounded because I had made a fool of myself so characteristically by not keeping with the official group. Perhaps he had even been informed how I had bungled around arbitrarily in the wings. Miss Klaassen, in spite of her good nature, had all the qualities of a quiet hen. I decided to stay where I was, in this crowd, which was the least concerned with the school and had not been able to capture a place to sit in the tea-room. I stood in the neighborhood of the bookstore. The lovely girl came peering out of the doorway. "Here is a place for two to sit," she said invitingly, and I went and sat next to her in the door. She smelled delicious, that girl, of hyacinth, I believe, if indeed such an odor exists, but on her right middle finger was a small golden ring. I at once raised my eyes again, afraid that she had been able to guess my indelicate thought and had misunderstood. The fashion show had begun. The models walked one by one through the other folding door. When they afterwards came marching through our corridor, where their course came to an end of brick-red mock-velvet, we got an opportunity to admire them also, a little bit second-hand it is true, because the high moment for them was the room itself with the podium, the alderman, and the seated and settled public. Most rushed to the end of the corridor, then quickly off with a perspiring blush of relief and all kinds of revived glances and inchoate gestures toward the watching classmates in the dressing room, now open, where Miss Freken was anxious for the good conclusion of all the turns. We, the standing audience, didn't count—"Smooth job," I heard the charming bookstore girl say pithily. But there were still, even at the last minute, a few who were worried and who pushed slowly by, even one who stood still and drew the gown around herself so that we could enjoy a single model, with her fantastically beautiful arm gestures, as in a slow-motion film or like floating plants in an aquarium. I no longer know how many pretty faces, how many elegantly dressed girls' bodies, passed by then. It lives in my memory as a whirling procession of fur coats, Canadian luxury, bicycling costumes, swimsuits, formal gowns. There was even a little bride, under a fairy-tale gauze veil and with a train a yard long, which was carried by two kindergarten pages, a little boy and a little girl, precisely like a cup with a flaxen forehead and a large bow. Different schools took parts of the show. I sat feverishly counting how many of the seven had already come past. Five. And Fran hadn't yet. But they couldn't leave out the most beautiful of them all! Beps had only spoken about singing, but also I hadn't asked about the show. Then my soul received a shock, and I almost got up out of my chair: Fran! Fran had appeared in the folding doors in a wonderful nightgown, pale, gold blonde, laughing, in a pale green sleeping garment with naked, shuddering, white shoulders, and her hands were movingly drawn keybones which made one think of an enigmatic tune with that dramatically twisted vein: strong and yet very nearly thin, and everyone, everyone had heard of her. Pale green, the color which was so becoming to her golden fringe of hair and her cameo eyelids, to her starblue eyes and her slightly blood-colored lips. I shrank back; my heart hammered itself to pieces. I did not want to let myself look when she came by us. I did not want to see her ivory eyelids again, this time I wanted to surprise her *glance,* to steal it, for *me!* The schoolgirl, the childish schoolgirl! By now she had surely received my book from Beps. Would there be any gratitude in her eyes? How womanly, how womanly, although maidenly, she looked now! There she was! I shoved boldly forward and applauded noiselessly, out of admiration, yes indeed, naturally, but chiefly to compel her to look at me. That's the way I had planned everything hastily. And yes, that time I surprised her. I saw the deeply fixed eyes on me for one indivisible moment, the womanly smile directed at me. Then she was gone. Her shoulders shriveled as if into each other, her body sloped forward somewhat, she let her head fall forward with a short jerk, just as she had always nodded. The schoolgirl, the schoolgirl! She was already past. The friendly bookstore girl said something. I grinned and shook my head yes and no, for I had not understood. But I did not dare look at the girl, I could not let her so much as see my murdered face. The string band struck up. Cubs and their leaders put things in order and blared everywhere. The laymen stood up, each as if to break his chair into kindling. The first lamps glowed on, a little ruddy because there was still daylight in the windows. The exhibition was at an end. Lemonade, beer, cigarettes, the scouts' leaflets, an intestinal rumble from the loudspeaker, the amiable bookstore girl—the whirling had begun; and whirled me asunder; and sucked me into everything again; me, the teacher stripped of his toga in a ridiculous boy's suit! At first I sat in the tea-room, at the large school table, under the malice of the faculty, with the principal of the school in the midst of them. It occurred to me that he looked at me repeatedly and inquiringly. I discovered that glance, but it didn't matter to me any more. I chattered with all of them, snorted with sweat, and drank several glasses of beer. I no longer gave a hang for the master! I bought cigarettes and clapped my hands deafeningly. There were little songs warbled by various scholars, piano pieces hammered, impossibly long poems dragged up from memory without a mistake. The scouts performed exhausting feats of skill. The alderman had already left. Work and strife had apparently called him elsewhere for the good of the community. Brantink sat a little backwards, his legs crossed, pale and urbane, and growled. The German teacher seemed to have forgotten the bare sheets of her writing display. She giggled weakly and ate ice cream. The English teacher, however, still retained his rennet color and looked snaky, not more so out of settled inclination than in remembrance of the assailed dictionary and the disputed phonograph. Behind the clear babble of the others I heard his bass voice grumbling like a horsefly. Beps said a beautiful poem. I did not really hear well, but her voice sounded emotional and her posture was so mature, so comprehending, that the careless audience might have been put into a mood as deep as that of the sad poet who wrote the piece. Then an exceptionally pleasant number was performed by all the seven together. They mounted the stage again in goose fashion and drew up in a fan formation, their arms linked, like a bevy of chorus girls. They sang down the row, and then together, opening and closing their eyes, dangling their heads, while their little bodies followed the music up and down and they stamped to the marked cadence with beating legs. The idea was surely from a film, but the text was of their own making. The whole audience, the faculty as well as the visiting strangers, unanimously considered it a success. I sat there disconcerted, viewing it wholly otherwise. There was nothing left of the little group with small shoulders and bowed heads that had listened so demurely to the master's address. Men are always children all their lives, and apparently because we want to be, but schoolgirls, no, the schoolgirls were already schoolgirls no longer. Suddenly they seemed women, women still concealed in the misleading bodies of children. They had fabricated the humor of their song, something about, "We, last year's students, we are one, two, three, four, five, six, seven"—of which each of them sang one numeral, quickly down the row, then falling together again: "They aren't at all sharp, but ready for a joke, those seven, seven, seven." Indeed, it seemed as though they had hired another seven, of cubs or scouts, sitting behind the string band, to echo them every time that refrain, which made such a clatter, resounded. For that matter, it also worked very contagiously on our vocal cords, and now, notwithstanding the great distance in time and what has happened since, I am surprised to find that I, writing, am sitting humming and beating time with my foot. There was a stanza relating to the master, and others to the most remarkable ladies and gentlemen of the faculty. K. K. K. was considered at length, and the English master was strained deathly fine. Brantink's name also appeared in the song, but without emphasis, which I thought then was very considerate, as did also the master, so watchful over everything: any shaft of wit would have sounded discordant with the melody of his departure, which, in contrast to that of these singing girls, was merely an end and not also a beginning. *My* name was not mentioned. I had not expected that it would be, so briefly had I been at the school. And yet how sad, how unreasonable—here only shall I admit it: I had all the same hoped a little, and it made me vexed, once more vexed, always only vexed, with all the rest. But I did not allow anyone to observe this. I clapped as noisily as all the others put together at the last. Fran wore again her pale green frock from before the fashion show. Her eyes were barred and nodding, and her legs were floundering like the others'. I even tried to hear her voice above the others', as if she sang in front of them, a silver-lovely, liquid voice. I saw her teeth, her purple tongue as she laughed, heard her bracelets jingle against each other, but she held her hands, her touching dark hands with the knotted vein, hidden right and left behind her back, on the hip of her neighboring friend. Afterwards I did not sit any longer at the school table. The flying eyes of the master now undoubtedly followed me. But I didn't care. I tossed the whole thing out the window. He could like it or lump it. I wouldn't care if they never wanted me back at the school. Why should I? And even if they asked me, would *I* accept? I tried to be friendly with a few boys I knew. They sat at little tables more crowded than that of the girls. Perhaps underneath they were amorous and sought to pay court to the girls. I connected myself with them; together with them I considered whether I should go to the girls' table. For that matter, did I not fit better in their company, with my millimeter-long fuzz and my boy's suit? I treated them to ice cream but continued to drink beer myself. I gave them all degrees in scholarship and even offered them cigarettes, but merely thirsted to begin. I proposed a game, a friendly game, in which the girls must be asked questions. There were already a few sitting with us. But the boys behaved with so little sensitivity, and the girls precisely the same. Childish and grown up at the same time, and dreadfully playful. Is it then true that modern technology has more than anything else made life into a delightfully free interval, in which the romantic heart belongs irrevocably to the museum pieces of the past, together with the curly locks of the periwig and the charming adventures of the buccaneers? There was nothing else spoken of besides camps, streamlined cars, and even airplanes. I tried to propose another game, also of a somewhat frivolous complexion, one that I was able, after great exertion, to remember from an afternoon that I had once spent outdoors with Corra and her two younger brothers. But I had scarcely explained the rules when through the croaking loudspeaker came the information that there might be dancing. Suddenly I sat alone. Everyone had flown up in order to help make a ballroom by taking away the chairs and tables. The string band was already rolling the drum, cooing, and stamping, as if in a movie. There was something in that music that made me think of the negress in the school museum, not so nauseating as in the hot sunny afternoon, but depressingly sultry. I dance like a slipper. I didn't give a hang for the master, but I didn't want to look awkward in front of him. The thought of seeing Fran cradled in another man's arms made my soul shudder, but that was nothing but jealousy. I even longed to be able to see Fran dance, because I found dancing itself very lovely, entrancing —only too beautiful. It seemed as though everyone was dancing and I sat alone. The light of the floodlamps quivered a harsh blue; next to them that of the ordinary lamps shone an amber twilight. Beps danced with Brantink. Over his shoulder she observed my loneliness. Perhaps it was merely a dance movement, but it really seemed as though she nodded to me encouragingly. Suddenly I thought that if I remained sitting here any longer, she would very possibly ask me for the next dance, purely from sympathy. I walked hastily away, toward the stage. What in the world made me think of that audacity? Fran was spinning around with the stalwart scout who had first spoken into the microphone. I stood next to the pianist, who led the string band, and proposed to him that if he wanted to dance, I would attend to the phonograph. Alas, I cannot play the piano, otherwise I would rather have replaced him. But with the phonograph I also liberated the other members of the string band, all of them large, handsome boys. They accepted; "for a few dances," they said. I remained at the podium, before the master and the faculty might begin to wonder what I was doing there. Between two dances Brantink and Fran stood close to each other in front of the stage, with their backs to me. I bent over a little, as casually as I could, but I knew that I did it in order to listen. Brantink said, "No, no thank you." Had Fran asked him for a dance? Then I heard the word "heart," but that was surely intended medically; and —*my* name! My heart was really horribly sick. God, must I now suddenly fall insensible off the stage, in the same place as K. K. K., who had held herself so stoutly on the brink of the precipice? But the master had surely drilled her a long time on that. I did not hear any more. I only saw Fran shake her head "no," friendly but decisively "no," no, *no!*—at the end not friendly any longer. Didn't that "no" strike at me? What question of Brantink's was she answering. Had he perhaps proposed that she ask *me?* Ah, she didn't want to, she wanted nothing from me, no felicitations, no candy, the book I had pressed on her as a gift, and I had had to steal her glance by surprise during the fashion show. Torn in pieces, I fled the stage. I saw everything as through a veil of red sweat. I could not read the labels on the phonograph records, nor could I get a new needle in the pick-up, my hands were shaking so. How long had I been playing records there? Perhaps it had been a long time. But it seemed very short to me. And then it grieved me that the string band was suddenly being recalled to play again. "The string band! The string band!" I could sit down again and be a wallflower. But perhaps now Beps had already forgotten me. I sat down on a chair near the girls' forsaken table. I suddenly felt so tired, so inexpressibly tired, as if I might glide right off my chair. I ordered beer, beer. Was I a little bit drunk? Brantink suddenly sat next to me, perky as ever, perhaps still affected and therefore so laboriously seeking for little offenses. He looked at the dancing girls and said something obscene, as he had often done since I had learned to know him better. I shouldn't take him amiss any longer. The worst scurviness—what did it really mean? Indeed, it had nothing to do with life. My soul was deaf to all this. As a matter of fact, perhaps it was very nice of Brantink, he had seen how lonely I was, sitting there; perhaps he himself felt even worse off than I and yet had come to cheer me up. I laughed, vacantly but gratefully. By this time in the afternoon I was able to see very well how soft the material of his soul was under that urbane, ironical mask, which now showed his well-situated position and his dignity, how well he deserved a good, long rest. But this graduation ceremony had now forever torn the edge from that mask, at least in my eyes. The blind favorites no longer moved so slowly; they danced themselves into a sweat, without even the least embarrassment about their milky knees. How incalculable it all was! The boys now suddenly looked as if they were becoming men, just as the girls had ceased maturing in order to remain schoolchildren, and yet there was something missing from the dancing of both of them which *I* had always seen in dances, or so I thought. Can it be that I was simultaneously older and younger than they? Younger because my soul had remained anchored in a between-life which they had omitted and would never know—older because I, notwithstanding my short hair (they wore theirs quite long—the bop haircut!) and my sports suit and all my effort, belonged irrevocably to the past? Younger and older—that seemed to come out all right: a romantic who secretly dreamed of dancing gloriously, for which they were too dignified, but was never able to dance; and who was the only one wearing a ready-made sports suit, while they, sportsmen in heart and kidney, at least then, with their feet and their bare knees, danced. I wanted to tell that to Brantink, covertly, and ask him what it meant, but I got confused in my mind; he shrugged his shoulders and began to talk smut. There was Lisa de Boer with the "pants-pisser" of an English teacher. The poor child was satisfied with anything, and he had surely not been able to dig up anything better. Yes, a "pants-pisser," with a breech-block in his pants, just as in the Middle Ages. And the German teacher was "a tub of lard," the alderman a "washed-out fart," and the master a "balls-for-brains." Brantink played in his favorite register, and I got to enjoy the most up-to-date grossnesses. There was Gussie Herikhoven waltzing, naturally, a waltz of the world. Or did I already know the definition of such a sleeping beauty as Gus? "The only tits she has are her nipples." My head buzzed. The floodlights cast their glowing white sand in my eyes, the music jingled in my eardrums on both sides, I had set down my beer glass too hard because my hand shook and I could not calculate the distance well any more. Fran danced indefatigably. I could no longer recognize Beps in the rioting crowd. Suddenly Fran stood before the microphone and sang the refrain of the song for the dancers. Beautiful as silver, clattering, almost bold. I looked as wildly as if I still had my job. But in vain. Her eyes remained obstinately on the dance-floor. She did not look pale any more, but luxuriantly warm, and there was a quality in her voice like something sweating. I couldn't contain it any longer. I looked around. I sat at the table at which she had sat before I came. She had drunk beer. I remembered that very well. And there, next to her half-empty glass—there lay my book, the book that I had given her! I recognized the colored binding, the sky-blue car, and the girl with the waving flaxen hair and the red neckerchief. There could be no mistake. It lay there soiled, there was beer spilled on it and a blot of chocolate stained it, as big as a chocolate drop. The beer that she had drunk and apparently a chocolate drop out of the paper cornucopia that I had bought Lisa and from which Fran had eaten, despite the fact that she still had to sing. There she was singing now, and she had not wanted any candy from me and had not once thanked me for the book. The string band paused. Then Fran sang "Le Lac," by Lamartine. I thought that Brantink's glasses grew steamy again. The tears swelled in my bosom, to my throat. Tears of deliverance, that on their way from soul to brain should bring alleviation and relief and bathe my poor, scorched eyes. And then Brantink said, "How stupid." I couldn't answer. I was too tired. I stood up, I felt myself tottering, but that would have been merely an internal impression. I walked out of the room. I couldn't leave yet, not yet, because when I left it would be forever, but I had to be alone. I walked up the stairs. There weren't any more people upstairs now. The lamps were all out. I walked into the classroom, our old classroom, of the snowy windows and the spring diamonds. A street-lamp cast its glow over the sea of German writing, while, in a dark corner, the twelve to sixteen volumes of the English dictionary stood imposingly by the school phonograph. Downstairs I heard the string band playing again. Swing. "Le Lac" and Lamartine were all forgotten. "How stupid!" And suddenly I thought of an old movie. Not of the book, which I had found boring and had never read to the end, but of the movie. *The Blue Angel,* with Marlene Dietrich, who was as blond as Fran, in the rôle of the heartless actress Lola-Lola, and Emil Jannings as Professor Unrath. No, I did not at all resemble Jannings, naturally. And, though just as foolish, as inhumanly and cruelly grieved as his, my senses had not yet been disturbed; it had not yet happened to me. And then I thought of him and felt that I myself stood there suddenly a little like him when he had fled, on the last night, from the carnival world which had made him like a pitiful buffoon, when he had rung the bell at the old schoolbuilding where he had been a teacher. The janitor had preceded him with his lantern and had magnanimously let him into his old classroom. He went in and sat in front of the benches, at his old desk, and laid his poor, mad head on his hands and burst into raucous sobs. He wailed out all his bottled-up emotions there, and then, at that desk, he passed away softly, liberated and sinking away in the most merciful of all solaces. I stood also sobbing, short, shuddering sobs, from my oppressed breast to my burning throat. I stood in the little corridor with coathangers and looked for the ticket under Fran's hook. Gone. Gone! Surely fallen down and stuck to the sole of someone's shoe. Then I burst into tears, into merciful tears. I laid my head against the cool, varnished wood of the hallstand, clasped Fran's hook with my hand, and kissed the place where the label had been, the ticket with her childish round handwriting. Fran! Fran! Frannie! Downstairs the stringband played, cubs, scouts, the faculty, everyone danced . . . and it sang in me, all my tormented, shrieking nerves sang, while the warm tears rolled down my cheeks: Fran is leaving school now! leaving school forever! . . . the old movie tune: Ich bin von Kopf bis Fusz, auf *Leiden* eingestellt! She stood at the exit, with several other girls. She didn't see me walk past. I stood outside, in the half darkness; lit a cigarette, to give myself something to hold on to, and acted as though I were waiting for something, seeing to it, however, that I intercepted none of the departing visitors. That was not possible; it looked as if they cherished the same hope with regard to me. Then Fran came outside with the other girls, but they did not separate. Had she seen me? It didn't look like it; they just kept chattering along. I strolled on a little, toward the first streetcar stop. Her group followed cautiously and then stood still again. What in the world could they giggle about so busily? Surely about camps and other vacation places. I had already let two streetcars go by. The girls must be looking at me now. Again I felt so inexpressibly tired. Now it was over, for good. That was the pitiful end. Now I had to go, I stood there all too ridiculously. Once more I looked a long time, in my countenance all the ardor of deprivation; I could still flirt with them with my patchwork person, with a last grim prayer of "Just look at me once, just come once!" They did not come, they cackled, they seemed already bored. The streetcar picked me up. I stuck my head outside, to cool it off, and also to look one more time. They were separating. Was I never, never to see them again? Was everything—and what had that "everything" been?—now finished forever? No, it could not be, it must not be. I had still not said a single word to Fran. Did I not, then, also have the right, the right of a teacher, of a colleague, of an ordinary mortal, at least once, as a parting gesture, to clasp her hand? Her dark hand, with the knotted vein and the bracelet? At the first stop I jumped off the platform. Oh, they probably thought I had forgotten something and had to walk back to the school. I began to step forth diligently and to whistle softly the march of the regiment in which I took my military service. God, how did it happen that I still knew that! Suddenly I walked very jauntily, with a boyish swagger, in my light suit, my sportive clown's uniform, for which the dark, sultry evening, already however permeated with autumnal freshness, pitied me. If my calculations were correct, I should meet with them now. Yes, there they were, Beps and Fran, walking together. The others had already gone their own ways. Beps and Fran! They drew nearer quickly, much too quickly, but that was the way things always happened to me. I did not dare to slacken my speed now; it was too brisk; I should have to change my posture. In the same way, in a car you can't suddenly put on the brake, or the machine will begin to skew. I tried to whistle, but my mouth was dry; I felt marbles of sweat along my close-cropped temples; it rolled down my cheeks. But they couldn't see that; and they too would still be warm, from the dancing and walking. Had I not been one of the most boyish of the boys? To that end, then, I should seem to be a siren-buoy of cheerfulness. The nervous tic around my eyes and in my chin had already begun, but Corra has often given me the assurance that you cannot really see anything from outside. Still, I felt my miserable smile sit on my mouth as unsteadily as a fluttering mask. There they were, and not under the streetlamp but still just behind it, so that all its silver-gold rays of light fell on their enchanting faces. A shudder ran through me, the siren-buoy howled in my breast, but I split my face into a laugh, into a monstrous grimace that felt as if dry paint had cracked on my face. The sweat trickled down my neck. "Hello!" I called out, "hel-lo, congratulations again and lots of luck!" I commanded my legs to hold still, but they did not stop, nor did the girls. We passed each other. Beps nodded in a sisterly fashion. Fran inclined her head forward, and they were already past. Past! We walked on, she and I, each his own way, for good, forever. Now I could at least weep, bite my nails, and cry out, and then everything would be over. But someone else was coming, someone I knew, Brantink. Still pale, with a derby, cane, and a small, ironic smile, a little laugh that certainly he could not take seriously, nor, surely, could I. But I had no desire to stand and talk. God, no! "Forgot something!" I grinned too rapidly. Apparently he also had no desire to stand and talk, waved briefly with his free hand, in which he gripped his dangling gloves, and we walked on. I looked around on the sly, still walking. Now he was under the streetlight. One moment more, and then he also vanished into the night which had taken Beps and Fran. The night which lay before me also. The night through which I crept, weeping inwardly, and which then closed itself around me for ten long years. I will not tell here of those endless years. It should be a story in itself, miserable and foolish, a shackling together of futilities, always narrower and more despicable, but which worked destructively on my always only comparative luck; which poisoned my whole existence as those smallest of all little animals or plants, the bacilli, underhandedly send a healthy and cheerful body to the ground. A story of which enough is said if one knows the dead black color of the binding and the grayness of the paper on which it should be written. With growing mollification and wonder I have looked around myself in those ten years, at the most ordinary everyday people, with whom you stand on the streetcar or who come toward you on the sidewalk. The people who walk with upraised heads, as if they admired the heavens each day anew, although what they see there is as dreary as a dishrag, as if they were rediscovering another pithy detail of the façade above, or of the rain-gutters. People who whistle through their teeth or hum as they walk; who always smoke pipes or cigars; who are not made sick by a morning cigarette; who would rather sit on the terrace of a cafe than in the dusky inside corner of it, and by choice acquaint themselves with others of those beings, who are chips off the same block, who are above scratching the fuzz on their heads. People who can undo their belts without ever losing their self-possession, even when one day is not the same as another. I have excused their luck all those ten long, monotonous years, without being able to taste a crumb. I have lived like a martyr, like the drudge of my task, growing steadily heavier. The automaton which sleeps in all those people and, sleeping, does everything so smoothly for them; that automaton, which I once awakened—but was that my fault? did I not do it with the most serviceable intentions, with great reluctance because I wanted to live as consciously and volitionally as possible?—that automaton has gone to work, the longer the less willingly. I had formerly been, thanks to my abeyant absent-mindedness in college, a good student. My probationary years as a lawyer were remarked even by my superiors. Then, once I had to stand by myself, I went to pieces spiritually, so to speak. I was able to hide it from myself for awhile, and for a still longer time from others. Slowly but surely it became more real, and always worse and worse, until finally I lost case after case. I have never had to defend really large suits, but however trifling they were and however much I exerted myself, it was a desperate muddle. Although the judge let me win a few very modest cases, I always felt myself that my defense limped pitifully, because I never had my preparation clearly in mind, notwithstanding that I found fewer and fewer clients and thus had more and more time at my disposal for each case; but, possessed by a critical fiend, I searched so much for spikes to nail water with that the single, simple, and solid arguments, which my colleagues grasped readily in all their cases, slipped hopelessly through my fingers. A few times Brantink was the compassionate judge, Brantink with his off-color face and mocking smile which I once mistakenly thought I could read. One day I decided to give it up. Corra didn't say anything but nodded silently. I can still see us sitting opposite each other in our kitchenette on a Saturday afternoon, each on a rattan chair at the white-scoured table. Corra looked pale and bit her underlip, as if to restrain her tears. She looked out the window across the canal at the Palace of Justice. It was late September, and the wind was blowing. The snowflakes flew through the sunless, silver-bright light like big, tired butterflies. I looked at Corra, and the tears trickled down my cheeks. We sat there for an awfully long time, almost taciturn. Then I got up by myself and, sobbing, pressed my lawyer's robe against my breast and against my cheeks and lips, before putting it away with marbles of white naphthaline in the large trunk from which, at least in my presence, it would never again be summoned to appear. Once the children wanted to play with it, but Corra rebuked them vigorously. A few months later we moved—Corra did not want to continue living on the canal—and I was given the lowly but regular position of clerk in the Palace which I had requested. I did not feel humiliated. I did not have any right to, considering that I had not appeared to my superiors to be in any position to do so. That is to say, I still believe, and it is really not false pride, that I had actually improved my status. How often have I not defended, alone in my study, the most difficult cases brilliantly, in hours of excitement, perhaps of over-excitement, but in which I felt that only then was I fully myself. In the daily exercise of my profession outside, on the other hand, something always stood in my way—always the same, and always more and more. A person's difficulties may arise from two things—from the work and from the working. And if someone wishes to make use of my misfortune, I give him advice with love and painful conviction: always look only at the work and never at the working. Don't pay attention if they postpone the object to the subject, which is you; in God's name, don't wake up the automaton, for it is a deathblow that you will inflict on yourself, on the working, and finally on the work as well. That is the abominable but expensive lesson that my afflicted life has let me teach others; the lesson for which, it may be, I have had to live. Hence, perhaps, that regular feeling and belief of mine, that I must not ever allow science to intervene in my disease, if it actually may be called a disease. It was something of the soul, and that will here and now smilingly smile, but do it carefully, and God forgive it—the soul is sacred ground, where the Lord alone may sow and reap; in my case I have even decided that weeding was not permitted me. We have, I reasoned, all of us our little or great sicknesses and mustn't desire to shake them off from us. There must be a reason why we have them, even if it is only to learn about these sicknesses. The world, life, is no dancing party, which is not to say that there is never anything which may make us hop; but above all it is a school, a school of testing. I repeat: I am certain that the notion of spiritual things which I have formed for myself is very hellish. But the pain of it which I have borne so openly and which I have therefore, I may indeed say it with some pride, carried so gallantly all these many years—isn't that hurt powerful enough to rectify my omissions and to purify my hellish spirit? Corra helped me all that time to the best of her ability. She was good, very good. I shall keep a grateful remembrance of her until I die, a serene remembrance full of pity for the misery I have given her to share. I don't feel guilty toward her; perhaps everything must be as it happens; but although I cannot feel a proper remorse, there is a repentance howling within me that I cannot assuage, the stinging melancholy of mourning love. In order that no one who will ever read me will misunderstand these pages: I love Corra very much, I have always remained in love with her, I still love her with all my soul. And I have been honest in that love, notwithstanding the great, dreadful occurrence which I must now impart. That catastrophe cannot be the punishment for a betrayal, for there was no betrayal committed. I have been only the victim of the tangle, the diffusion of the things of the human soul, as I have had to experience them, alas, always worse and worse. Those ten years were a night for me, black night, so that I kept dreaming of the ideal landscape of my existence, my evening planet of bliss. Black night, without any consoling caress of wind, which I always liked so much because it, and it alone, in autumn, in the season of my most propitious constellation, could blow away some of the torment of golden or ashen cloudstuff and the droning, like that of a telephone pole, that sang in my neck. But let me now, as I intended, be silent about those ten years. Let me let that tale of death rest in its black cover. For the end of this report of my life I merely have to open it once more to the most recent pages, when, after those ten years, my night has opened up, not for the sunrise, but by a tragic flash of lightning in the gray dawn. I will now attempt to write somewhat more rapidly, for I am growing tired again. Writing has always cost me so much effort, and this most recent time may well have been the most difficult of my life. I shall endeavor to make it not much longer, for myself and for others. I had calculated it well: a few dozen pages should suffice, I thought, but once more, the most recent time, I shall have been wrong, miserably wrong. I have already covered 93 sheets, and I must still tell the most important part, the worst. But I have wanted to be complete. Not unnecessarily complete, but as necessarily complete as possible. When everything is done, I must still have the strength to read it over and over, to think of the most suitable names possible for all those who are mentioned in this confession. I do not want my word to be considered untrustworthy any longer by the director, whom I have promised to let bygones be bygones. But it was stronger than I; I believe I have heard a higher command, to write down everything here first before I do as the director wishes. I think that I must note all this down, so that a few should know how everything really happened. For although I have made my horrible confession already in public, as honestly as possible, I had to dress up a few facts even then, with an eye to the others. These pages, however, I shall send to a literary publisher, anonymously or under a pseudonym, and in any case without mentioning a home address. For that matter, I no longer have a home. So then I can write everything down on these pages, without having to suppress or embellish anything. It will resemble literature and not actuality. No one has to feel himself concerned by it, and to a third person he can always say, shrugging, that it is fiction. Thus in the last analysis it has only minor importance if I cannot read my composition over again; I should be in danger of making myself sick, and the piece would be improved only a very little. Perhaps there will be an obliging literary soul in the publishing house who would do that for me, and with finer results than I could achieve; also the substitution of *all* names by others, chosen as suitably as possible. If the story of my life appears then, Corra will perhaps accidentally take it in hand and read it, and later Doos and San, and—Fran! They will guess the truth each for himself, who the writer of this was, without daring to say so even to each other because they will not be sure. That is as it should be. I must tell them everything, but so that perhaps it could not be from me, so that it is not publicly and distinctly from me. That will make my message to them gentler, although not very personal, but as if whispered to them by a distant voice from the sky. Then it will have reached the greatest beauty that I have always dreamed for literature: to bring an airy message, a little unrealistic, and because of this of a higher truth, with something of God's universality, no longer so directly human and therefore always a little mendacious or treacherous, and in consequence provoking obstinacy and resistance. And if the publisher won't publish my work, that is good also. Then the piece goes into the wastebasket and, by means of an amiably calm charwoman's hand, it will become entrusted, along with the other contents of the wastebasket, to the hallowed blaze of a sunny stove. Then it will be fitting, and the best for everyone; only messages which God approves and deems necessary reach their destination. I'm no postman, I satisfy only my last desires, although I intend by this to perform at the same time my last duty: this imperfect letter, from an unhappy dead man to other, perhaps happy, people, in order to tell them how admirable I have found them, how much I held them dear, and perhaps in order to bid them goodbye until we meet again in a heavenly body, where we shall all be without distinction, without disease, even without grief, and may dissolve into whiteness and coolness. Forward, then, several dozen pages more, if I am not mistaken. One last exertion, and then everything, everything, is over . . . . After those ten years I received a phone call from Professor Mato. I had never seen Fran again after the school celebration. That is to say: once on the streetcar, from the platform, I had glimpsed, in the sunny whirl of a spring day, an auto going past in the opposite direction and thought I saw in it a blond girl with golden bangs and pale green clothing, who sat next to the driver; she reminded me of Fran. I was so startled and so moved by this fleeting appearance that I did not have time also to look at the man. I had heard nothing more of her. For although I had been summoned to my clerical job, the work still claimed all the strength of my oppressed soul and my heavy head, so that outside of that I still led only a dull life. I went nowhere any more, never had company, and seldom spoke to anyone, for I had become at the same time shier and humbler. More than before I now saw Brantink, my superior at the Palace of Justice. Indeed, he had even tried a few times to use his old jovial tone toward me, but I myself was not agreeable to that submissiveness, and finally we were entirely estranged from each other. Only with Professor Mato, a celebrated medico-legal authority, especially expert in inquests and exhumations, did I stand in an almost friendly relationship. He had shown me marks of sympathy and yet had never endeavored to push into my spiritual depression, to understand what was inside of me. I was even more sincerely grateful to him for this. My job brought me gradually more into contact with him for the administrative portion of his work. It was fortunate for me that everything in

Professor Mato's work stayed on paper. For even no matter how great the admiration and affection I entertained for Professor Mato, his work itself filled me with a terrible, irrational fear. I had, however, never dared to acquaint him with this, and from this, just as in a Greek tragedy, everything else resulted. So as not to let anything of my horror show, which, I thought, must seem insulting to Professor Mato, I had a few times, it is true, expressed my very cautious interest, in the form of some timidly curious questions, about his work. Fate willed that Professor Mato took them literally. On a Saturday morning he called me up. A little case, but an international one, called him to a village right on the border, and he wanted me to accompany him out there. It would certainly interest me. On the way he would tell me about the case; the various points of it would form the subject of our conversation. Professor Mato was going in his sedan, his assistant was also going with us, along with the laboratory chauffeur. Thus there was just one seat open, for me. The expert asked me to stand alone punctually at half-past two in front of St. Evermarus's Church, where he would drive along to pick me up. The invitation proper was not put in the form of a question; I could only stammer a word of thanks and that I should gladly and scrupulously be at the indicated place at the hour set. Considering that it was Saturday, I would not have been able to pretend that other work prevented me from accepting Professor Mato's generous invitation. Saturday afternoons are time off at the Palace, and I could always arrange to do urgent extra work on Sunday. For that matter I know that, however much I was filled with fear and loathing, at the same time both horror and dread attracted me inexplicably. Surely even if I had not refused the invitation, I would not have gone to keep the appointment. Alas, later, yet before the next day had begun, it became evident why everything had to happen this way. No one escapes his fate, and my destiny had waited patiently for ten years for this conclusion. Still, I am happy, now that I know everything, that it was nothing morbid that attracted me then but the veiled and delicious fate which awaited me and which would lead to such disastrous consequences. At the hour determined upon, I stood waiting in front of St. Evermarus's Church. The car drove up very punctually, Professor Mato shook hands with me heartily and introduced me to his assistant, whose voice I remembered from the few times that he had spoken to me on the telephone instead of the professor: an expert still young, yet it seemed to me somewhat older than Professor Mato; the easily laughing type of peasant-boy-making-good, so entirely different from the professor's smiling eminence. It turned out to be an undeserved honor for me: I enjoyed the privilege of being permitted to take my place on the cushioned seat in the back, next to the professor, while the assistant went to sit up front with the chauffeur. The car ran noisily. I calculated that at the speed we were going the long ride that lay before us would last scarcely two hours. It was broiling hot, the sun scorched the landscape. Large clouds of ash-gold material flew up before us. The little windows scarcely cooled the oppressive air under the roof of the car. I sat as far away as I could with delicacy, wiping the sweat off my head. I still wore my hair cut short, even shorter than before, for I had become for the most part bald on the crown, so that I had had it millimetered even finer—"sheared" would almost be a good word. Professor Mato did not perspire. In spite of his youthful appearance, he had a dry skin, on which this temperature apparently had no effect. The well-fed, red-necked assistant was really getting warm too, just like the chauffeur. In an amiable, conscientious tone Professor Mato began to tell about the case. At D— a bank messenger had been missing for six months, properly one of our fellow Belgians, but he had last been seen at D—. All investigations had been futile. Until a month ago there had been washed ashore at D— a corpse which it had not been possible to identify because of the greatly advanced stage of decay. It had been buried provisionally until all administrative formalities should have been completed. That was the case at present, and Professor Mato had been entrusted with the exhumation and post-mortem, in order to try once more to establish the identity of the dead, as well as to examine whether he possibly had been the victim of murder. The word "decay" made me tremble deep in the marrow of my spine. I stared through the little windows, but the landscape, although beautiful, with its high hedges of poplars slanting on the ends, brought me no invigoration. Something steely lay over everything, under ashen cloud-stuff, and the grass was too deep a green. I like only the tender light green of spring; that of the summer grass I have always found brutal, annoying, and gloomy. After that the assistant entertained himself by discussing some affairs of their profession with the professor, to do which he sat half turned toward us. The chauffeur lit up a cigarette, without lessening speed. It was Oriental tobacco, which the peasant boy regarded as exotic. It made me sick, and I quickly lit up a bitter cigarette in order to combat the sweet fragrance. I still thought about that "advanced state of decay" and asked the professor whether that was a usual occurrence. "Yes," he answered calmly; "after only a few days the action of the water has already had a frightful effect." At that I wanted to know how far the natural course of mortality could be checked by embalming. From Professor Mato's answer it appeared that there were properly three types of decomposition. The first through rotting, which is the least preventable type. Secondly by means of mummification, such as occurs sometimes in the hot deserts of Africa, or by artificial embalming, which the professional embalmers surround with all sorts of mystification, but which is simply the injection of a solution of formaldehyde with long needles into the blood vessels and into all the body cavities. Finally decomposition can also, in the temperate zones, occur with the formation of corpse wax, particularly in the case of dead bodies which remain for a considerable time in pure running water or in cold, damp ground. Then a white, soapy material, *adipocere,* forms on the skin; this cuts off the air, by means of which the body dessicates and can be kept for a long time in a very handsome state. The complete phenomenon requires several years and is moreover so dependent upon the climate and the nature of the soil that it must be considered a rarity. The professor named a monastery, the name of which has gone out of my head, but which is known in the scientific world for the remarkable collection of waxed bodies which was found in its churchyard. Usually, however, corpse wax forms only on a few scattered places on the body and for the most part furthers the usual variety of rot. I learned, moreover, that in our climate, even without artificial embalming, the new-born which live only for a moment mummify very well. If they have lived longer, then decomposition mostly occurs according to the usual process of rotting, apparently because then, by means of the food introduced into the little body, the intestines become polluted. The assistant turned half around again so as to sit facing us and told us of a case that he had met once. A new-born baby was suffocated by his mother, who had afterwards concealed it in a cupboard. Two years later the little corpse was discovered there by the court, in a basket, under some handkerchiefs. It was really a beautiful specimen of mummification. If it interested me, the assistant could let me see the dessicated head of the child in the laboratory at F—, where it was preserved. I nodded as gratefully as I could. The chauffeur had driven energetically. A half hour before the calculated time we came to our destination. D— is a small municipality lying on the right bank of the X—, just before it empties into the sea. Professor Mato suggested that we should make use of this unexpected half hour to drive around a little and go inhale a supply of fresh air now at the beach. The car climbed up on the dike; in front of us suddenly lay the wide water, rippling free and wild under the sun. There was a stiff wind blowing. We walked along the paved bank. The wind played in Professor Mato's long hair and made the two ends of his tie flutter around his neck. The chauffeur had asked permission to go drink a glass of beer. The assistant wore a felt trilby, which he pressed somewhat more firmly on his pink head because of the strong wind. Professor Mato lit up a cigarillo and breathed in the sea air with scientific satisfaction. The assistant asked a man, who sat on a little heap of stones killing time and was obviously a native here, whether the water of the river was already salt or still tasted sweet at this height. The man answered that it was half and half. The stones along the shore went under the water at a soft slope. It was high tide. Three girls were playing in the water, two large, with feminine reserve, and one still very small, who walked naked in the water and continually came out again splashing and romping. She had only a handkerchief knotted in front of her little abdomen. Immediately I thought of the corpse wax and felt a shudder pass through my heated body. Although the sun shone no less brightly, the wind was as cold as the breath of the dead. We walked up the pier. It wasn't long. At the end there was a beach and a little open tower made up of girders. I think that the pier was really a landing place. Professor Mato and his assistant went to sit on the beach. I leaned over the parapet. Connected to it was a wooden stairway, which descended with broad, quiet steps, almost confidentially, to the water. Every hundred feet in front of me bobbed a red-and-black buoy. Suddenly I grew dizzy and imagined that I fell into the water. Then I thought that I was a strong, bold young man who swam to one of the buoys, but when I got there, I was suddenly sucked up by a whirlpool and drowned. The water washed my body back to the wall with quiet, bobbing movements as if I were still swimming. And there on the steps of the stairway sat a young blond woman, who was dressed in black and who was watching me. I glided thus, dead but as if living, into her arms. She sat partially in the water. She sobbed softly for a little while as she kissed me long and slowly. It was like a new-fashioned version of "The Two Little Princes." And the young woman wore a golden fringe of hair over her forehead, like Fran, like Frannie of ten years ago, who by now, in the meantime, must also have become a woman. But then this sorrowful beauty suddenly disappeared. A storm cloud had darkened the sun, so that everything now lay in a gray and melancholy light. Again I had to think of a corpse which had washed ashore, but this time the corpse of the murdered bank messenger, who, as long as a month ago, had been found in an already far advanced state of decay. "Come on, gentlemen!" said Professor Mato, in his affable, conscientious way. "I believe that it is time," and he stood up and carefully threw the stub of his cigar over the parapet, into the water, as if he were afraid the wooden scaffolding would catch fire. We turned back. The chauffeur was already waiting for us at the car. And a few moments later we rode into the little churchyard, which lay around the little village church like a garden, between two state policemen who had caught hold of both sides of the opened gate. We were welcomed by the mayor, a tall, stout polder farmer, who assured us in a very inappropriate manner that he was happy to see the monotony of his village existence broken for once by this intellectual inquiry. Professor Mato nodded cordially and reprovingly at the same time. The police magistrate, a little man with an accent, in gray and bareheaded; the deputy marshal, a tall man in black; and the clerk of the court, who was certainly also a scholarly farmer in a townsman's suit, were already in place. The mayor introduced us to each of them. Almost at the same moment two witnesses also arrived, relatives of the bank messenger—an older man with a goatee and a man still young, both common people, who made a favorable impression on me. I heard the police magistrate, while Professor Mato showed certain papers, whisper something about a large sum that the bank messenger had in his possession when he disappeared. Professor Mato nodded solemnly and pensively. A moment later the gathering grew still larger with the addition of an aged nun; I have never known in what capacity she was there: perhaps she had known the bank messenger, or perhaps she had been present at the burial of the body which had washed ashore. The mayor preceded us to a neglected outer corner of the churchyard, formed by boarding off a little shed which served as a charnel house. Through the open door I saw a couple of whitewashed walls and, in the middle, a rickety wooden table. A few meters in front of the little charnel house, under the overhanging foliage of a willow, the body had been provisionally buried in a dirty wooden coffin, which now was again removed from the ground with an eye to the post-mortem of this afternoon. At either side of the pit lay a heap of beautiful fresh earth, and on one of these two heaps rested the coffin. Impassively, with their pipes in their mouths and leaning on the handles of their spades, two farmers stood so as to watch more closely. "First the oath," said the police magistrate. Professor Mato naturally knew it well already, because of his long years of practice. The magistrate raised two fingers, Professor Mato did likewise and said rapidly, but clearly and solemnly, that he swore to complete the task assigned him dutifully and conscientiously. The willows rustled; the sun burned on the hedge; the farmers sucked on their extinguished pipes. It was all very still, and yet not boring. I even breathed freely. Then the witnesses had to swear that they would tell only the truth, nothing but the truth, so help them God. After that the silence was over; cigarettes were lit up, and everything began to run together a little. The magistrate gave a hasty reading of a verbal process, wherein certain identifying marks of the bank messenger were named: the right leg terminated in a club foot, the ring finger of the right hand displayed a lump at the height of the second joint, the teeth were perfect; the man was very large of frame and in his forties. Professor Mato nodded approvingly and did not ask him to repeat. I had hardly been able to follow and in fact doubted whether I had remembered everything well. The assistant made a few notes for the report. Professor Mato had meanwhile stripped off his coat and laid this on the hedge. Then he tied on a large rubber apron, then a smaller one, also of rubber or celluloid, and next his white, his beautiful white autopsy coat, on which even yet there was an old bloodstain. After that, helped by the assistant, he stuck his hands into the thin rubber gloves, the clean, pale color of which seemed to signify that they had just been boiled again. All these items of clothing came out of the black suitcase which had been behind the back seat of the car. The state policeman walked around with the chauffeur in the little paths of the churchyard, between the crosses. The marshal and the clerk of the court stood idly by, looking on, about a dozen paces from us. Then

Professor Mato asked that the grave-diggers open the lid of the coffin. I went to stand very close beside him, as if drawn by the awaited spectacle, and at the same time in order to find in his clear, scientific, and official presence some support and courage in the face of everything that was now shuddering and swimming inside me. Indescribable horror! The corpse already seemed to be not much more than a skeleton, bedecked with crumbly pieces of rust-colored cardboard that seemed all sodden. A smoke of decay arose from it, and it was all full of innumerable little white bars which grew parasitically and in gigantic numbers on the inner walls of the coffin. "What—what is that?" I shuddered voicelessly, while I was involuntarily forced to think of the photographic image of bacilli seen through the lens of a microscope. "Mold," explained the assistant, while Professor Mato nodded and still, scrutinizing, continued to look in. Then he walked back to the charnel house. I followed in his footsteps, like a child. For that matter, even the assistant walked almost equally humbly after his master. During these few minutes a deferential silence had again fallen over those present, but almost immediately afterwards most became themselves once more. Professor Mato then requested that the grave-diggers carry the table out of the little house and set the coffin down on it. The body floated in a loathesome white fluid; it was not possible to raise it out of the coffin without its smearing everything and even crumbling it completely, Professor Mato explained cordially, turning to me. The whole afternoon he addressed himself to me in particular, while I stood beside him, following everything with big eyes and nodding like one of his youngest students. It was all so horrible that for two hours I felt almost nothing of the miserable condition in which my body and my poor head found themselves. The heaviness of the sensations then must have temporarily deadened my soul. And just for that reason I was most fearful: that I could have tolerated everything, that I did not fall faint, which would have kept me from horror to spirit and body, but that on the contrary I had to behold everything to the end, the hideous vision of which I carry with me forever, like a poison that you have swallowed by impulse and that begins its relentless working only a short time after taking it. I have always been subject to such inexorable after-effects. I came to my examinations, as I have said in the past, very pleasantly, although they demanded much pain and exertion from me; but later, much later, ten and even twenty years afterwards, sometimes at night I have been suddenly frightened, clammy with sweat; I had dreamed again of the examinations when I had studied for several days and almost never, never would anything come clear for my miserable preparation. Also other forms of phobia have often rooted themselves in my life's happiness, which has always been so relative. An initial little fear, sometimes only a foolish, doubtful notion, took later on a terrible form and grew to uncommon dimensions. When I once sat preparing for an examination in the sweat of pain—I must have been in about my third year then —I intended to establish that my little pipe, so sociable and comforting, stimulated my salivary glands more than, for instance, a cigarette. Hitherto I had even been able to smoke my pipe dry, like a cigarette. Well, now, from that moment on, I have never again succeeded in doing that, however much I regretted it and have tried repeatedly, even with new courage and with all the power of self-persuasion I could muster. Finally I could no longer even think of my pipe again, or my whole mouth filled with saliva. I have always liked to lie down after lunch. In fact, I needed to; the day was too long for me. I had to divide the exertion in two parts and between the two try to recover myself with a nap. I had to be able to interrupt that stroke-of-twelve-o'clock-one-right-after-the-other; not to think any more for a little while, half in dream, for I dreamed regularly. But dreaming isn't really logical thought; it is loose, almost impersonal thought; almost becoming-thought, like being read a relaxing story. And then I have already entrusted to these pages that the noon, the hour of the highest point of the sun above the earth, when the "copper cad" (as the East Indians call it) plays hide-and-seek with the clouds, has always been the most hellish part of the day for me; the hour in which

I have felt myself most ill at ease here on this earth and have had as much nostalgia as possible, or rather: was the most miserably homesick for another planet, that far, cool heavenly body, rich in shadows, of my soul. Sleeping meant a brief deliverance from that, fifteen minutes, half an hour of sweet unconsciousness, even consciouslessness. The moment that I lay down was the greatest of all the worldly paradises I knew about. I may say that I shall never be able to taste greater, more tangible happiness than in those poor minutes as rest finally descended over and in me; as I saw the sun darken between my eyelashes and saw the daylight, the cruel middaylight, extinguish between my eyelids. To myself I have referred to these hours of frequent little silences as "under the wing of Death" of the lost Angel with whom my soul will sometime be able to fly to her evening-planet. Well, now, on a nasty day still another phobia attempted to rob me of the innocent necessity of this noon nap. I had intended to remark that whenever I stretched out on the bed fully clothed, every time I waked up again after a moment because of a tormenting little need. I began to worry about it and therefore sent my robot off his head again. Experimenting, I found that my abdomen felt cool every time. Perhaps the cause lay there. And even that was perhaps the result of the binding of my trousers, which, as I stretched out and lay down, were much too tight in the groin and therefore possibly obstructed the circulation of the blood locally. How could it be that that silly little occurrence became such a daymare that I was never again able to close even one eye when I dared to go lie ununclothed on the bed; as soon as I was upright again, it was to drain only a few little droplets. And it was useless to fight against it. In order not to lose my hour of bliss, for years afterwards, after my lunch I had to remove my trousers and creep between the two uppermost blankets in the bed, with a warm woollen scarf over my ears, to help me cut off all the gloom from outside. At first sight it might seem surprising that in my rest at night I never found the same need as during the noon hours. I always had to, or wanted to, work on my daily tasks, which I never got rid of, since I was never satisfied with them, to finish them as much as possible. What I permitted myself at noon signified to my soul no more than a pause. The day was not yet at an end; afterwards I would go to the battle again and possibly with better results. The evening, or the night, on the other hand, I saw as an endpoint; with it elapsed a day that was now past forever, irreparably. To repair one was impossible; tomorrow would always be another day. Hence I could decide only with difficulty to take a rest; I was already, around midnight, often more dead than alive from exhaustion. And then when I went to lie down at last, sleep would not come, on account of overexcitement and dissatisfaction. My ears buzzed, my head throbbed, my squinting eyes melted like lead, but inside there was a burning eye that would not close. I lay thinking, if it can be called thinking, in my delirious manner, more snarled up than ever, and yet there were over-acute alertnesses in me: how often haven't I heard, through the wall of our bedroom, the ticking of my little wristwatch, that I had laid down on the desk in my small study, in spite of its double glass case. But come, all that is now far away. In the clean, whitewashed little room where I sleep now there is no clock. The window must be open summer and winter. Now I always go to sleep early and get up early. I still dream and sometimes wake up screaming. But then I listen to the rain outside or to the summer wind in the trees in the garden. And the great, huge nostalgia that in the beginning often wept in my throat for that little watch of my former home is now as well suppressed as it can and must be. Professor Mato began with establishing, and the assistant took careful notes of it, that the notorious club foot was lacking from the corpse. The police magistrate, from a little distance away, gave a significant look. The nun stood motionless on a little rise between the two relative-witnesses, at a still greater distance. The two farmer-grave-diggers, with their spades between their legs, sat on the earthen mound on the other edge of the grave and silently sucked at their extinguished pipes, with children's eyes of forget-me-not blue in their brown leather faces. The flying horseflies raged in the hot shimmering light. The little steeple clock of the small church struck so suddenly, on behalf of the vicinity, like a storm carillon, that I was startled by its violence. Long after the clangor, the cells of my nerve fibers still continued reverberating like an invisible chime throughout my whole body. The assistant handed Professor Mato his lancet, which for this case served half as a dagger, half as a spatula. Then Professor Mato, still with delicate, calm gestures, took the skeleton's hand in his—the corpse's right hand. He did so not at all "with the fingertips," but in a scientifically direct manner, as if he was confronting a living person or a sleeping one. The skeleton's hand dropped off and became a little heap of damp, filthy brown cardboard fingerbones and sticky gunpowder. Professor Mato dictated to his assistant, who was writing it all down, that it was no longer possible to identify anything from the right hand of the victim. Then, not with his lancet but with his index finger, Professor Mato removed the cardboard lumps of the skeleton's cheeks. They fell along both sides of the head, with short little splashes and spatters, into the hideous suds that swam in the bottom of the coffin. With two last skillful incisions of the knife, the cheekbones were freed. There reposed improbably long, dirty, yellow teeth, but these, in the skeleton fleshed with life, must have formed a fine set. Professor Mato picked a few little green leaves from the hedge and shined the biting surfaces of the teeth as well as he could. With his bright eyes he looked slowly at me. "It is *not* the bank examiner," he said calmly and pointed with his lancet to the various lead fillings, as also to the black holes of two broken molars. The police magistrate had walked even closer in order to determine it also. The witnesses were likewise requested to come look and solemnly testified that their relative, the bank messenger, had never had to have a single hollow molar filled, and that moreover he had a full set of teeth. Professor Mato looked at me thoughtfully. Thereupon the witnesses, including the nun, might leave; Professor Mato did not esteem it necessary for them to have to undergo the terrible spectacle any longer. The magistrate himself made use of the occasion to disappear also for a little time. The farmer-grave-diggers—they sat there so motionless that we almost didn't notice them any more—remained undisturbed, sucking at their pipes, on the little pile of earth by the grave. Professor Mato began a detailed description of the victim's teeth, which, like all that preceded it, was carefully written down by the assistant. That would, Professor Mato explained parenthetically, and in the confidential tone which he always directed to me, eventually serve to discover the true identity of the victim; he would now investigate farther whether there was the possibility of homicide, or whether the man was drowned by accident. The professor estimated the age of the victim between forty and fifty years. The skeleton was large and strongly built; and the degree of wear shown by the edges of the teeth, which Professor Mato especially called my attention to, served very well to deduce his age approximately. The dagger-like knife sank into the throat and laid open an unsightly black porridge of blood, veined with pink and white strings. Professor Mato buried in this his thumb and index and middle fingers and groped around, kneading. It looked rather as if he wanted to pulverize the infected clay in order to determine its exact composition and the degree of its slipperiness. The decomposition seemed, however, as predicted, too far advanced. Professor Mato pulled his hand back and shook his head softly, as if he wanted to make it known that the investigation in this direction was to no avail. Still the head sat firm and strong on the trunk of the corpse. I saw the knife, already completely polluted, carve repeatedly, until the dead man's head was finally cut from his body. Professor Mato stuck a finger in each of the muddy eyeholes, lifted the head out of the coffin by them, and went, carrying it, to one of the three buckets of water which he had requested and which had been set down by the hedge. Carefully he plunged the dead man's head into the water and began to wash it with his hand. The decayed flesh was washed away like mud, the water in the bucket became filthy brown and began to scum lightly. It was a handsome, round, strong skull that Professor Mato finally raised on high and admired thoughtfully in the full sunlight, on his upraised arm. "It doesn't look like any skull from around here," said the Professor, and he informed me of certain anthropological peculiarities, while the assistant stood nodding agreement. Be that as it may, there was nothing to notice that could even to the slightest extent lead us to assume homicide. Professor Mato laid the head respectfully back in the coffin, by the single foot of the corpse. I saw his eyes go slowly, several times, again and again, over the left calf, as if he felt the roughness of that dark brown, wholly fleshless piece of skeleton with his glance. Then he looked at the assistant, went to the hedge again, and pulled off a handful of leaves, dipped them in the still scummy water of the bucket which was now polluted, and cautiously began, as with a sponge, to wash the shinbone of the corpse clean, after which his other hand removed the fibula with the same ease with which he would have broken off the stem of a clay pipe when it was clogged with nicotine. The shinbone did not change color very much, and only a little filth came loose from it. It looked, indeed, as if the filth softened, as if it were baked on. The professor gradually stopped washing, bent lower over the piece of bone, and remained for a while thoughtfully contemplating a certain spot in the middle of the bone. Then he stood up straight again, turned halfway toward us, and silently pointed with his finger to a suture, almost unnoticeable, but of a somewhat lighter color than the rest of that part of the skeleton, an insignificant zigzag line, which sat there like a ring. The assistant nodded and said softly, as though he spoke to me on behalf of Professor Mato, "An old break." I betrayed my ignorance by letting fall unthinkingly, as a matter of fact only to have something to say, to give the gentlemen a selection of my grateful thoughts: "Then this means the description was wrong!" But the considerate professor did not answer me with an insulting laugh. He shook his head slowly and said cordially, while he still looked thoughtful: "I shouldn't go so far as to say that. The break is already very old; the bone was set by a very skillful hand, and the pieces have knitted together very well, thanks also to the victim's strong constitution. He probably had almost no limp at all, and therefore it is possible that no one knew of the injury." In the meantime the assistant had made a little sketch of the piece and had written on it a few careful notes. It seemed to be an important discovery, for Professor Mato stood beside the assistant for a moment and cast a searching and approving glance on the page of his notebook. Then the professor turned to the coffin again and began to remove the leprous crust of crumbling, rust-colored cardboard from the trunk of the corpse with a few flicks of his lancet. The stale jacket fell off in large slabs; the smaller bits, which adhered more firmly, the professor loosened with his fingers, without aversion, while he stood bent over the coffin, investigating. The chest displayed two gaping black cavities, which were covered with a fine black mire. Professor Mato's knife glistened no longer, it was so thickly smeared. The substance into which it sank was less soupy, and as the professor cut deeper and removed the exposed tissue, with gestures as graceful as they were efficient, it seemed as though a good many anatomical parts were still in very good condition. It is almost unbelievable how many layers of tissue there are in a human body. The assistant caused a huge bag to appear out of the black trunk and stood next to Professor Mato. It looked at first glance like an ordinary sack with a strap, but when the assistant had pulled on the strap, the rubber lining, which served to ensure that it was watertight, came into view. Professor Mato cut loose countless tangles of flesh and other anatomica and let them fall into the sack, which the assistant held open for him; after that he also threw the lower jawbone in the sack. I learned that these slices of flesh were under the walls of the lungs, and that in his laboratory, by first boiling them and then examining them microscopically, Professor Mato would be able to make out whether the victim was still breathing or was already dead, thus murdered, when he had come into the water. In case he had still been breathing, the microscope would reveal the existence of little pieces of very tiny aquatic plants in the lung tissues. Then the abdominal cavity came next in order; with a gash of the knife it lay open. I stepped backward a pace on account of the spattering and the oppressive appearance. "Yes," nodded Professor Mato, "nature is indeed tenacious, as you may observe, Mr. Antfield." Indeed, indeed. There, in that monstrous corpse, everything was still wholly recognizable: the white intestines, the butter-yellow, thick-grained stomach fat, the internal genitals, I don't know what else. Apparently not in the state in which they could be met with in a new-born child, but still exceptionally well preserved. Everything floated in a fluid that was colored differently in the various cavities: here yellow, there rose, yonder colorless and almost clear. Professor Mato, with his customary placid efficiency, each time with but a very few movements, mostly gentle, sometimes for a moment more vigorously insistent, removed the various organs, held them out before him in his half-raised arm, at eye level. Sometimes the fluid dripped off them and fell in thick, dull dribbles back into the coffin. The professor let me see the liver, which was black and foul. The kidneys, on the other hand, had certainly remained fine and made me think of large red figs. Professor Mato cut one of these, on the palm of his doubly gloved hand, flat through the middle and remained looking intently at the clear-cut surfaces. Then both pieces were added to the others in the rubber sack. Finally the criminologist shoved the point of his lancet into a rose-colored stripe and followed it up to the top. It looked as though he cut open a sodden reed, entirely crushed and half decayed. "The great artery," he explained as he nodded happily. The victim must indeed have been a healthy man; there was not the slightest trace of arterio-sclerosis to be found—even the assistant looked laudatory. "And the heart?" I whispered. It was no bigger than a child's fist, yellowish brown, shriveled up into itself like a spongy pear—it vanished in its turn into the sack. Professor Mato had still not found anything unusual. He remained for a little while looking pensive, with his arms in front of him, his hands on the edge of the coffin, as though he had a little list before his mind's eye and was crossing off which investigations he had completed, in order to see more clearly what he still had to do. That was at least twenty years ahead of my naïve, scrupulous manner of working, and a person is always inclined to think only of himself. A heroic scientist, such as Professor Mato is, would surely have smiled if he could have read my constricted, clerkly mind. "The back," he said softly. He laid his knife, which had become repulsive because of the filth which adhered to it, down on the table and groped with his two hands firmly in the carrion. He must have strong arms, Professor Mato; you could see that by the manner in which he attempted to turn that heavy skeleton in the coffin that surrounded it, which was like a leaky barge, without jerks or unnecessary movements. It did not go easily. The professor's dry facial color became even darker and slightly clammy, and he had to scrape the corpse's bones. With my usual resignation, although I stood nauseated by the loathesome sight, I made the damned proposal that perhaps I could help him with it. Professor Mato shook his head no, but in a friendly manner, without looking up; the assistant did not move; a prickling hot surge of blood went to my foolish head from embarrassment: how could I have helped, I, without gloves, without apron, and unhandy as I was! There lay the corpse on its left side. But even while Professor Mato turned to his assistant, it began to slide back again in its grease, first slowly and then rapidly. It was as if the cadaver suddenly wanted to lie on its back again. Luckily I did not scream, but I, who had just offered to help, sprang backwards. Professor Mato grabbed hold of the stinking specter with both hands and forced it to lie on its side again. At an invitational wink from the professor I went, not farther over, but to stand next to him again, on the same side of the bloody, muddy tub. That back, that back! That was certainly the most horrible of all the spectacles which I had had to observe that afternoon. *That* was really rotten. Black, full of pale particles like swollen, moldy cardboard, liquid and yet solid, festering and suppurating, with blisters and blains and boils, like leafing bubbles of stench on a morass of ordure, strewn with armies of microscopic bacilli, like so many white worms stretched to little staves and stiffened, and dripping, leaking, with black, red, yellow fluids, foul as half-digested vomit with strings of saliva and a froth of mucus. This time Professor Mato did not insert himself into the examination. One straight stroke of the knife, and the back of Lazarus lay ripped open from top to bottom. Nothing, however, fell off the skeleton, as had occurred with the crumbly cardboard jacket of the trunk in front; it remained tenaciously cleaving fast. The cut, a good centimeter deep, gaped like a longitudinal profile of rose-white alluvium. The professor now carefully scratched on the shoulder blades with his knife; scabby slabs of filth fell splashing into the water at the bottom of the coffin. Just then the point of the lancet displayed a white spot: "Corpse wax," Professor Mato elucidated. I nodded, shuddering. Then, suddenly, the professor and his assistant simultaneously sprang forward, with their faces less than two hands' breadths from the rotting back, and did so although neither wore a mask. Professor Mato had explained to me that this was entirely unnecessary; when a corpse is in so advanced a state of decomposition, there is no danger of sepsis; the decay bacteria are always ordinary saprophytes, with which name, roughly speaking, the beneficial antagonists of the parasites are denoted. Professor Mato pointed, this time with his gloves, to a little spot of skin, more or less clean, on the victim's shoulder. In the middle of it I soon noticed a little round black hole. The professor looked up and evidently sought the police magistrate, who had not yet returned. Then Professor Mato looked at me, who had stepped backwards a little again when he and his assistant had stood so close together over the body, and winked affably at me. "Perhaps a bullet wound," he explained quietly, pointing to the black hole. He asked the assistant for a pincers. A sort of long, rounded pincers made its appearance out of the black trunk; the professor inserted the points in the hole and proceeded to rummage around in the porridge under it, searching carefully. But he apparently was not able to find anything, not even when he went to work on the other side, that is, from the front side of the trunk outwards. He even groped around in the murky tissues with his fingers, gently and slowly, as though he was simultaneously kneading the porridge fine between thumb and index finger—but in vain: there was no (more?) bullet to be found. Professor Mato finally came around to my side again to stand and began very expertly to loosen a fragment of the skin of the back, as large as the palm of your hand and with the black hole, which had now grown somewhat larger, in the middle, and to cut it out squarely. The piece was at least half the thickness of your little finger, very soft, and looked dark brown on the outside and somewhat lighter on the inside. I had never thought that human skin formed such a heavy covering; although the conditions here were naturally not normal, because of the influence of the water and the operation of decay. The specimen disappeared into the rubber sack, and then suddenly the autopsy was over. Professor Mato laid his knife down in the grass by the hedge, before the second bucket, with his strong arms turned the corpse again on its back, and winked at the police magistrate, who had now suddenly popped up, in order to give an appearance of being very industrious, under the overhanging leaves of a willow at the end of a little path. "There is little to be deduced from the investigation," Professor Mato said calmly, without even the least sign of disappointment in his voice; I have repeatedly been able to admire that serenity in real scientists. Even when their investigations reach no conclusions, or when the results do not answer to their expectations—they are seldom perplexed or crushed. They seem to find everything interesting, and even a negative conclusion is a result for them. "I am afraid that the laboratory examination won't yield much either," Professor Mato continued, "but we'll see. The corpse may be reinterred. I won't take the skull with me," he added, still softly. The magistrate thanked the criminologist and gave a signal to the grave-diggers. The coffin was nailed shut in the twinkling of an eye, and two round holes in the head and foot end were plugged with wooden bungs. Afterwards the whole thing was tilted up and let down into the hole with two ropes; and the heavy, healthy, fragrant earth fell, pitying the lamentable remains of what had once been a man. The steeple clock sounded the hour again, but the sound was already less nauseous. Professor Mato took off the gloves he had used, which were saturated with filth from the corpse; I thought that he would throw them away, but the assistant held open a piece of gray paper, on which the professor laid them jauntily, the assistant folded the paper shut and let the packet fall into the notorious sack with the anatomical pieces. In the second bucket, then, the professor washed his rubber gloves clean. The water turned the yellow-rose color of plasma and began to scum over slightly. The gloves were carefully stretched out, inside out; then the coat was untied and finally the rubber under-apron. Professor Mato rolled it all together, the assistant unfolded another gray paper, and this bundle was also stuffed in the sack. In my imagination I saw the chauffeur open the package the day after tomorrow or Monday at the latest in order to cook everything or to disinfect it in an antiseptic bath. My spirit was tormented by the disproportion between the short time in which everything had become hopelessly besmirched here and the long hours of labor that would be needed to get it clean again. The assistant had already packed in the knife and tongs; the sack vanished into the black trunk, and the professor now stood over the third bucket, washing his hands, slowly and carefully, but still not at all so hard and long as I had expected, and only once, with a fresh bit of toilet soap that had been laid down in the grass by the hedge on an ironed bathtowel. Professor Mato rolled down his sleeves again, buttoned his cuffs, took his coat off the hedge, and put it back on. "Job done," the assistant smiled at me. I walked away with him, after Professor Mato and the magistrate, yet without looking at them. The assistant carried the black trunk; I didn't want to have any more to do with it if I could help it. As a matter of fact, on the arm of this stalwart scholar, the trunk looked as light as if it were empty. The other men waited by the car: the deputy marshal, the clerk of the court, and the cheerful mayor. Professor Mato was now invited to the town hall for a few formalities. I said that I would remain by the car while he was gone. The assistant stuffed the trunk in the back seat and walked to the town hall with the little group. The two state policemen still, or again, stood at the gate. I saw the mayor walk up the sunny little street with his guests and disappear into a small building. Just across from the entrance to the churchyard, on the corner of the lane, there was a café. An opulent waitress was looking out of the upstairs window, leaning on the round, rosy elbows of her arms, bare to the shoulders. She seemed to be interested in the sky. One of the policemen seemed to be telling a joke, for the other stood laughing hahaha. When I attempted to walk past them, they stopped me. "There is something stuck to your shoe, sir." I started; the voice sounded serious. It was as if a flash of crackling lightning had shot from my brain, along my backbone, to the soles of my shoes. I knew at once what it was. A piece of intestine from the corpse! A black remnant, striped with rose and white; a horrible shred, tenacious and durable. I had the feeling that all my blood began to flow in the opposite direction; I glowed with loathing and nearly howled: that such a thing should happen to me, *me!* Desperately I kicked the wretched thing away and went to scrape the hollow between sole and heel clean on the edge of the sidewalk. The policemen laughed again, but not openly, as it seemed to me. Ordinary people are more sensitive than intellectuals to the transcendental powers which direct our fates, to the mysteries which exist before and after this life, and to the enigmatic hints of these which are given us sometimes, perhaps continuously, in the course of our existence, and which they notice and understand better than those trained in "logic"—that is, in hyper-worldly thinking. That piece of intestine must have fallen out of the coffin during Professor Mato's labors, apparently during the difficult turning of the cadaver on its side, without our, without my, having paid any attention to it. And I, just I, had had to step on it! What might that hideous sign mean as omen? I could not then understand it or foresee it. I could only fear, as I had not done all that afternoon and for that matter all my life long, and dread the worst. And that I was not the only one at least to feel the same and to dread it is indeed shown by the unaccustomed behavior of the policemen, their unnatural smiles, which attempted to take the incident as droll, and also to make it pass for such, but which in fact stimulated inward shuddering and betrayed human compassion. I walked hastily into the café. A little girl of thirteen or fourteen years, barefoot, with untidy blonde hair but with a roguish nose, came out of the kitchen; she didn't ask me anything but seemed to wait for my order with a mischievous little laugh. I vacillated. I wanted to let the child alone, but it was stronger than I was, decidedly I needed something hearty: I asked for a large gin, a double gin—"just put it in a beer glass," I laughed unconvincingly. The child laughed convincingly and with the expertness of a professional bartender poured a beer glass three-fourths full of gin. "Is that enough?" she asked mischievously. "When," I laughed back and drank. I also bought a package of bitter cigarettes; my old one was almost empty. Apparently I drank the explosive liquid too quickly on an empty stomach. I had not been used to taking anything afternoons because of my excitement about what might happen next; together with the heat and the terror I had endured, which had emptied me completely, the alcohol actually did operate in me like firewater. I paid with a banknote and said that that was correct. I wobbled slightly when I started to walk outside again, but the policemen did not let up on me; they still stood there growling. Or rather, they acted as if they told stories all the time, perhaps in connection with the buxom farm girl with her naked arms in the upstairs window of the café, surely the mother of the free-pouring little blonde barmaid who had served me. Perhaps they were trying to find the way to attract the eye of this rural nymph, although she remained staring adamantly at a point in the sky, above and behind the churchyard. But, however short a time it might have lasted, it had not eluded me that her eyes, very very briefly, when I came out of the café, had gone to my shoes, rapidly and stealthily, and as if against her will, and that she, while she did all this, for one indivisible moment had ceased to smile. I went to sit and smoke on the runningboard of the car, without a thought in my mind but with a longing eye in the direction of the town hall in the lane. I do not know how long it was before the group finally came into view again. I sprang up at once and went behind the car to where the spare tire was kept. Everything that was oppressing me was, I saw, lying against it. The men took leave of each other. The pompous mayor still stood on the threshold of his little building, apparently sorry that this intellectual investigation was now finished. The police magistrate, the deputy marshal, and the clerk of the court walked slowly down the street, away from us, while Professor Mato and the assistant came back to the car. When they stood before me, I thought I realized that they also had needed a little pick-me-up; it gave me a more peaceful feeling concerning their eventual judgment of my own action, although I could not suggest that the learned autopsist would ever survive anything so excessive as I had just done. His brown eyes looked, indeed, even brighter and clearer than ever. The assistant also looked even a touch redder and fleshier than in the beginning of the afternoon. Suddenly the chauffeur came out of the church, looking somewhat odd and creepy, although I do not know precisely why. Had he sought protection there against the investigation which went on in the charnel house, with the farm-girl siren in the bedroom window? You see what evil gin-thoughts drifted through me. Professor Mato imparted to me in a friendly but bored manner that a telegram for him had arrived at the town hall from a colleague at A—, Professor Zijsma, who had heard of his coming to D— and suggested that they meet each other that afternoon or everning at H—, the large city between D— and A—, where they would eventually stay the night. The professor thought that he could hardly decline that friendly offer; his assistant was in fact very eager to make the acquaintance in person of his celebrated foreign colleague. Professor Mato apologized that he would thus have to leave me behind at D— without transportation, the more so since, as he had been informed by the mayor, there were no more trains leaving D— today by which I could return. It would be a pleasant solution if I would accompany them to H—; then we could return home together in the car tomorrow. Tomorrow was Sunday. The professor and the assistant would notify their wives by telegraph from H—, as I could do also. Without consideration I accepted. I was under the influence of the beer glass of alcohol and almost did not dare speak so as not to betray myself. Therefore, without hesitation, I then nodded that fateful "yes," simply from shame. Although what had happened had in fact so shattered my soul that my strength of intellect and my will power, even without alcohol, were in not much more than a condition of passivity. Thus everything happened together: one innocent circumstance after another trapped me, a poor, volitionless, unconscious plaything, in the path of my corruption, because now it had to be. It was in the month before that in which my birthday fell. I don't know much about astrology; but in heavenly space my constellation was approaching; perhaps in the sign of Virgo, driven by the last decree of my predestined fate, it was accelerated toward its realization. We sat in the car again, going just as fast as in the afternoon, perhaps even faster; the sun blazed just as volcanically; and the landscape was also to a large extent the same as when we had come: landscapes along freeways always and all ways greatly resemble each other. The roof of the car glowed above my head. I perspired excessively and tried in vain to cool myself in the air from the wind wing. Professor Mato and the assistant were involved in an expert conversation. I held my mouth half open, as inconspicuously as possible, I thought, and my head turned a little away, so as to let the wind play through my nose and pharynx in order to rinse them and take away the smell of alcohol, together with another, more terrible odor. The professor and his assistant seemed to have noticed my gesture and to have guessed at one of the reasons for it. "Are you still smelling the corpse?" the assistant asked, smiling. Yes, I nodded, but I did not dare say anything about my shoe sole. "It used to be that way with me," he added cordially, "but after a little while you get so you don't smell anything at all any more." Then Professor Mato wanted to know whether the afternoon hadn't turned out rather better than I had expected; the case couldn't, it was true, be called very unusual, but I had still had a first look at what an autopsy was. I assured him that I had found it terribly educational and was very grateful to him for having wanted to ask me. He smiled also while he asked whether it had not been too terrible. "Rather," I said hesitantly. "You get used to that too," the professor said with his amiable earnestness; "at first, naturally, everything seems very bad, because then you're still looking at it with a literary or philosophical eye; that is to say, because you are still thinking too much about the person that the corpse had once been, and about yourself, knowing that sooner or later you too will have to go the way of all transitory matter. But later, and even comparatively rapidly, you go over to a clearer knowledge, and then finally you don't find anything gruesome about it. As a matter of fact, then you even come to see the beauty of it, in its way. Then a wound isn't a mutilation any more, but a sort of peephole into a delightfully ingenious piece of construction. Something that at first was a bloody lump, that the layman calls by the butcher's word, 'flesh'—which is also the flesh of the novelists, the poets, and the pulpit—becomes tissues, muscles, sinews, all kinds of well built, organized forms of living matter, each with its own existence, with a personal aspect and almost, I'd say, an individual soul, and each more remarkable than the other. And the 'death' of all that is just a crude word for a wonderfully fine and multiform phenomenon, because death is only a postponement of life to new forms of life. 'Decomposition,' 'decay'—that is the wonderful world of bacteriological life and the perhaps even more mysterious one of chemical life. You see, there is the whole difference between the expression 'stink' and the concept 'smell of H_2S.' And I don't mean that it's only a question of words." I nodded. I thought I was able to understand it, although I could not accept it so sympathetically then as I do now. My acquaintance with this scientific world which had just been exposed to me by the knife was recent, and then it had all happened so suddenly and violently. I wasn't a young student any more, with an incalculable life ahead of me, so that death, impermanence, decay, did not still seem to me merely improbable curiosities. Professor Mato and the assistant were in that enviable time of life when they had received this worldly knowledge, and they had many happy years available to them to learn to think "scientifically" and to learn to feel that way gradually. When I raised this point without any preparation, because I was still not wholly free from the influence of drink, the conversation turned to detective-story matters, through my questioning the professor about his personal conviction or suspicions concerning whether or not the case that he had examined this afternoon was homicide. He answered thoughtfully that it was difficult to make out. He thought it somewhat suspicious that the family and the nun were so unprecedentedly well informed on the victim's teeth, that not one was broken or filled with lead. Such things the family did not usually know with so much certainty; would I, for instance, be able to fill out a chart properly with the tooth formula of even my own wife? No, probably not, I confessed, shaking my head. Moreover, that large sum of money which the bank messenger was carrying—where did that come in? Suppose that *he* had embezzled it; then the family's attitude would become somewhat more comprehensible; rather a disappearance than bankruptcy or a swindle and bringing scandal to all who bore his name. The missing foot, which must be a club foot but which might not be, and for which a search could be made thereabouts, also sounded suspicious. The constable who had discovered the corpse after it had been washed ashore had probably let himself be bribed to remove the annoying corpse from the little charnel house on a dark evening before its burial. The foot, the club foot, could also have remained in the water of itself, naturally. It was possible that the drowned person had got stuck somewhere or had knocked against the keel of a boat, by which that part of the body had been torn away. "And the hole in the back?" I asked. Professor Mato was not wholly sure that it was a bullet wound. It could also be a bruise, sustained when the body floated in the water and had rubbed against the pier; a bruise caused, for instance, by a large spike; or when the drowned body was stranded on the paved bank where we had walked that afternoon; or even by the coffin. I thought that the microscopic examination of the skin sometimes could serve to identify a bullet wound by establishing the presence of traces of gunpowder, invisible to the naked eye; had Professor Mato cut out that little patch of skin and put it in the rubber sack for that reason? Of course, but he seriously doubted whether there was still anything to be identified with any probability; the state of decay was, as he said, too far advanced. From there the conversation went on about bullet wounds and bullets. I learned to my amazement that to be fatal on contact a shot in the region of the heart must have a caliber of at least 9 mm. Naturally the distance from which it is fired plays an important rôle here; but with a well aimed, forceful shot, as when the weapon is held against the body, as must occur in the case of a suicide, this rule bears no exceptions. The hole bored by the bullet in a heart wound is then so large that the cavity which surrounds our muscle of life fills with blood immediately, and in this the heart dies a sort of death by suffocation, what the German criminologists call "die Herzenstamponade." The victim lives at the most only a few minutes, but numbed by the blow, completely without consciousness. While a caliber of 7.65, for example, causes a much narrower opening, which is almost completely closed by each muscular contraction of the heart, so that the blood flows but slowly. The person who is shot is usually still conscious quite a while and retains his power of movement. He can revenge himself on whoever has waylaid him, or he can walk away, even as far as fifty meters, even clamber to the top of a wall, and impart the name of the assailant or give his personal description before crashing down. And when it is not the heart that is struck but a neighboring organ, death often occurs still later, sometimes only after days, and is then almost always the result of the previous loss of blood and inflammation of the lungs. That was indeed somewhat less romantic than in books and films, where the villains are at once and for all eternity brought low by a pellet from a little pistol carried in a lady's handbag. The professor found only the writings of Conan Doyle as authentic as they were entertaining. At that the assistant, turning again half-way to us, called up the example of I forget what country, which once lost an important war, against all expectations, only because the caliber of its soldiers' guns was too small. Its army was splendidly equipped and also fought excellently, but . . . the enemy still had the strength to knock down the opponent in return. And, the assistant added, smiling, the huge dimensions of cowboy guns or of American police revolvers, not only in the films but even in reality, because lighter calibers were often evidently used in the fights with Indians or Negroes, gave only a very slightly higher capacity for doing damage than blanks. I said something in admiration of the tenacity of the human constitution but still wanted to know whether the brain did not form material susceptible to death. Then it appeared that I had forgotten myself here also, and worse, for what the professor had said about the body applied equally to the head, and possibly in an even less romantic manner. Naturally, with a heavy caliber, shot from nearby and right into the brain, the irreparable immediately followed. But Professor Mato had met with countless other cases in which the victim had merely lost consciousness and finally succumbed only after the passage of days in the most wretched circumstances. Since the bullet had surely damaged the center of the brain, the customary awareness of what was going on outside and of the direction of life was impaired: when something was given him to drink, he swallowed wrong, the water did not come into the gullet but directly into the windpipe and lungs, or perhaps he swallowed his own vomit again, so that often the chance of poisoning occurred. And therefore the person shot through the head finally died in a pitiful manner, by suffocation or pneumonia. "Yes, nature is indeed tenacious," the professor concluded again . . . "and yet at the same time so frail," I completed his thought under my breath. Thereafter both scholars preserved the silence. Perhaps because of the glass of strong drink, the ride seemed shorter to me, although the distance from D— to H— is really longer than the first part of our journey, to D—. The sun had still not set but had begun to shine more softly when we arrived in H—. Professor Mato looked in his notebook and commanded the chauffeur: "Hôtel du Lion d'Or," he said, "near the marketplace, on a canal." The chauffeur nodded and stopped. He stuck his head out the window and asked a passerby the way to the Hôtel du Lion d'Or. The one he spoke to directed us, straight ahead and then turn right. A few hundred meters farther on we reached the marketplace. There was the canal, with beautiful gold-and-green plane trees in the evening sun. And on the corner rose a hotel, a handsome, spacious, and tall building of an international type. Surely it must contain many rooms, the upper windows of which shone beautifully, while through the open windows we could see that the breezes were billowing curtains of warm, rich materials. The high façade was whitewashed but covered with a soft patina by the years; the steps must have been recently painted, just like the gilded writing in flaming, buoyantly cut black-letter type:

HÔTEL DU LION D'OR

Everything gave the whole an appearance as pleasant as it was intended to be; modern, but well bred and with tradition. And so were the few people who sat on the sidewalk, raised with wood, at little round lacquered tables on chromium legs, enjoying refreshments in new wicker chairs under colored umbrellas. The canal, with its quiet green plane trees, ran along the side of the hôtel, where, on the corner, as was shown us, the only entrance for travelers was to be found. We proceeded at once to the desk in order to send telegrams. Professor Zijsma, Professor Mato's colleague, had not yet arrived. Thus we could go to our rooms for a while so as to refresh ourselves; dinner, we understood, would not be served for a little while. The professor and the assistant were shown their room first; the bell-boy walked on a little farther with me. My room was at the end of the corridor, on the same floor. The boy held the door open for me; I thanked him and went in. I was really so filled with other things that I did not notice then much more of the room than the open window, the golden glow of the setting sun in the panes, and the soft waving of the plane trees outside along the canal. As soon as the bell-boy had gone and the hallway was, I thought, empty again, I also left the room, swiftly. I had surely not gone in more than one step; I did not want to contaminate it for the whole night with my horrible shoe sole. I walked downstairs and washed my hands several times in the men's room, with much soap. After that I wanted to go buy a few pairs of new shoes. In the lounge it was becoming all dusky; a knight in uniform snapped on the soft lights under the shades of the lamps. But outside, in the twilight, I suddenly felt so languid, dead tired, that I had to sit on one of the wicker chairs in front of the hotel, on the terrace with the umbrellas. The umbrellas were not necessary any more. The sun, a dying bitter orange, still bathed the upper façade of the luxurious building, but the steps were sunk in the shade of evening. There weren't any more people; mealtime was drawing near. I sat in a little corner close to the glass wall along the side; but I could still feel a caressing breeze, which probably came from the canal. The plane trees, already darker, rustled. I ordered coffee. I wanted to go buy the shoes at once, because the stores would surely soon close; I only hoped that I could still find one open—it was, after all, Saturday evening. I drank my coffee hot and was so soon refreshed that the alkaloid must become steadily more operative at high temperatures: so that it dispelled my weariness and the last of my alcoholic fog all the better. But I must have fallen asleep then —a dreamless sleep for once. When I awoke with a start, the sun had completely disappeared. Surely it was dinner time now.

I shivered. Had I caught cold? No, it was my soul, which must have had a presentiment then of what was now at last finally going to happen, of the delicious and so miserably inescapable conclusion to the impossible history of ten years in the life of an obscure man. I called the waiter, paid my check, and walked shivering back into the hôtel entrance. At the same moment someone descended the broad stairway, with wrought iron banisters and thick carpet, to the lounge, someone half in the dusk and half in the muffled glow of the floor-lamps, a woman in a pale green evening gown, with bare shoulders and arms, in a tepid, heavy, yet strangely moving and sharply stimulating cloud of powder and perfume, with the quiet, silvery rattle of bracelets and a blinding golden fringe of hair—Fran, *Fran,* FRAN! I stood thunderstruck, stunned, transfixed, a rooted block of trembling stone. She looked so rich, so glorious there; and I so fishy, the down-and-outer! I still always wore my poor hair short, now I had it shaved shorter than ever, my "crown"—the ironic word—so as to conceal how bald my crown had become. But the more closely to the skin you have your hair taken away, the clearer it becomes when you have not been to the barber for a little while. And for a long time I had not taken care of my appearance with the concern that I used to expend on my exterior in my youth. The laborious work of my head and the grief of my soul demanded all of me; the ropelashes of daily life had finally broken my pride; I did not still feel entitled to be flirtatious, and I neglected myself, like a fighter who lacks time and strength, because of circumstances, and like a defeated one, out of humility. Moreover, because, with my modest situation and the expenses which Corra and Doos and San needed or deserved—for they, so healthy and handsome, were worth at least a certain small extra expense—I could not afford as many visits to the barber as I should have liked. Only once a month, sometimes only every two months, was I able to sit in the chair where I had sought my innocent pleasures so often, before the spacious mirror, with the colored flasks on the little white porcelain rack, wrapped in the wide white mantle, allowing myself to be worked on by a caressing hand. And now naturally, with my usual adversity, it occurred that I had not had my hair cut for a long time, so that I must have looked awfully untidy, with a fleecy coconut beard on my bald cranium, above my ears and on my neck. In passing, my appearance must indeed have produced the impression that I was old in body and stale in visage as in vesture. True, I was still big and strong, but wasted, with something stiff between my shoulder blades from the bent posture in which I had sat for so many days and nights, year after year, over my recalcitrant work, and which I had even accepted outside it, humbly, in order to conceal my shame from people, in order to diminish my body, which was too big in proportion to my ability, and to cause them, as well as that Lord who is equally—inconceivable paradox!—my Creator and my Judge, to forgive my continuing inadequacy. And grooves and pits had appeared in my countenance, at my temples and under my eyes, and my color was a mixture of excited spots with the gray of fatigue and exhaustion. God, how could I stand to think of myself! Still, I saw that everything was the same with her, everything, and surveyed her eagerly and respectfully. She was simply clad, but it surely must have been expensive material, her pale green gown. The same rich, noble sobriety as Francina vander Zwalm—and as Judge Brantink—I thought hastily. Just as before, around her wrist, on the arm which was hanging down, pressed against her pale green clothing, I clearly saw her golden bracelet glistening again, but this was no girl's jewelry of silver—now it was a golden armband, gold as pale and warm as her "suicide" hair, which must be a term from an American movie which I heard from the mouth of Doos, who found it amusing; but I, who tried to laugh with him, I experienced that word as a stab of cruel beauty. Even her body itself was no longer that of a child, but rich and full. She had wonderfully beautiful breasts, with a soft groove between them, the beginning of which was just visible above the brim of her gown; and her arms, too, her light-brown tinted arms, were luxuriously fleshed. Her shoulders looked strong, without having completely lost their earlier soft rounding, and her neck also offered a touching view of strength and delicate femininity. However, I could not see her hands: one, on the arm which was hanging down, pressed against her side and was hidden by creases of her gown, while I still held the other clasped in mine. I was well aware that *she* already no longer gripped my hand, but still I could not turn her loose. Therefore I could not see whether that hand had kept its little, dramatic knot of vein. But of course it must have, for however beautifully her throat had been sculptured, even there, in its rich flesh, the play of muscles could be marked, with a light, convulsive movement, and a vein throbbed softly. How giddily sweet was the fact of that concealed, intimate, passionate pulsing, in an animal tissue that would otherwise appear almost too abundant, under the cool bloom of a maidenly skin. But equally I saw her eyes. What was their first expression? I am still asking myself that. But they were a deep blue, full of blinking mystery. Astonishment? Hasty searching in her soul, under old, untidy memories, before remembering me? Surprise? A little fright? But why afraid? I, who had never, never ever, told her? There was still, just the same, or for that reason, a little laugh on her blood-red lips. Those lips were now very certainly painted, as for that matter her whole white face was, about which a touching irresolution could now no longer exist as it had for ten years. But that did not annoy me any more. Just as previously arose from that doubt, now from this certainty arose an equally great, a now perhaps even more vehement temptation. Her eyelids were now no longer ivory colored but painted blue, aquamarine mixed with the silver of shells. She still had the dimples in her cheeks, too, but they were no longer childish little angelic paganisms, rather soft stigmata, silent, tender wound-symbols of the same good-hearted affection which I had dreamed of being able to read from that sinew and that tiny arch in her neck. God! Just for one moment then I took the glance of those eyes in mine; then with a short jerk, she let her head nod foward the least little bit. The schoolgirl! the schoolchild! it screamed through me like a hurricane of golddust and heavy gray clouds along a line of telephone wire in an autumn storm. Taller than she, I looked down then for the space of a breath on the crown of her head; which seemed suddenly to become golden in the circle of light from the floorlamps. A wonderful part ran horizontally, from left to right, through her coiffure, which must have been parallel to the sweeping of hair from her bangs to her forehead. I did not spend any time, however, in unraveling the puzzle of that touching, almost foreign, transverse midway stripe, which certainly was seldom noticed—she raised her head again. She still wore her bangs. Was her hair dyed now, too? It was even more blinding than ten years ago; nevertheless, there had been ample time to make it so in my intense memory. I had kept it in my memory as pale gold, perhaps on account of the fog of a hazy recollection. But now it was beaming matchlessly, at the same time lighter and more full of light, as if of an inexpressibly soft but inextinguishably beaten metal. Were those darker places, those stolen, fiery, glowing spaces, introduced into it deliberately? Perhaps she was now looking at me as well. But I could not catch her glance. Her eyelids, with their silver-blue shadow, and the inky black rays of her eyelashes, which were stiff and had been spread apart with cosmetics into a taut network, barred me from entry. Through the pomade her eyelashes looked as though they cleaved to each other by being accustomed to weep. But that cleaving was so regular, with such well spaced, beautifully ordered, balanced distances, that it must have been a work of art, and what artful work! I even saw her teeth, in a broader laugh, or rather in a rounder little laugh. It looked as though even her lips were somewhat stiff from the paint, and for that reason she could laugh only in the painful shape of a cramped heart. Oh, those sparkling teeth, so strongly set together, with their milk-blue appearance against the young, salmon-colored rose of the gums! I still see them as they were then, and I should not think of them, I should not, my spirit is apparently not equal to it, for it must have been changed, it is a violation of the memory of so sweet, so dear and gentle a departed one, how those teeth, whenever I dare to think back on them, bite me and wildly tear the stuff of my soul. Her laugh, her little laugh, was it—oh, so completely—mocking? I had finally loosed her hand. Both her arms now hung at her sides, as if they were hiding there, in the happy folds of her sea-green gown, something shameful, or, for me, the intruder who stayed, something too precious. What, if that actually were true, could they want to withhold from the eye of an unfortunate beggar who never, never could be intimate with her? The now passionate abode of a gloriously human knot of vein? The cruelly beautiful nails, which had surely been filed long and sharp, and lacquered blood-red or varnished with amaranth, and sticking out of the white roses of her flesh like ten dagger points from a Mater Dolorosa heart? Or her rings, hard and frivolous pieces of ostentation, perhaps, with the fiery shame, not to be extinguished, of so many adventurous memories which contrasted all too painfully with the shabby schoolgirl of childhood days? Or possibly only one ring, one small, flat tubelet of dull blond metal, around the usual finger, and therefore, forever, around this strange heart and around that whose body, given away to a single chosen one? Oh, that band, that one ring she was surely not wearing now. Someone like her must naturally have been asked often by enough claimants who had something to offer, and why should they always have been refused, in the supposition that she had said "no" at least once, and although the exchange was still, then, so unequal; although there could never be found a common measure for these two commodities, so mutually different as heaven and earth themselves? No one, in fine, is in a position to see himself, for to do so he would have to step out of his soul, to which the substituted trick of looking in a mirror, even a Venetian one, is not equivalent. So that, indeed, no person, just as little as even the most beautiful flower, will ever be conscious even of the wonder of his own consciousness. Perhaps he feels that she and he, an ordinary obedient earthly stalk, both drink their sap from the same muddy ground along his thirsty roots. Why should that flower refuse the hairy, grasping hand which longs to pluck her? Doesn't she think the hand is friendly, related, made of the same stuff, and doesn't he promise to raise her above her grubby sisters and let her drink sparkling water in a flamboyant vase until her early or late death? Perhaps only to the poet, like a third person placed between the two of them, with the flower in one eye and the hand in the other, is the sad inequality, the tragic mismatching, visible; perhaps she herself exists only for the destruction of his soul, and truly it is as beneficial to the flower as to him for her to leap from behind her shield and even to extend the hand of charity, and so from the third suddenly to go to the second. Although I still believe that, and although during his whole absurd and futile existence nothing except a hopeless avalanche of words has flowed from his stuttering lips or from the bleeding veins of his pen, there really must be such a poet "by the grace of God." Forgive me, Lord, for the conceitedness of this self-abasement, for it is alleged that the kernel is still formed from human arrogance, similarly as for all *les miserables;* but, when Thou hast ordered whatsoever is good and necessary, Thou hast still made me want to cross my stumbling path of life with that of Fran again, and there, in that foreign, dark and brilliant luxury hotel, beneath a wrought-iron balustrade, in my week-day clerical togs, embarrassed by my polluted shoes, I stood on a little throw rug laid on the thick, endless carpeting of the hallway, as if on a humble atoll of exile in a sea of luxury inaccessible to me from other climes, to be confronted with a schoolgirl who had wholly outgrown me, who had once been my student, but for whom I had never been of any account, even as teacher. That was the way I felt then, like the poet, the third who does not wish to become a second, torn between the flower and a pale gold tubelet which I cannot see but with which a hairy hand surrounds beauty in exchange for such a vase-like choice of attire and for the sparkling water of seas of luxury, the international hotels springing up at their seaweed-rustling shores. And the purchase must have been concluded long ago, to arrange that trap for the noble, almost negligent ease and the scattered looseness to which she, Fran, had come, with her one hand like a slow white bird soaring above the wrought-iron railing, without touching it, and between the double, rising hedge of veiled lanterns. What had I said to greet her? "Fran . . . *Fran* . . . Frannie!" I had stammered, partly to her and the rest apparently stifled inside myself. And now I had to speak again, although at the most only a few seconds had elapsed. But I have never, in a group or on the other hand even when alone, had to maintain a longer silence. I have never felt in myself the right or the daring to do as those eminent men who even know how to make conversation with undertakers, whom they undertake calmly and whose reactions they laughingly describe with gestures. I have on the contrary even considered it my obscure plight to pay the costs of conversation, as it is called in French with a very sober but painfully just expression; for often in my life, now so little social, there has come to me the same, perhaps naïve feeling of being guilty of something, three or four times, of paying for someone's entertainment who has scarcely thanked me and has never repeated it to me. Corra's realism and my later habit of staying at home have in time reduced these occurrences a little, but still, in the days before the wretched events which I shall have to tell at the end of my confession, I remember clearly having my streetcar ticket punched by an official who happened to stand there beside me on the platform. His income was almost three times as high as mine, but just because of my lower position he seemed to find my affability just as obligatory as I did. What must I, what could I, and what might I say to Fran now? Hastily I asked, "I may still call you Fran, mayn't I, Miss Veenman?" That "Miss" slipped out because of the habit of those few months, ten long years ago, but still stamped so firmly on my soul! I did not find time to make an excuse for having called her "Miss" now, for it was more urgent to add something to my question about that so dearly beloved and tender nickname with which I had addressed her, which still had some importance for me but which she possibly found foolish. She no longer remembered, her little friends were always committed to calling her "Fra," after the second syllable of her beautiful, old-fashioned first name, while "Fran" had been *my* secret name for her! and why? Well, because of the golden fringe of her bangs . . . and frou-frou! . . . Because of the sound, and because of the color, and by way of wordplay. It must indeed seem extremely confused; I could not say everything I must and wished to impart to her, and did it, too, heels and heart over head, while almost in the same moment she answered my question, whether I might still speak of her thus: "Of course, Mr. Antfield, naturally." But brusquely and yet with an eternal softness, for what I made was almost an entreaty, interrupting myself and her: "Govert, Godfried, please! we're—we were—friends?" She laughed again; did she laugh mockingly? "Now that sounds nicer," she said, "don't you think so? Not so—restless." God, that *she* had to say that now! No one else had ever done it before her, maybe no one, even Corra, had ever even thought of that possible pun on my name, of that dreary witticism on that fate over which I had myself so often . . . ranted: *Antfield* *, the ant-like unrest that had devoured my soul and my whole being, and the disconsolate field which had made what my whole life had been—and that to somebody who had to be called Godfried, Godfried, the freed of God! Oh, Fran, Frannie, that *you* were the first of my fellow men to utter that to me. I still weep whenever I think of it. Yes, you said it laughing, but that was perhaps only a pretense—wasn't it?—a form of politeness; how could you have been able to say it to me otherwise, in the fleeting moment of that chance meeting, when we sent each other a greeting by light, like two cruising ships in the night—without that light, without that laugh, without that formal pretense, it would all have been impossible, wouldn't it? Then suddenly there was a gentleman standing beside her. I had not seen him coming. He must have come down the stairs too. A gentleman of an international type, dark, well dressed, sporty

* Translator's note: *Antfield* is a literal translation of the Flemish *Miereveld.*

and at the same time urbane. He had frizzy, very heavily pomaded hair, an olive-colored complexion, and a movie moustache. There was an inexpressibly Israelitish cast to his appearance. He must have been nearly ten years older than I, twenty years older than Fran, and yet I felt myself, with miserable clarity, the most elderly there. He looked well next to Fran, I will admit that, while I made not much more than a discord by her. His whole expression must have appeared friendly to everyone, but I, I felt myself overwhelmed by his height. He seemed supercilious, so supercilious, to me. He remained standing very close to Fran, and she had turned half toward him, half away from me. Otherwise there was nothing changed in her external appearance. For that matter, what was there in the coming of this man which must change anything in an expression which had been only barely friendly to me? Thus he looked, her man, elegant and fortunate, indeed, certainly with a car, jewels, and a luxurious life in his one hand, as compensation for the other, with hairy, grasping fingers, in which she, in ratification of the sale, had laid her shimmering white, dramatically veined, but not in the least hesitant hand. "Rouben Vaclav," she said, and then followed something about impresarios, or managers, I know. Vaclav merely inclined his stiff neck a little—a nod of barely a centimeter. Then she introduced me to him as her old teacher, "Mr. Antfield." She pronounced that "Mr." almost with emphasis, it seemed to me. Was that innocent friendliness? The idea that she should have received just from my inglorious professional decline, even from the most inconsiderable height, naturally contained an obvious absurdity. Was Vaclav now laughing softly, scoffing, in his conceited little moustache? "Honored," he said, almost without moving his lips, but otherwise irreproachably and by no means in a foreign accent. The three of us stood there; suddenly I saw it as if with the eye of a fourth, how we stood there, both of them as if out of a movie, and I the clerk who had been "Mr." once. How insane! While I stood there surveying us, I was made to think of a book by Julien Benda: *La trahison des clercs,* and that it should have been called the other way round: *La trahison des maîtres.* But out of what need am I noting all this down here? I must be like a sickly child who sings a horrible song of longing. And perhaps that is partly true. But understand me, reader, try to understand me. I am summoning all this up before my mind and in my soul for the last time. As I am writing it down, I am taking farewell of it forever, as I promised the director to do earlier—and no matter how much a pity it is, how unnecessarily tangled it is too, and how terrible it will be in the ending, still it is my life, everything that I have set down, and that I have loved so much, so much! We did not speak. I stood, trying to find words, but they scrutinized me quietly. Were they laughing, or weren't they? Sometimes that is hard to make out on a whitened face, and an olive-colored, bluish, shaved and powdered man's face with a movie moustache cannot be read any better than a masked one. It was my turn to say something again, I, the lesser one. I brought out something confusedly about a post-mortem, hastily because I tried to tell everything in the hope of being able to hold them with at least something, and awkwardly as I appeared to myself at that moment because it was nearly the dinner hour, the luxurious milieu, and especially the subject that I was standing there imparting, unasked, which obviously was completely improper, because of which I had awakened my robot for the nth time in my life. Fortunately a bellboy hopped past then and saved me with the proclamation: "Dinner, ladies and gentlemen, dinner!" He almost sang it, the lad, though he surely could not have been instructed to do so but was a self-taught announcer. In distinguished hotels it must be almost rude to break off conversations among guests, and apparently because of such a brutality more than one wretch of the hotel staff had been shown the eternal revolving door. The guests themselves knew perfectly well when they had to eat, and in fact there could be no question of "have to" in their level of social pre-eminence. I felt compassion for that frisky youngster with his red-and-gold livery, who with a flick of Mr. Vaclav's hairy little finger, on which there was a thick ring with a heavy, ominously glittering stone, could be pitched into the wide world and the descending night; but at the same time I was sore at the jerk because he intervened between Fran and me, Fran, whom I should certainly never see again, because fate is not so kind as to repeat herself with such wonderful *wiedersehens,* and it would be many times ten years that would elapse before the Great Master would perhaps trouble himself over the least of His clerks. Still, that cruel little squirt was a lifesaver. I became silent at once about the autopsy; she did not ask about the result—perhaps she hadn't even been listening—and then I stammered only, I the first again: "Excuse me." Twice I said, "Excuse me," and pressed my side, away! although I did not by any means stand in the doorway to the dining room. Excuse me, rich, healthy, happy man—and excuse me, my Frannie of days of yore and from never more! They nodded, he, again, scarcely a few centimeters, with his fleshy, stiff neck, and then she, this time *not* like a schoolgirl, but with a friendly shake of her golden curls, which if they had actually been of metal, would surely have jingled in lively fashion. She seemed also to give me a fleeting wink with her eyelid, but how could I know whether that wasn't because of the fitful, complicated illumination of the floorlamps? Perhaps they had even been shoved then by somebody's foot, or even moved with the upper part of the body—that would have been enough to discompose the faint circle of light and to make it flicker. But at the same time she said, and this can never be taken away from me—so ordinarily that it sounded soft, but precisely because it was so very soft, it could not have disturbed me more deeply if, instead of having lisped those three words, so completely incalculable to the ear, she had imprinted the ten glowing red dagger points of her lacquered nails in my soul—"See you later," she said then. That was all. There were no handshakes. They walked into the dining room. I breathed deep, deep breaths. "See you later!" What might that mean, what *could* that mean? A little civility, a friendly stop-gap? Through a new cloud of intoxication, this time no longer to be blamed on alcohol, I trod in turn into the dining room, where I was introduced to Professor Zijsma, who was already seated and rose before me. He looked like a very simple but very learned man, with a fatherly beard and glasses that twinkled with cleverness. He shook my hand cordially, holding it firmly and warmly while his glance descended as though into my soul. I had made the gentlemen wait. Dizzy, seething with all the alternating currents of joy and misery which that strange day had awakened in me, more violently than ever, I meekly asked the gentlemen to excuse me. They only smiled, with complete amiability, and all the more delightfully because that smile from them was just as pure as what I sincerely felt for them. But they were scientists, scholars, with understandings and hearts full of heavenly calm and brightness. They remained smiling, so that *I* thought it was necessary to set the conversation going again. I stammered something hastily about an old student I had met accidentally after many, many years. "Oh," said the professor with the white beard, "I didn't know you also used to give lessons in a drama school, or a music school!" I answered confusedly that indeed I had never done so. "But the lady you were talking with in the lobby, I suppose she's your old student, isn't she Franny Veen?" the old gentleman asked, with a sort of scientific persistence, while he looked at me again with fatherly examination, and afterwards his glance went openly and yet delicately to a corner of the large and stylish room, where, at a little table of beautiful damask, decorated with silver, crystal, and flowers, Fran and Mr. Vaclav, on either side of a rose satin lamp, were having dinner. They were talking, it occurred to me, sparingly, and did not look at each other much; but also they did not seem to pay any attention to us—not even once, as long as the meal lasted, did I see them vouchsafe our table even one glance. And so then I had to learn the truth from the mouth of a stranger, from a gray savant learned in the study of the exalted riddles of life, that Eufrazia Veenman had now become Franny Veen and for several years had appeared in concert halls and theaters. Professor Zijsma's spouse, and especially his daughters, were particularly captivated by her; he himself, to his regret, had not found the time really to attend one of her performances. But perhaps this evening offered an opportunity, he added humorously, as he regarded me affably. My heart began to bounce, but "bounce," "batter," "burst"—do these words really say what I felt then, all that whole afternoon? I am afraid that my poor vocabulary may not stretch to the end of my confession, though now it is growing near. Perhaps in the beginning I have done violence to my style, so that near the end it will shoot too short to scream out my farewell to this world, to all the swords that I have loved and admired, the highest beauty and the last terror, from the disaster which has ruined my soul for good. However, our imperfect human language, unless it was my unskillful and accidental authorship—does it not always remain below actuality? Although the tone, from the beginning of this long confessional, might appear to exaggerate, in fact the feelings which in turn caressed or tormented me were inexpressible. And perhaps that is only for the best. What may still follow, dear creatures, beloved known and unknown fellow men, shall reach you all as an echo, as a muffled, misformed shriek of a soul, more easily acceptable to third parties, like the deaf redoubt of language, like the inevitable type-trap of literature, thrown down into your soul. It will seem to you as though I had made up a story, a depressing, horrifying story, of which only a few of the softer features were borrowed from life, and, so thinking, you, on your side, will perhaps let this whole depressing, horrifying thing go through your imagination, but at the most only a few of the softer features of it, those which you think are actuality, will you allow in your own soul. Then if you follow me with any emotion, it will never be to the perilous edge of the ravine, on the bottom of which am I, the dead man who still lives, agonizing because of all too much actuality. Let me then say that at Professor Zijsma's playful utterance on the occasion which was offered to him that afternoon to establish the soundness of his wife and daughter's admiration for Franny Veen's art—that then my heart, instead of still "bouncing," gave me the impression that it was pressed flat in my tormented bosom, as flat as a heart with only two dimensions, clipped out of cardboard by ivory hands with glowing red nails—the heart of a gigantic playing card, with painfully torn edges. "Waiter," the amiable scholar asked, "do you know whether Mrs. Veen will appear anywhere this evening? Or maybe she isn't on tour?" How could the waiter remain so calm, so indifferent in his high seriousness, while he respectfully answered—but did that respect apply to Fran or to Professor Zijsma?—: "Yes, sir, *Miss* Veen will conclude the summer season in our municipal auditorium this evening. The performance begins in half an hour. The auditorium is on the other side of the marketplace. In case the gentlemen would like to go, I can call up the management at once and reserve as many seats as necessary. That can be done even yet. The hotel always holds some seats reserved until just before it begins," he added, smiling, with a modest professional pride. Professor Zijsma's roguish glance inspected his colleagues. "Miss Veenman!"—it flashed through me just then. The professor had said "Mrs." in his question, but the headwaiter, with a touching truthfulness, all unstudied, to the details of actuality, had, with tactful emphasis, corrected him: "Miss!" Thus *not* married! Thus there was no trade—at least not officially; the flower had not sold itself to the hairy, grasping hand, at least not before God and men! Thus I had not misheard: Rouben Vaclav was only the director or the manager, the producer or the impresario, or however they may be called, perhaps even also the lover, since so often it happens that the one is the inevitable concomitant of the other, but still not the husband, still not the *spouse,* of Frannie. "Won't you be my guests?" I heard Professor Zijsma's friendly appeal to his colleagues. Professor Mato and his assistant looked at each other and then nodded, "Glad to." I—was not consulted. The cordial graybeard perhaps deemed it superfluous. Had he not read my soul, or did my posture speak clearly enough for me? "Now," Professor Zijsma then replied to the headwaiter, "if you would be so kind, four tickets then." Four, with me then, without my having said yes—it spoke for itself, didn't it, that the clerk would gladly accompany them, that the ex-teacher would feel fortunate to be able to applaud his famous former student? I do not know anything more about the further course of the meal. I must have eaten something, although I still cannot understand whether I was in a fit state for that or whether I was able to take in only a bite because of my knotted intestines. But indeed it was not I who did this, but my good, pitiable robot, which, no matter how defective I had made it, still always lay in wait to refresh my soul or feed my body, profiting from my least inattentiveness with its interfering, industrious brains. The gentlemen talked among themselves. Sometimes one of them looked cordially in my direction, and then I nodded bashfully, hastily, something between yes and no. I sat so that I could observe my fellow guests and the little table in the corner at the same time. I looked without looking, for I was afraid I might give someone the wrong idea. My behavior was, for that matter, unusual enough already. And what I saw—oh, perhaps only quite the most ordinary scene in a restaurant; little white tables, a silver chandelier and blossoming table lamps, neatly eating guests and noiseless, heavily laden waiters, and, in the light from the high windows, between the Bordeaux tapestries, a violet evening sky above the rose-lit city—completely everyday, as the motionless headwaiter perhaps saw it, who stood in the middle of the room with his hands behind his back and his head pressed a very little bit backward—it came to my eye in just the same way, I look at it now as a summons, but then my retina was just as battered as my heart and suffered that clear and peaceful image like a final shipwreck in my turbulent brain. At a certain time Fran and Vaclav got up. He arose first and bestowed himself behind her chair in order to pull it out, gallantly, but without disturbing so much as a muscle in his face, while she stood up. Then I did not dare to look any more for a few moments, on account of my tablemates. I just saw her leave the room, her back toward me, her half-naked back in the pale green gown, with her golden hair above her ivory shoulders and her beringed arms, next to the international man. We were scarcely at our dessert, and there was still coffee to come. The gentlemen chatted pleasantly about scientific things; I had sat so taciturn at their side that they understood well that they might converse about all that captivating stuff, to which I could not contribute anything but which caressed my ear like an exalted secret language. Then finally we were through and stood up simultaneously. Professor Zijsma and the assistant desired to go to their rooms and took the elevator together. Professor Mato lit a cigarillo and went to sit for a while in a comfortable clubroom area in the lobby, inviting me to do likewise. He must surely be weary after the activities of such a day—but although his face looked slightly gray, his expression was still handsome and even brighter. He appeared to me even especially cheerful, probably more, I considered privately, the result of the important interview with his excellent foreign colleague than of the prospect of going out for an evening with the very idle art of a beautiful young woman as its highpoint. Then, encouraged by this unexpected tête-à-tête with just the man who had given me repeated glimpses of how well he intended toward me, I blurted it out hastily: as obsequiously as possible I imparted to him that I could not accompany them to the theater. Almost pleadingly I looked at him: I was so tired, I informed him, it had been such a dreadful day, it had all been so overpowering for me; would he then excuse me, for himself and also to the other gentlemen? How very pleasantly he smiled then, how sympathetic was his reaction, really that of a beautiful, scientific spirit. "Naturally," he said, nodding. "Certainly." "Then I'll walk around for a while, the coolness and the darkness will calm my nerves, and then I'll go to bed," I assured him deceitfully, with a very short-lived revival of some long-lost boyishness in me. He extended his open hand to me, and I shook it silently. Then, without waiting for my hat, I walked outside in great haste, into the beautifully dark, warm, and yet fresh summer evening, the clear, rich night of the strange city. The plane trees had now become black, but in the water of the canal, trembling slightly, lived a softly colored, feverish world of lamps and other enchanting reflections, which were called up on that smooth and somber surface by a glorious accident on the other bank, where a string-band blared. I walked through the plaza. For a moment I remained standing, pressed against the wooden shutter of a newsstand: there was the Theater, with its white columns bathed in a strange, bright glow against the velvet night, with its golden windows and the neat, black silhouette of the many visitors, arriving without interruption. Behind the enormous curtain, dark as ripe lilacs, Rouben Vaclav surely stood, with his mysteriously sparkling oriental eyes, now worked into that canvas by the little round church window, peering into the room while the hairdresser and make-up artist and costumer were nervously working on Fran, Fran, whose destiny was reflected in her mirror, and in the orchestra the instruments were tuning up, like so many plaintive chords of my frightened heart, oppressed by death. I walked on. Glistening cars snapped past, without the least exertion accelerating or decelerating their speeds and describing graceful curves around the corners. There were still many people on foot, and the store windows sparkled with rich and variegated displays. The stores ought to be all closed now in a little while; in fact, in this distinguished part of the city I did not venture to put my intention into execution. I walked through many streets and arrived finally in a modest neighborhood, with only a few store windows still lit, the showcases of which looked meager and bare next to those of the main street. After a little while I finally discovered a shoe store. The pane was a little steamed over; the nauseous white shrillness of the deathly, naked lightbulb, which hung on a miserable cord above the rather untidily scattered display models, was somewhat dim. The models themselves seemed, however, on a closer look, not much uglier than those in the expensive stores, which in fact, as is commonly known, order from blind alleys in the slums the costly and sought-after handwork that they exhibit to people in their glittering displays for so much money. The door of this simple store was closed with a venetian blind. I looked for a doorbell, found it, and pressed it.

It looked, however, as if there was no current, for I heard nothing and no one came. My heart leaped against the walls of my throat. I tried to ring again, waiting whenever a few lonely passersby appeared out of the misty halo of the last streetlamps. In vain—nothing stirred in the house. Then, determinedly, I risked a few blows on the blind. Three, four, the first soft and the last a whole lot harder, so hard in the sudden stillness that it made me tremble like a blow from a fist on my own heart. A shuffling foot neared, the doorcatch was undone from the door, a woman from the lower middle classes looked speechlessly out at me. Yes, the visit must certainly have seemed strange, first because of my dumbfounded appearance and then because of the hour. But I had talked myself into taking heart, all the whole way: that no one knew me here, that I was only going to ask for a few minutes' work, that then I should have peace, and that in the morning I would leave the city again and certainly would never return any more. Still, while I stood there before the woman, I felt my resolution drain out of me again; but then I did as I had intended; I thought back as vehemently as possible on the loathesome piece of corpse that my heel had picked up that afternoon at the little churchyard at D—. And then I hesitated no longer. I stepped inside boldly, tried on a pair of brown colored shoes, the most attractive of those on hand, and said that I wanted to wear them immediately. I had my old pair wrapped up in the box that the new had come out of. Since it was a poor store, the box was not wrapped further in soft tissue paper with an elegant crease in it but in a coarse, torn sheet of gray paper, around which the young lady obligingly lashed a thick end of twine with a loop for a handle. That's the way I wanted it. I had already seen the price in the display window and computed that after this purchase I should no longer have money enough to pay my hotel bill in the morning. But I would get up early and go to the assistant, while he was still in his room, to borrow it from him. I did not dare ask Professor Mato. Monday, before I went to the Palace, I would pay it all back to him. I shook the young lady's hand because I had left my hat in the hotel and wanted to salute her with emphasis, in one way or another, in order to show her my gratitude for her kindness. Upon which I fled again into the dark street. It was a long time before I found—without leaving this lower middle-class section, from which I did not want to depart yet because of its sparse lighting and the undisturbed loneliness which prevailed there—what I was looking for: a canal. I went to an opening in the shrubbery along its banks; then I looked around hastily—no one!—and with a short throw and a dull splash the gray, nauseating package disappeared forever in the muddy depths. I hastened back to the hotel. I did not remember the way—it was, in fact, possibly best that I did not return through the same streets and alleys—but I did not want to address any of the rare pedestrians. I shuddered at the thought that I might meet a talkative person who would walk a little way with me. I wanted to leave this ghetto, where I had thrown off my defilement, alone and tracelessly. Soon I began to run. The three scholars would now surely be at an intermission and surely would not return for an hour and a half. Therefore I didn't have to fear meeting them now. But would the barber, would the barbershop in the hotel still be open? The possibility served me for a while. I don't know how, but suddenly an alley brought me back into the main street, where there was a great deal less movement of cars and pedestrians. The beautiful shop windows were now chillier, although still just as glorious as ever; or had it actually become cooler in the meantime? I could not feel it, I had been perspiring so much. After a few moments I stood once more in the lobby of the hotel and walked down the marble steps to the glitteringly lighted basement. The barber was just now leaving! But had he perhaps heard, just like me, the leather of my band-new footwear brushing on the steps, creaking on the steps veined in flaming red? He bowed cordially and immediately reopened the door of the barbershop for me. In case I also wished a manicure, he could have the girl called for at once, he informed me, for she, like him, lodged in the hotel. I grew a little dizzy from so much unfamiliar luxury but allowed everything to satisfy me. Scarcely had I sat in the lovely chair, soft and high, with the white barber cloth on, which gave me so much innocent pleasure, as if its impeccable white essence was made for a calming and divine dreamlessness, to which it has always known how to bring my soul—when the manicurist was also sitting at my side, a very pretty little girl, barely full grown, with mischievously curled hair and maybe also mind, freshly dressed and washed as if it was not evening but still only morning. A young barber's helper in full uniform was also propelled into appearance, as if by magic, in order to fetch his boss and the girl whatever they might need and also to observe accurately, and yet tactfully, wrong strokes of both activities in the mirror. I had to dabble my fingertips in soapy water, the cuticles were smeared with an odorous pomade and then cautiously clipped away, and while the manicurist began to work with my hands, very skillfully, with a long, limp file, my carefully millimetered crown was washed, dried in a stream of warm air, and smeared with fragrant oil. With childish regret I saw the end of these silent works of enchantment drawing near. I tried to find an excuse to make it last; a pretense that for that matter was not a complete lie: "I have a little headache," I said as casually as possible; "we came such a long way, and it was broiling hot in the car!" The barber nodded sympathetically, and yes, then what I had fancied so mischievously, or at least with as much mischievousness as someone like the writer of these dreary lines could be expected to have, was brought out. The barber took an old gadget out of one of his drawers and inquired whether he should massage my neck. An affecting memory began to sing through my whole body, but I did not let anything show. On the contrary, I acted as if I had absolutely never heard of that superannuated instrument. The barber expostulated with me about it confidentially: he had only to plug the cord into the electricity, he explained, and the soft rubber knob would quickly begin to rotate; when this was pressed against your neck, in an upwards direction—the spinal cord, sir!—you feel yourself revive at once, more surely than under the most skillful fingers. On the face of it an antiquated remedy, but proved by experience—they had never found anything better yet! I let everything soak in. I didn't really have a headache, but there were so many other illnesses, tremblings, and deafnesses in me that longed for relief. And again, as ten years before, it brought a short-lived calmness, or at least the illusion of it. When everything was done—I could not make it last too long, either, the gentlemen might return earlier than I had counted on!—I gave each of my caretakers a large tip and walked out again, up the stairway, with its gallows-colored streaks and flesh-white marble, as thick as a muscular biceps, to the lounge. I had now spent the last of my money. A bellboy sprang towards me with the question whether I wanted my key. I nodded. The boy ran to the board to fetch it. I thanked him and said that I would find my room myself. No, he did not have to call for the elevator, I would rather walk. I was a little bit afraid of those pleasant, brutal chaps in red-gold livery; those whose hands were always stretched out. I have heard that they had to live exclusively on the tips awarded them and sometimes they had to give up a part of them, like the waiters, too, for that matter, as a sort of fee, for they "hired," so to speak, their situation in the hotel. And now I didn't have any more money to give them. So I walked upstairs alone, but quickly. But when I was in the corridor of my floor, I regretted it. Surely, the *information* about which I had been excited the whole time—I had intended to ask the boy casually, in case he led me to the corridor. I had been such a child, there on the floor; I should at least have thought of *that*. How was I to manage it now? I began by taking a bath, as hot as possible; that always did me good and often helped me decide things. Then I hesitated. It is said that a cold shower after a warm bath is also very beneficial. On the one hand I was afraid that I would now quickly become tired again, just as before dinner; that I would suddenly feel totally exhausted again and that sleep would overpower me at once. And that could absolutely not be; no sleepiness could be allowed to thwart the plan that was now, hand over hand, taking clearer shape in me! But on the other hand I must admit here that I was always especially hesitant about cold showers, and that I had avoided them for a long time. The stream of icy water gave me such a disproportionate shock that I had once vomited a dinner that I had digested hours previously; and once I had broken out with many painful body sores. That was in a swimming establishment where I had gone when I was laid up in the hope of being able to strengthen my body and soul by daily exercise to improve the no longer smooth action of my spirit. When, after that incident, I gave up my resolution and imparted it to Corra, I expressed the opinion, in order to convince her and to comfort myself, that my nerves were perhaps closer to my skin than other people's, and that my whole sensitivity and vulnerability was nothing more serious than that. But to speak honestly, cold water has always not only given me superficial pain—actually everything does that, more or less—it also literally goes like an icy sword through my soul. And when once a quality or an illness, here really an illness, lies so deeply placed, what avails the mere desire to help it? You are beaten before you begin! Still, that evening I took a cold shower. I clenched my teeth, counted to three so as not to think any longer, and then once more really to three, shoved the door handle, and experienced the freezing stream for a few moments. Shivering, I rubbed myself for a long time until I finally began to get warm again. Was the tension in my soul so great, or had my system already absorbed so much that day, that it could react to this new punishment as it did? I experienced no ill effects from the shower, but felt, as I had fearfully hoped, in some measure refreshed. I dressed again hastily. The same linen, the same suit, but I was washed, barbered, shorn, and manicured, and I was wearing brand-new, beautiful brown shoes. I felt a little bit, a very, very little bit, as much as was still possible after ten years, after the ten years *I* had endured, young again. And then I had a rather clever, I think, idea. I walked silently back and forth in my room, grinning once to myself in the mirror, and lit a cigarette. No, I would not ask for anything on the house phone, that was too blunt, and I could not hope that no one would remember! No, I myself should. . . . I walked downstairs. The bold little bellhop was fortunately invisible. The headwaiter stood a little drowsily and pale by the keyboard; he apparently replaced the usual employee. One more stroke of luck, for people *ad interim* are almost always easier than people *ad hoc,* and when they leave their temporary posts again, any trace of the appeal you have made to them vanishes also. "Didn't Miss Veenman leave a message for me?" I asked, as casually as I could. It was naturally possible that the question would be mentioned to her when she returned; but she had said, "See you later," which I could at least partly answer for myself, my so entirely innocent behavior. And it was certainly less indecent, and I supposed my silent purpose would be less likely to meet naked failure, at least by opposition from the manager, as mysterious as apparently passionate, Rouben Vaclav—when I asked for a note than directly for that which I burned to know. In fact, before I left the headwaiter again, I politely suppressed a weary little yawn and negligently but still explicitly added: "No? Thank you very much. Then I'm going to bed. I'm about to fall asleep. Good night!" The man asked me the number of my room. "Seventeen," I said. Then he turned around and looked for the number on the keyboard. That board was only a cupboard with a great number of little pigeonholes, which were constructed like the squares on a checker board and into which letters and even small packets could be stuffed. Above each pigeonhole a number was painted, and the keys of guests who were out hung with the same number cut out in a copper tag on a little chain. Such boards are in use in all large hotels, but I render this one particularly because it had so much importance for me on that ill-fated evening. Everything that must follow now before long, all so glorious and disastrous, is in great measure dependent upon it. Without that keyboard perhaps it would—But come! That's the way it always is, the cruel and beautiful—too beautiful to be only cruel. Perhaps sometime I shall be permitted to feel, and not only with my dark soul but even sunk in the Father's radiant truth, that suspicion as an actuality. Then will I virtuously begin my death on earth as the punishment for my indefensible crime. I shall never see my dear ones again, the days lose their names and the years their numbers; but my deliverance has already commenced with the inexpressible sadness of that farewell. It would perhaps be blasphemous to confess that I am now already happy, or am becoming so, no matter how eternally melancholy that happiness is; but I am at least no longer unhappy. With the little dirt path that I rake and the flowers I tie up, I am perhaps more necessary to a handful of mortals than I ever was to human society as a failed lawyer, as a miserable clerk, and, as I once was, a worthless teacher. I have thought for more than forty years—I wonder pensively whether my simple, gentle father or my solemn, kind mother or my honorable teachers ever taught me that, but I think their schooling must have always implied this—that a person becomes necessary and happy only when he exerts himself, when he tries to reach above himself, when he beats himself to excel. But now I do not think that any more. On the contrary, all our calamities come to us from this; our personal sorrows and all the miseries of society, the material as well as the moral. We must not desire to make, from our souls, from our bodies, from our minds, more than God has endowed us with; we do well when, on the contrary, we always have something more in reserve. Each flower has a vocation when it appears, and it will stop nowhere else but when it has grown naturally; no matter how useful and pleasant it might be to do otherwise, it will be compensated for it simply, perhaps doubly, for what is true for the good things of the earth, the shortage of which raises their value, is surely so in a yet higher degree for the joys of the soul. And who told me that a modest happiness was less meritorious? I have always, at every racetrack, felt something cruel, something that is especially human, but yet not permitted to me, to see the God of Love as the great pacemaker. They are indeed many, the little dirt paths which are continuously beautiful to rake. If I, from the beginning, had found that, my modest and sweet vocation, another, more suitable teacher would have stood once before the school benches and would have been able to awaken the frail lives that sat on them. Which is still not to say that Fran would never have come through my garden even once, but what I would have offered her then would perhaps have been a flower without consequences, but also without blemish or calamity. Let me then without delay complete this composition, written by a dead man on the softly piled earth beside his grave. Let me try to enter the great mystery not without anything, although with only the luminous, blank whiteness of the last page in my black-bound autobiography. The portion already written has been gray enough. Perhaps I am producing in the reader the impression that I am padding it out, and indeed, as I always meant to have said, and no matter how much pain it may cause me, I can do no other than to linger over that which has been my miserable but unique possession: my own little, disastrous history. Perhaps I do linger here, not only because of the ending, but also in order to describe the evil with which everything finished: the short, earsplitting conclusion, after which everything became a soul-splitting, deathly silence. Yet, next to that, I desire, with all the fibers of my emotions, to be able to recall that soundless point before long in this melancholy document, with my dull pencil. When I dispatch my story, to bestow it anonymously for possible publication, it will be somewhat as if I have torn away, out of that black-bound manuscript, the part described as gray. And thanks to that last irregularity, then I shall be better able, wholly able, to keep my promise to our beloved director, whom I esteem so highly. However, with my intention to send these pages to people, I act once more out of personal, selfish motives. It will be forgiven me on account of the many sorrows that I have borne from others. My "case" is easily not what one usually requires, and properly so, that the art of literature should deal with: something universal, something human, as they call it. I stand on the so-called seamy side, like a man balancing perilously on the farthest point of the thinnest edge. But as a caricature does violence to reality in order to make it better appear, perhaps not a few would be able to recognize their own portraits, precisely in the overwrought state that I have been in and can only offer here, just that, in my *folie raisonnante,* as though under a magnifying glass, and, before it is too late, be able to draw from my experience a lesson never to allow themselves to drift irretrievably away from that path. Perhaps—O final dream!—I, the disinherited, shall by this have been able to add out of my shabbiness a very, very little something to the luxurious and harmonious world, on which I have gazed with shuddering awe and glowing love: to the world of science, which is the highest truth, and of which it has been given me to have been able to draw near to some of the white-aproned servitors, in the person of scholars like Professer Mato and his assistant, like Professor Zijsma, and even like Judge Brantink, and like the man whom I see now, occasionally several times a week, at the end of my raked paths, behind a clump of the flowers or vines I love so much, our director. Perhaps through me they would be able to add something, even though only a small amount, almost nothing, to the temple which they are erecting—their temple of science, their work of centuries, built with all the gold of the earth and all the blood of our hearts, in order, when heaven and earth touch each other, to be able to invite God Himself in, as our common answer, ours and His, to the riddle that perhaps He has put to Himself as much as to us. In this spirit I have thought over my case a few times, very deeply, and a few days ago the following notion came to me: science brings distinction to young men and old, who themselves are like the former, but considered at a later period of their lives; history speaks likewise of young cultures which in due course become older and even die; furthermore, someone has tried to bring people into all kinds of typological categories, and now I ask myself whether, at the same moment in society and apart from their real, "bourgeois" ages, there aren't men living different types of lifetimes, of an older, dying type, and of a younger type, up and coming. At first glance, we are all playing, with greater or lesser success, the same game, but the latter laugh before the mirror and disguise themselves with comic masks; while, as when the play is over, and the musicians, the fragrant ladies, the urbane gentlemen, and even the stagehands have journeyed back home, the others stand on the darkened stage in the gloomy, empty hall, gazing, with a gray moonbeam falling through a crack in the dilapidated wings on their clammy features, painted the color of corpse-wax, above which, but pushed back on their balding foreheads, appears the howling mask of tragedy. I must not add anything to that with relation to my case. The reader knows very well where I think I myself stand in this strange world of disguises and masks, in this deathly dreary Threepenny Opera of the soul, with "this one in Darkness and the other in Light." For already old Moritat has lamented: *"erstere sieht man nicht!"*—I think that their darkness, their clumsiness, their antiquity must be connected with the miraculous removals of souls or bodies, with a slow disincarnation to other, new regions—perhaps to that beautiful night planet of mine—under the cryptic slogan: "Mission here soon accomplished." And it would be all too presumptuous, no matter how accurate regarding my penitent self, to dare to write it down. Perhaps the notion of this typology also is not completely new. The elements which compose it, which I have enumerated, are all familiar, but perhaps, perhaps my possible construction of it lies in an insignificant amalgamation of otherwise plagiarized elements—even in the history of chemistry that has sometimes happened—or at least in providing a starting point to take up a new illumination of the soul of matter. It might be, then, that I could shed at least a glimmer on the matter of soul, on that material so painfully rooted through, on which I myself, one of these dawn people, have found that notion like a small, fresh birth, shot upwards just like a funeral pyre out of the old lumpy earth of my inconsolability. I have plucked it newly here, reader, and offer it to you likewise, together with the last black pages of my story. Farewell, little blossom, sole harvest of my existence, farewell! The headwaiter looked for my number on the keyboard. The key wasn't there, naturally, and there was also no message in the corresponding pigeonhole. "I'm very sorry, Mr. Antfield," this chief of waiters said with deadly earnestness, as if he actually did regret it, at the same time emphatically, with self-taught enjoyment, addressing me again by name. I tried to do my best just the same. "Oh, that's all right," I said. I had already prepared to leave; then, very offhandedly, as if I had just thought of it: "And in Miss Veenman's pigeonhole? Would you please look there, too? But I don't know the number." The last words were the hardest. Had I not betrayed myself by the foolish, puerile tightening of my lips, which had suddenly stuck together and dried? Had my voice sounded satisfactorily indifferent? But yet not so much that it should lack its irritating effect on the worldly wisdom of the experienced headwaiter? "The number of Miss Veenman's room is 21, sir," the man said quickly, as though with his mind's eye he read off a solemn register-page, at which he—fortunately, for my face was one blazing exultation—turned round again to search the pigeonhole above which her key hung and in which, naturally, had been stuck not the least little note for me. "No, nothing, Mr. Antfield, but the young lady apparently isn't going to stay here much longer. If you wish to speak with her—" "Oh, no," I cut in, as hastily and yet as unnoticeably as possible. "I'll see her tomorrow morning. I'm too tired now." I knew her number, I had her number! Room twenty-one, *twenty-one!* I had to restrain myself in order not to climb the stairs again too rapidly. TWENTY-ONE! And I had seventeen, thus apparently on the same floor! I stuck my hand in my pocket, looking for my cigarettes, but I remembered in time: they were so bitter, the headwaiter would surely think badly of me. Still, I was too happy, I had to do something. I absolutely had to say something. And then, recklessly, I asked, "Just a minute, look at Mr. Vaclav's; maybe it was put there." But the headwaiter did not turn around this time. He shook his head negatively. "Mr. Vaclav has had all his baggage loaded into his car, Mr. Antfield. This evening is Miss Veenman's last performance, and when it's over Mr. Vaclav is leaving for A—, early in the morning; he's going to attend the dress rehearsal of a play that's having its opening night tomorrow. You know, Mr. Vaclav never rests. Miss Veenman, on the other hand, she's going for a few weeks' vacation in the South of France and won't leave till Monday morning." "Of course," I said, and struck my hand against my forehead, as if I had known all that a long time but it had slipped my mind on account of my weariness. And then I yawned once more, as I had intended, said my little sentence about falling to sleep because it had been such a busy day and so impossibly hot in the car. "Thank you, and good night to you!" "Have a good rest, sir." This time I jumped into the elevator, the bellhop wasn't in sight, I was still dead tired, and I especially wanted to be alone again. Room twenty-one. Yes, it was on the same floor. When I stepped out of the elevator, I noticed that from that corner on, the numbers decreased in the corridor. It began with thirty. I slid noiselessly over the felt carpet, and here was 21! I stood still a moment, the whole building looked deserted, I heard only my own gasping breath, and, oh so silver beautiful and soft, the ticking of the perhaps expensive little clock in Fran's room, a clock that surely could have been heard only by me, since I was actually living only at the farthest tag ends of the fibers of my soul. Then I walked on hastily, like a drunk. Our rooms almost next to each other, and Vaclav away, Vaclav, who had never been her husband, at most had been only her lover, for his opening night counted more to him than she—his work, his plays, his *money!*—for didn't he let her go, all alone, on a vacation to the South of France? Monday, Monday morning, she was leaving, when I was obediently going home again with my wrinkled face and with the worn briefcase from my days as a lawyer, in which now there was only a sandwich for lunch and the thermos which Corra had fixed for me silently, faithfully, it seemed a year and a day ago, in addition to a few wretched pages of night work, a fruitless attempt to become independent of arrears in day work again by encroaching into the hours of my sleep. Monday! But today was still Saturday, and a night yet separated us from the new parting that this time would be for life. A whole night, which was the most incredible gift that fate ever granted someone like me. The unexpected is the most beautiful—and the cruelest. Back at my room I smoked half a cigarette with a few greedy draughts. How sweet was that bitterness to my beaten, always exhausted soul. I ordered coffee over the house telephone, and a little glass of gin. I wanted to ask for even more strong drink, in fact, a bomb as explosive as the one in that mess in the little bar across from the churchyard in D—. But here was no twelve-year-old barmaid to spur me with her moist, mischievous flirting. Moreover, I was not thirsty because of the hotel bill, for which I should have to borrow money in the morning from the assistant. Scarcely had I hung up when a maid brought my order. This was apparently a very distinguished hotel. I went to sit and smoke before the window, in a deep, soft easy chair, and drank the coffee, which was as hot as it could be; between whiles, drop by drop, I sipped the gin. It worked like oil on a fire. One half of the window was ajar. Thanks to the curtains in front of the other half and the warm drapery around it all, which were now wholly dark because of their reddish brown color, I had the deliciously mixed impression of sitting safely inside and yet, emotionally, face to face with the wide outside world of night. In the white window frame the dark canal stood silent, with its black plane trees and the colorful reflection of the glittering places on the far side. These danced on the rocking pulses of music from a string band which played loud and soft by turns. And despite the dark night everywhere else in the great stillness all around—or was it for just that reason?—the music shot again through my soul a new, caressing golden cloudstuff, burning me all raw. I dreamed sweetly and turbulently, in the fashion of perhaps all sharers of companionship: in the beautiful world of my imagination. I saw myself standing there, leaning on a white-stone gallery in the last station at the edge of the West, as did Lt. de Saint-Avit during the night before his mad drive back to Antinea and death. But immediately I had to remember also, and it comforted and strengthened me a great deal, our old professor of philosophy, now dead, who considered such dreams most precious, because through them we are able to raise up our always miserable existence to a higher life on earth and the eternity of Heaven. For that matter, I wanted to think—I had known it already—of nothing else, clearly, of nothing that could be called even in the slightest systematic. My intention had a singularly great longing: shoes, barber, bed, and one particular desire: for the number of Fran's room. Beyond that I considered everything a violation of salvation: Fate had cast an adventure, unheard-of for me and perhaps even in the comprehension of those endowed with ordinary wealth, of a meeting such as one seldom comes across except in a film or in books. Didn't I then have to behave in a worthy manner toward it, that is, in a manner that lies between dream and deed, as a child is born out of desire and love-making, as the French say—a brutal expression, on the face of it, but indeed from a surprising romanticism, as exists in no other people in imagination or actuality—much more than out of thought and execution? So I let myself fly away on all the wild ponies of my most delicate feelings, in the western storm of that last night of my soul, toward *my* Atlantis and *my* Antinea. I would go, I would speak—how and what, I did not have to figure out beforehand, as I knew already—it would not have been beautiful, and it was also at the very least unnecessary: hadn't everything been, hadn't everything stormed within me already for so many years? Once, just this once, then, I would once more, I would now be completely the boy it had been given me to be, the boy of over forty years! I smoked carefully now, I would barely have enough cigarettes to last till morning. The coffee was all gone, and the last drop had been sucked out of the glass. It was too bad that I hadn't dared ask for more. And then I fell asleep there, into a sleep that lasted several hours. I awoke with an infinite grief for the clear and reproachful realization that I had slept. Apparently the coolness of the night and of the canal water awakened me. I did not awake with a start—but hastily grieved myself awake, quietly and gnawing. Was it still night? Hadn't the time of my dead-solitary life's adventure, trapped relentlessly between two unadjustable limits, irrevocably elapsed? I asked myself this question silently. The plane trees were still dark, and the canal shiny black, but the sky was very gray. In any case, there still weren't any people on the street and the birds still slept in the trees. I had not dreamed—also a rarity. But it seems that even the longest dreams flit through our enchanted brains for only a few seconds, so that even if I had dreamed, I would not have had any time in doing so to treasure up the time that had irreparably vanished. I could, of course, look at my watch. But I didn't want to. No! No figures now, no figures yet! Still, it couldn't be so late, so early, already. And then time is, to the inner man, only a fiction, a logical fraud. Everything depends on me, how I want to experience time, how I dare to use it. I did not feel any more as I had before I fell asleep. The golden cloudstuff had left, but the fear and the trembling remained. A cold, miserable, and terrible storm now prevailed over me, but even that was adventure now. Oh, cruel-sweet romanticism of the butt-end of a soul! The multicolored reflections in the mirror-like canal of the glistening place on the other bank had disappeared, perhaps because of the later or all-too-early hour and the pertinent police regulations. The sounds, apparently only by sporadically pushing the light, gently pressed again, as if from far away, through the subduing windows and drapes, the now blaring, now predominantly lamenting, lullaby. And yes, anew, too new, something sang in me, it has already been realized, perhaps, that the night was still not over, that the night was still here! They were dancing over there now, all of them pressed closely against each other, with pale faces and intoxicated souls, and therefore with magic spaces of adoration between each other, which, sober, in the lifelike separations but spiritual covetousness of the day's actuality, would never be, or could never be, so beautiful and sure and real. I felt again a miserable sadness that I had not dared to ask for more to drink over the house phone. But now, away with all that! I stood up. I closed the drapes. Now I would go, without counting three times to three! I walked on tiptoes to the light switch. Suddenly there was light in my room, and I still knew it well: it didn't blind me. I went to stand before the mirror. God! how little youthful I looked any more, despite the barber and the cold shower. I washed again at the cold-water faucet, rubbed my cheeks rosy with the hardest of the handtowels, and massaged my head with it. There was already so little hair left that I felt only a slight trace of friction. Suddenly I was ready. I stood by the door, looked again at everything here that was so familiar, so friendly, so secure, in comparison to the unknown of No. 21. Then I put out the light and pushed the night-latch down. Only one wall lamp of weak, translucent pearl burned in the hallway. Noiselessly, on my tiptoes, I glided over the carpet. Number 21, *twenty-one!* Suddenly one of my new shoes creaked. I started violently and froze. Must Professor Mato see me now! But she, Fran, had actually said, "See you later," and I will think only of that. "See you later, see you later," I whispered to my own soul, my nerves, and the circulation of my blood, my feeble windpipe, to my stiff muscles and my feet, heavy as lead. See you later! Perhaps she meant by that "later in the theater"? Theatrical people, they say, are often rather conceited creatures; that is the way their profession damages them, I read once. When you have to depict heroes and heroines evening after evening, something of that gradually rubs off on you, and after you have felt looked at by thousands, millions, of eyes for several years, it is apparently inevitable that you are presently deluded from your proper perspective, and finally you can't meet anyone any more in the last half hour before the performance without instinctively believing that he is, just like you, on his way to the theater. So perhaps Fran hadn't meant anything more by her "see you later" than that she, through a very forgivable professional warping of judgment, which she no longer felt as conceit, and thus ought not to be judged as such, perhaps believing it automatically, thought that I was going to applaud her that evening in the theater—yes, that my appearance in this city could have had no other cause than to come admire her in her last performance of the season. What sense did it make, then, that I was here, now, scared to death, standing in this dark hallway? Any minute a sleepy maid or an audacious bellhop who had night duty might appear standing in a doorway or shooting around a corner. With my pale, distorted face and feverish eyes propped open, they would certainly not doubt for a moment that they had trapped a burglar redhanded. The maid would begin to scream and the bellboy would make the alarm bell rattle. God, no! I still had as much right as anyone not to be able to get to sleep in the night; to walk downstairs and get a little aspirin tablet from the night staff. But what sense did it make, about Fran? She had said "see you later" mechanically, and afterwards hadn't thought any more about it. She must be sleeping restfully now, contented with the success of this last night and dreaming of the South of France, of the sunny, soft vacation days that were now ahead of her. She was naturally completely ignorant, and it had surely never occurred to her for a moment, that I had *not* gone to the theater; that I had not satisfied my great appetite—for she and Vaclav had certainly noticed, even without looking, its prominent appearance!—to hear her. What sense did it make to disillusion her, in the supposition that by a miracle, which still seems improbable to me, I might have the happiness of speaking to her once more for the last time in my life? Disillusion? But her conceit was only a professional mechanism, and what did I matter to her, whose impression of my comings and goings must have been, at the very least, that I was a dull, ridiculous fool, a distasteful bumpkin who disturbed the best part of her night's rest? But *I*, then, did I still have the right, just once, one last and single time, to be myself, someone with a little too much inconsiderate conceit, with melancholy dreams and meager visions, a lamentable, twisted automaton? Wasn't I ever permitted to misunderstand a situation and to dream up a meaning from a flippantly said sentence, as would have been so dear to me to do? That she had meant it a little bit, oh, only a little teeny tiny bit, ambiguously; ambiguously because of the pleasant memories between us, who were older acquaintances than she could have been with Vaclav, although he had, on the stairs, stood so close by her, so divisively between us two. But if she had possibly expected to meet me after the performance, tête-à-tête, in the lobby downstairs, or even, best of all, for the time of a cigarette and a little cup of tea, in her room—then, then wasn't it much too late now for that? The night must be almost over; she must still be asleep, and all insignificances of my sort are forgotten. Oh, fool! The tears suddenly stood in my eyes. What a stupendous, what a monstrous illusion was I cherishing with my last soul's blood! After ten years, and what a ten years! I was still treating her, and how completely ridiculous that was now, as I had that hastening little scholar at the school celebration. Suddenly I saw before my eyes again that smeared book, my foolish little present to a high-spirited girl with cruelly laughing lips who stood before the mike to sing or who danced cradled in the arms of unromantic athletes. I stood there singing again, "Fran-is-leaving-school! Frannie-is-going-away-now-forever!" to the old tune of that mad Professor Unrath, and tearfully kissing a bare clothes hook, from the beloved vicinity of which a name ticket had fallen. And I saw her vanish, vanish for ten immeasurable, hopeless years, with her dancing golden hair, away in the night, away in my darkness. No, that was enough pretty foolishness! Back to your room, for a few hours anyway, and then back to your house of grief yonder in the gray city; to your kennel and your miserable paper rubbish in the Palace, for a few years anyway. Back, astern, into your gloom, miserable clerk! A few steps more, I would not allow myself any more; soundlessly, silently I could take farewell of a door as of herself; I wouldn't kiss the door, as I had the clothes hook, but once more, one single time more, think of her, violently and conclusively, and then onwards, not on my tiptoes, because then my shoes would creak again, but shuffling along as flat as possible with my feet barely moving over the soft felt carpet. I would not startle her in her perhaps already lighter morning sleep. Suppose that she, still half dreaming, thought that a criminal sought to rape her; or wanted to extort from her her jewels, the ostentatious gifts, glowing from passion and shame, of wealthy adorers or lovers! She would naturally scream, and then Professor Mato would come. The hotel guests would gather in a crowd in the hallway; the professor's assistant would look at me, shaking his head, and the manager would invite me to go downstairs with him, to his office. The scandal! The last, crushing blow of my evil fate, on the pitiful, shorn head of the wretched, of the punch-drunk ex-lawyer and ex-teacher, of the humblest clerk of all the clerks. But no, no, I did have the right, as well as the richest guest in this hotel, to go stand in a corridor at night—it was no crime, with a catch in my throat, with quivering lips and clammy, nerveless hands, with dizzy head and sobbing soul, but without sticking out one finger, without making one sound, to say farewell to a *door!* I stood before No. 21. And oh God, there was a light shining through the crack at the bottom! There was a strip of light, which pierced me like the stroke of a sword; that made all my sensible resolutions nothing; that cut me loose from all further thought and consideration, from everything by which I was still attached, though still so deficiently, to rational life, so as to push me irretrievably over the precipice. I listened, but I could not hear the least sound. Was it possible that she was asleep with the light on? Theatrical people are extraordinary, oversensitive, with all kinds of habits which others consider strange. In any case, she didn't have anyone else in the room with her—with two people it would never be so quiet. For that matter, Vaclav must now have been in A— for a long time already, for the dress rehearsal in the morning. Perhaps, after the success of her last performance, an exciting show, sleep had eluded her, and was she now sitting reading? Or—God! could it be, was it really possible? "See you later," she had said. "See you later." Then I knocked. Softly, but clearly, *two* times. I did not hear anything, there was no call of "Come in!"—suddenly she stood in the doorway. I likewise said nothing, I went in, and she closed the door again. The curtains were closed—the same drapes as in my room, I saw—then I covered my face with my hands and laughed and sobbed together, with short shudders. I do not know, I shall never know, whether she said anything nice then, or perhaps made a comforting gesture and possibly rested her fingertips softly on my arm, as an invitation for me to sit down. When I looked again, I saw first of all the lamp, the intimately veiled floor lamp, also the same as in my room —and then, just then, the other permeated to me, to me, the ungrateful, who had not paid any attention to it at the door: she was wearing exactly the same nightgown as ten years ago, at the fashion show at school! The same, breathtakingly beautiful robe that she now wore so much more luxuriously because of the sweet bloom of her body. I had to swallow and avert my glance—the surprise was too great, too affecting the thought that—since that strip of light seemed not to have been an insane illusion!—this circumstance was perhaps, perhaps, actually meant as a surprise! My averted glance accidentally met the bed; I started a little bit, but looked at it hastily, quickly, yet still for a moment. Unslept in—thank God! She had not yet gone to sleep. She had been waiting, waiting! She sat down again now, in an armchair across from me. Between us stood a little smoking table. But there was no book or newspaper lying on it. Thus she also hadn't been reading. All that time she had sat there, like me in my room, dreaming or meditating, but I could not suspect from her unimpeachable eyelids—shyly my glance stroked them—that *she,* even for only a moment, had slept. All the time she had been waiting! My eyes flew through all the room again. How wonderful! Precisely, precisely the same as mine, in construction and in the furnishing. I saw the small differences in detail, her delicious little personal things spread here and there, which made it completely *her* room. But it wasn't possible; I felt dizzy for a moment and asked myself whether I really wasn't still asleep, whether this wasn't all a cruel deceit, a desperate dream image; whether I had really left my own room, my room of which this was only a feminine variant, for which transposition Fran's actual or imagined presence was essentially and even completely responsible! But I clasped my hands on my knees, worked my clammy fingers through each other, pressed my nails, which I had not only had manicured but also, with a comfortable feeling of real pleasure, filed so beautiful and handsome that they *felt* clean, in my flesh: no! *no!* it was all true, it could have been so earlier, but I had bathed so long in the most unexpected gift of fate, in the most magnanimous hour of overwhelming, actual luck that time and chance had ever allowed me. I wriggled in my pocket, in the skittish paper packet in my pocket, for the little white support that soul sufferers habitually seek and find in a poor cigarette, although it is also every time like a new little candle of death that they burn for their slow ruin. I didn't dare to appear to pull out the little pack to offer Fran one of my bitter, cheap cigarettes. Bashfully I asked whether I might smoke. But at the same time I saw that she herself was smoking and, without widening her painted, smiling lips, nodded silently, as if to say cordially: go ahead! I lit up hastily and threw the match in the ashtray on the smoking stand, the identical ashtray on the identical stand as in my room. But her ashtray was a great deal fuller than mine. There lay there, in hers, a dreadful number of half-smoked fag-ends, nervously stubbed out and snapped. Thus she had certainly not slept, but all that time, all those long hours, sitting there, meditating, dreaming, and—God! God!—perhaps indeed waiting for me! Suddenly I started at a stealthy thought inside me. Anxiously I looked at them again, more sharply. No, fortunately! They were all the same cigarette butts, cigarettes with mouthpieces smeared bloody red, with golden mouthpieces like those which had been fashionable in my young years; and perhaps she, from a touching coquettishness for old elegance, as a very personal eccentricity, now never smoked anything else. And smeared with blood from her mouth, sharply incarnadined. Blood and gold! Gold as her glistening bangs, and bloody as my heart! "Blood and Sand," like a heroic film from my youth. Could it be that she cherished that old romanticism, that old-fashioned, disconcerting charm, as much as I did? Thoughtfully, she let the smoke from her cigarette curl out of her half-opened mouth. I saw the white of her spotless, evenly rowed teeth. I could not, I dared not, look more deeply. But there, in that warm, tender, soft cavity—did there also, behind the first white row of teeth, a heroic intimacy of gold and blood-red prevail? She was still young, but still certainly thirty already, and it bothered me not at all to consider that at the back of that beautiful mouth certain teeth perhaps had been filled. I asked myself only whether she, who liked golden cigarette mouthpieces, just as I did, also gave preference to a denture that, as it were, seemed to have bitten into a golden material and borne from it the remaining, flickering trace, to the darker silver, or the sickly pale imitation of it, of new-fashioned dentistry. I could not see that now; for that she would have to laugh more happily or painfully, with the corners of her mouth more separated, and the head tilted somewhat backwards, and the light of the lamp wrung between her torn lips and the biting surfaces of her teeth. But I did not want to think any further about that. Perhaps that also would yet be granted me: to be permitted to cast just once a quick, innocent glance into that lovely throat, that rose, moist passage so near to her soul! I did not want to, I could not proceed further; it was a too dizzying, an all too exciting idea, with perhaps something involuntarily indecent in it, such as occurs when a person descends in his ideas without preserving a sense of actuality and through it the strange power, which always commands respect, that is sheltered in the perceptible, externally existing reality of things or creatures. And then today—how long ago, how fantastically long ago that afternoon seemed already—I had already spent more than enough time on teeth and biting surfaces and lead fillings. The monstrous, dangerous remembrance of that now slipped into me for a moment; I knew well that it was present in me, that I should never again be able to rid myself of it; I saw it there in me, on the bottom of my memory, lying low, sleeping, but *itself,* that remembrance; it was not now arguing; it lay there unconscious; like an invalid under the veil of a wonderful narcotic—God protect me from waking up that horrible specter!

Then I made a great effort and, as the diver who has descended, floating, to the floor of the ocean, pushes himself away from it again with his foot, I tried with gripping arms to reach back to the rational upper levels of my soul. Altogether the golden fag-ends, smeared with the lethal red of her lips—none otherwise, none from a possible *man*—showed that she had spent all those hours in complete solitude, entirely *alone!* I should be happy now, so greatly had I feared that she had perhaps *not* sat there thus. And I was happy, I smiled and nodded—I swam again for a while on the upper surface of myself, in the light of a soft lamp and of a matchlessly beautiful face. My cigarette was almost done; it was one of the cheaper kind that are usually not so firmly packed, but yet—I felt that I was going to have another pain: did she smoke then so much more calmly than I? I remained on the defensive. We sat across from each other, with the smoking table between us. Her eyes, a little narrowed because of the smoke, did not rest directly on me, but on the portions of my armchair which were visible to her. It was like a motionless wink, like a soundless communication, which I suddenly began to understand. How was I also going to sit? I completely forgot that I had done something, that I had pushed the chair, though even only half a centimeter, closer to the smoking table, or with my face directly toward her. Thus had I been standing there, just before I came in—thus was I perhaps still waiting for something? And on that smoking table I suddenly noticed now two finely blown glasses which had the form of two large inverted cones and which must actually have been there the whole time, for Fran had not moved other than with the ritual gestures of smoking. Two goblets—two again! Each and every side of a crystal carafe, filled with a plum-colored liqueur, the glass stopper of which, in its innumerable glittering surfaces, like a precious prism, divided the light into the most startling colors and then melted them together again. The carafe wasn't full to the neck, but wasn't that perhaps usual in an eminent hotel of the international type? Must wine or other glasses always be poured full at select tables? Concerning this,

I was still so eager, was certain, or . . . ? But Fran's fingers took the crystal stopper out of the neck, you would have sworn unconsciously, and yet with the indescribably soft handiness of well-to-do people, for whom such a ceremony is a daily occurrence. She poured the glass on my side three-fourths full —three-fourths! My glance flew from the glass to her eye, but I could see only the downcast ivory lids, and also that her mouth now barely bordered upon a smile. Three-fourths, and she had asked not a word whether I desired to drink; had not even consulted me with a glance to see whether I was up to a similar quantity! Perhaps, perhaps she had drawn the wrong suspicions from the shabby impression which the sudden reappearance of my woeful figure after ten vile years had undoubtedly made on her this evening downstairs on the wrought-iron steps; and perhaps my wild eyes, and possibly a certain atmosphere which still remained about me, the result of that steinful of gin that I had ordered in the country tavern across from the churchyard at D—, had set her in the opinion that there was, between my apparently having got into low water and the evident indications of dipsomania, a relationship of cause and effect. But when she had poured her goblet, just as full as mine, suddenly it didn't matter to me any more whether she supposed me upon that evil course. I was for a moment jubilantly happy for the unasked-for drink that she had poured me, and for the comradeliness, the brotherliness, which which she had measured out precisely the same amount for herself. But then I felt a touch of sorrow: I had thought of so many confused things alike that I had lost sight of the starting point of my sorrow. My thoughts had strayed, first to the carafe, then to the quantity of liquor in the glass—and now it was too late, the dark drink was already in her glass, the chalice already sparkled on her lips, it was now no longer possible to see, I would never, never know whether she had been drinking already that evening, that night, while she had sat there before my arrival, or whether she had awaited me in everything and also in that! We drank, without clinking our glasses, which I approved of: for the first time in my life

I realized that clinking is bourgeois, both undistinguished and uncomradely. She nodded her head, at which a floating glitter stirred through her bangs, and blinked her eyelids. I no longer know whether I answered her, but that was apparently unnecessary: I had the distant feeling of associating in such an extreme state of incitement that everything material had become as if transparent to me, and my least meditations could be read immediately from the raw wall of my soul itself. We drank; it was a heavy liqueur, much less sweet than I had feared and than I knew women usually choose, which is treacherously able to make the beauty of their comradeship too soupy; and moreover breathtakingly spirituous. I did not see the least convulsive jerk in the handsome, pure flesh of her throat; she assuredly drank less greedily than I, and yet when she set her glass down again after the first draught, the darkly brilliant mirror of the liquid was clearly lower in it than in my goblet. There they were, resting near each other again, our chalices, closer to each other than previously, it seemed to me. Whispering, and it was our first word, I believe, I said, "Thank you, . . . Fran!" Nothing more, and without my glance rising from our glasses. I did not count, like our principal with his stage manager's soul at the time of the commencement ceremony—and then I felt, over my bowed head, the smallest units of time brushing past, while I almost wished that she would not, especially now, break her silence. When she did not answer, she encouraged my gratitude, and with it myself, and everything that I had imagined of her waiting, of that comradeship—everything! She did *not* answer. Then I looked up again and saw that she was barely smiling. Encouraged, she had encouraged everything! Now I could look straight at her, now my glance could encompass her as no physical embrace of people has power to do. And she looked at me, too, meditatively and intently, darkly and yet softly. Now we could speak. And we did speak, we spoke. What we said to each other then, in that fatally beautiful night—now that I have come so far, I am intensely frightened at having to try to write it down here. The loveliest, the most terrible dialogue of my whole life, which was at the same time a conversation with the dead—how would I be able, how would I dare, to want to reconstruct it here? Each word of it stands carved in my soul like an indelible wound and will always remain twitching there, whenever I think back on that farewell. How should I then, out of the distorted marks of that injury, be able to record faithfully here that dialogue between heaven and hell? For that matter, wouldn't the attempt at such an endless task contain something desecrating to the revered memory of the soulfully beloved departed? Let me therefore try only to summarize on paper the principal matters which were then discussed between the unforgettable ex-student, the celebrated artiste, and the fallen teacher, the shipwreck of a clerk. Thus I shall not exercise external completeness and precise rendering of the chronology of our statements and replies, as they might have appeared to an outsider—my poor disturbed head, my tormented soul would at any rate fall too short for that. The content, the material of our dialogue, veined and arteried with blood and nerves—that hardly matters. Forgive me the metaphor; perhaps the dream of a horrible afternoon still haunts my brains, forever scorched by it: but the substance of our conversation I will not even try to open here, in its last articulation, once quivering with life, although I could no longer describe it as a beautiful, rounded whole, with composition, from which death has now stroked away the external wrinkles and notches. Let me then cut our interview straight across into not more than two halves, her half and mine, so as to let just the inextricable entanglement of two lives of solitude and affection, of adoration and inaccessibility, of glory and vilification, be read from the two bloody inner surfaces of that incision in all the divine-human splendor of that soul-destroying night. First, then, here is my half, since the opening word, if I remember correctly, was spoken by me, but I no longer doubt that this resulted from the necessity created by her remaining silent. I looked almost at her luminous head, my hands roving restlessly in my lap or around the arm of my chair, my lips perhaps electrified, but I spoke, I finally spoke! And I said: "Fran, Frannie, if I can still call you that, if I can finally call you that aloud—do you remember, Fran, what you said about *my* name today, this evening, downstairs on the wrought-iron steps? They talk about fingers that are cut off in accidents—which almost always means something painful and harmful, as if it wasn't only that the finger was cut off in a sensitive place, but rather vengefully, as if it was done on purpose. Well, Fran, you, you cut a finger off my soul by accident, and for that charitable contact with my troubles, I want to say thank you. Do you remember? I've held it to myself all my life, but yours was the first living mouth that I've ever heard say it aloud, as if I'd said it to myself. And you did it so cordially, the way you referred to the sad contrast between my first name and my last. You thought of Antfield, of any unhappy worry-wart, doomed to wear himself out with all kinds of anxiety about his whole existence, as foolish as he was pitiful; and you'd rather call me Gopher than Govert, which isn't so bad, or God–fried, which suggests that sooner or later, finally, I'll find my freedom in the Lord, Our Father. You know—yes, *you* know, Fran, don't you, how well you read me; how clearly you understood and summed up all the tragicomedy of my whole life, deeper and sharper than anyone else seems to. And I have no doubt whatever that you didn't say it just because you wanted to make fun, like rich and contented but not unfriendly people who can hurt less fortunate people's feelings so often without meaning to. Should I, Fran, should I doubt that, should I? I'm sorry, but let me just this once tell you everything, confess everything, ask you everything that's been eating me up for ten years, for the ten years since I knew you and you went away from me again, but I tell you, my health and salvation depend on what you answer, everything that my first name promises. Listen, Fran, from the very first there has been something in my life that I haven't been able to explain. I won't get off the subject by talking about that, I don't want to burden your rich, active life, your beautiful, well-deserved peace of mind. Don't misunderstand me when I say you are blessed; I don't mean with success, not even that you've made something fine out of your life. I'm looking at you, Fran, by yourself and all alone. Do you know how beautiful you are? You're so beautiful that you surely must know it, not from the mirror or the love speeches from your admirers and suitors, but because while your beauty may have a physical origin, spiritually it reaches so far, beyond any limits, that it must be *in* you, and all I can do is 'servilely'—I like that word because it has both 'serve' and 'vile' in it—'servilely' bow down before you. So now you know why I adore you, Fran, and I don't have to be ashamed of that word any more; you can't understand me any more; you know now that I don't mean it only one-sidedly but infinitely. For me you're the incarnation of Beauty itself, or else an inhumanly beautiful person—I don't know which, because those two ideas go together, they're both in me, to me they have equal weight, one as deliciously painful as the other is cruelly sweet. There's your blessing, Fran, for yourself and others. Your blessing—oh, you're like a mansion to me, like another Beau Domaine of a little Meaulnes. My wild ride through life has brought me to you now for the second time—and the last, for the holy number three must be reserved for heaven. I stand outside your lighted windows peeking in like a tramp in the night, but don't be afraid, this hobo isn't any thief or arsonist, what you have is outside the sphere of social wrong and revolution against the aristocracy; that mansion is mine, too, our only property—as a French writer has said, 'Illusion is the only treasure of the poor.' That's why, Fran, just as one of the faithful respects his idol, I won't, I can't make any trouble for you. I'll leave when I've finished my drink. But just the same, let me sit in your golden light for a little while, the first time I could do so fully, and for that reason also the last; afterwards the tramp will hurry along onwards into the night, with one last sob, taking with him the memory of that light of years, just as Jean Valjean, when he was on his deathbed, burned the candles that Monsignor Myriel had given him in that stormy night that purified his soul. This afternoon, I must tell you this, I went through a horrible experience—a post-mortem; I think I was so rude as to mention it to you before dinner. I'm sorry—I won't come back to that again. But I just wanted to say that it was a bad mistake for me to endure that terrible spectacle. But I couldn't refuse Professor Mato's invitation—he's my scientific friend; it was my own fault for having foolishly laid so much importance on his particular calling—and now I have to live with the results. But I believe it was too much for me. I'll tell you everything: there was always something in my life, from the very beginning, something like a sudden, painful boredom, a tingling fear, that throws clouds of gold and ashen material through my poor head by turns, and that's the reason I keep having my hair cut shorter and shorter, in the hope that the wind and the rain and the cool of the night, the breath that sometimes blows here from the planet I've promised myself, will bring me peace. My abilities are like a ball of tangled yarn that through the years has gotten worse and worse and that I have made worse by trying to fight it, by playing antics with my name, ANTics, Frannie, until the good robot who holds us all on the straight and narrow has lost his head. I don't believe in 'demons.' It seems to me that the concept of 'devils' is almost like blasphemy—it just isn't possible that the Lord of so much beauty, in his wise and merciful dispensation, would also create evil monsters. That's why I'll only believe in angelic powers, but they can turn against us sometimes because of our own stupidity. The robot in us is one of those angels, and with my eternal worrying, just to take one example, once I had him so paralyzed that just by playing antics with the cold-bloodedness you've got to have when you're speaking on the radio so as to ignore the temptation that seems to come swinging out of the microphone like a naked, idiotic rejection of good habits, so as not to blast out some idiotic noise—I lost control of myself and started to yell into that terrible machine! Thanks for not laughing, Fran. It's always been so abominably miserable, for so long. But I don't want to go through all that. I see that you've grown serious with the thoughts that my story and I have given you. And I won't be an ingrate; I won't take advantage of it, because I can't offer you anything in exchange for what you're giving me except this pitiful *de profundis,* a raw cry of admiration, which won't enrich your life, because you don't need it now, and it can only serve to remind you of the existence of abysses of darkness and grief. I'll try to be brief. There have been six, only six, completely happy months in my life, Fran. The months I spent teaching in your old school. Your last months in school, Fran, and they were the end of things for me, too. Because—this afternoon, when we met each other suddenly downstairs on the steps, I asked you whether you knew it, but how could you know it? You have so many other, more important things on your mind and in your heart—I'm not a teacher any more, Fran. I haven't been at our old school for a long time. If you've ever gone back, you didn't find me there, and a good thing, too. Because I didn't want to see it again without you. And I'm not a lawyer any more, either, Fran, no 'mister,' as you wanted to call me today, before Mr. Vaclav. Now I am just a common, ordinary clerk, like hundreds in the Palace. That's the career, Fran, that your old teacher has made for himself. I was already married when I was your teacher. I have a good wife, a brave and loving wife, and two dear, bright, healthy, and happy children, a boy and a girl, Doos and San. So far none of them has had to go without the necessities, because I've been working myself to death, but there are many, very many, things that I haven't been able to give them, things that other fathers seem to be able to bring home, not, of course, without effort, but with an effort that I'd call 'playful,' that is, through a use of their powers *within* the limits of their normal capabilities, which they apparently know how to draw on and even enjoy doing. Doos and San don't realize all that yet; they're still young, and so far Corra has been beautiful in adversity, bringing them up in all innocence of heart. If they could just keep that forever! It's better than wisdom, it makes success unnecessary, because it provides the purest joys and gives us the liveliest kind of happiness. When I say 'better than wisdom,' I'm thinking especially of Corra, for it can't be anything but wisdom that makes her so patient with everything, that makes her accept things so quietly, walking beside me in my darkness every day, without even once neglecting even one of her duties. It is beautiful, and I'm so grateful to her for her companionship that I don't know how to tell her. But no matter how elevating the sight of such wisdom and virtue may be, every time I look at her my heart bleeds. And without me, Corra's wisdom wouldn' t have any reason to exist. For her, life without me might not have been so meritorious, but it would at least have been happy. So at home I'm always living under the silent accusation that I have failed miserably even in building my family. I don't know how many years I still have to live. No matter how dilapidated I may seem, I'm still healthy—unfortunately, but fortunately too. Unfortunately because I feel so weighted down. Fran, I'm so tired, Frannie, I wish so much I could just lay down my foolish head and doze off forever. But I can't do that, I can't just yet, and that's why I say 'fortunately,' because I couldn't leave Corra alone with the whole burden of the children. It doesn't matter how imperfectly, I'm going to do everything I can to fulfill my obligations. I hope God lets me live until Doos and San can stand on their own feet and can look after their mother. Then delivery may come for me, and that will mean that Corra will be free as well. Maybe then, at the end of her life, she'll be able to find such a happiness in life at the side of her children, when they're grown, as everybody has a right to and as she has deserved more than others because of her patience, which has hung like an eternal light over her beautiful life and, no matter what others have wanted to do and tried to do, and although it has frustrated her all these years, which will finally bring her a spring and a summer blossoming out of the soil of her own unlucky nature itself. Because her virtue and her wisdom are flowers of the autumn and winter, and she deserves all the praise in the world for them, and *I* bear all the blame for such premature seasons. There, Fran, you have the whole dreary life of the man who is now, once more, after ten years of anguish, grief, and fruitless effort, sitting across from you like a tramp looking into the window from heavier and heavier adversities, warming his unhandy hands and his soul with its paralyzed wings at the glowing gold of your blessed and forgiving presence. I had to confess all that to you so as to get it off my chest, and I mean it also from an obligation to be honest with you. Maybe you don't think much of me now, for more complete and certainly sounder reasons than before, during that graduation ceremony at school, when you begrudged me even one little glance—or at least that was the only way I could interpret your attitude. But maybe your attitude has changed, Fran, and you will remember your Dostoyevsky, and there is a warm echo in your heart of the voice that was harsh but that was pleading for all his destitutions and humiliations. Maybe you also cherish compassion and a little love for destitutions and humiliations. I wouldn't go so far as to say that this is something that goes with your beauty; I think that what we can see of it is of course only the physical aspect, which is only the beginning, and its spiritual background must go infinitely deep. But beauty is so mysterious, it is so completely self-contained, that I really don't know whether its immaterial face may have something to do with compassion and charitableness. Time and again, when I let my obscure face turn toward your light, in my most solitary thoughts, I have anxiously asked myself whether that action wasn't wrong; whether there wasn't a shadow that fell over your splendor, which formed my only comfort. Why should beauty, which is so beautiful, have to have anything to do with goodness? They're both children of the Father, but why do we try to make a monstrous Siamese twin out of them? And yet, and yet! Is there any beggar who has never dreamed of standing, or even tried to stand, peering in at actual or imaginary windows on a winter night? Oh, Fran, I can see and hear just as well as you can that what I am now is what I've been all my whole life long, and always worse and worse; every day I work myself deeper and deeper into the tangle of myself, because of my fruitless antics! Only the other day I was waging my battle far from your beautiful glance and your radiant head; I can't tell you how miserable I was. Once a friend tried to pay me a facetious compliment. He said that I thought like a microscope. And I've carried that around with me ever since. A microscope fragments life; when the scientist looks away from it again, his genius joins together all those little pieces anew, into a more meaningful whole, from which science can gain some support in its explanation of the universe for the benefit of us all. And there's a microscope sitting in my head, I can't get my mind's eye away from it, and so I am endlessly fragmentating, without ever even once being able to turn back to life with a tangible, wholesome conclusion. When I understood that, at least, clearly and definitely about myself, I was honest. I confessed to myself and others that I was not equal to my task and looked for a more modest job. Good clerks are always needed, too. But even that was an illusion, because my human pride told me that surely, unquestionably, I would belong to the category of good clerks. But what bitter disillusionments, what painful humiliations and insults were in store for me, not from other people, because I'll take to my grave only a good and grateful memory of my fellow men—but out of the most miserable depths of my own inadequacy. Well, anyway, I've done my best, I've done my best inhumanly well; I've never spared myself, not for a day, not for an hour. I've literally put myself through the wringer, Fran; I've loaded myself up with work until every night I simply collapsed under it; and then the next day I went out and did it again. And that, that *is* still something, isn't it? Even though nobody else has ever had to supply any of our needs, maybe I'll be blamed for that as well, as the least important of all human rewards; but I've never been afraid to try, not even when I knew all along that I was lost beyond hope. Fran! Why I have done all this isn't clear to me. I think it's from a sense of obligation, from sorrow and from love—out of a dark, miserable, unreasoning love for the belief in a Father, for abasement before His wonderful power, and for His inexpressible compassion toward life itself and toward mankind, even the least of mankind, as I myself have learned to know. I don't believe that it's out of a depraved desire for self-pity or in the selfish hope of earning a place in heaven through this submission. I do hope that maybe I'll seem worthy of it; the beautiful mystery of heaven does captivate me more than some other things; but I want to say one last time that I might have made a tragic mistake; even the smallest door into Paradise may never open to my knock, or the Hereafter may not even exist —well, I still won't complain, I won't feel embittered or rebellious; then sleep, Frannie, endless rest, will be welcome and sweet to me. See, Fran, there's the 'something' that's always been in my life, and that I've told you about—I really can't describe it more closely—and I won't bother you with it any longer. And at least you do know the results of it. I consider it as my ordeal, as a punishment if you insist, more than as a disease. Don't you agree, Fran, that it can't be really a sickness? I've never been able to accept that, and that's why I've never been to a doctor about it. I can't put it into words, but this is the way I feel, it would be unfair in a way, a little like doping a horse or any other kind of dishonesty in a race. My problems have always begun in my soul, Fran, and that can't be sick, can it, because that's a part of God in us. *God!* I am saying so much to you about Heaven, Fran, about that wonderful mystery that captivates me more than anything else, because if it actually does exist, everything else, which you see can only be the result of that cause, will become clear to us on the disclosure of that secret. At the same time I have spoken to you, Fran, of a sweet, nocturnal planet that I dream of as the home of my soul. Well, now I'm coming to the most important thing that I want to tell you, the most important thing spiritually that I want to ask you about; something that gave me a golden stab in my very heart at the same moment I saw you for the first time in my life; that I have turned over in my antic thoughts in exhausted, sleepless nights and through the restless, anxious hours of so many days of drudgery, and into which now some clarity has come, extremely slowly, so dreadfully slowly that it seems almost imperceptible, as if ten long years hadn't passed. I say clarity, and by that I mean only that little bit of clarity that I need so that I can at least have a subject for my statements and an object for my question. I see myself as an impoverished soul who has lived for ten years in the deepest, blackest night and who can scarcely move from its place because in that complete darkness everything it touches hurts it. When it raises its hand futilely to break out, it never knows whether it would be better off if it did. And if that's impossible, it doesn't have anything else and can only reach out for nothing at all. I think that's why I didn't come to you any earlier, of my own volition. Of course there's always been ground to move on, but I wouldn't have been able to express it, for your sake as well as for mine. Now, Fran, I hope I have the strength to do it. Because it's an overpoweringly beautiful thought how just at this propitious moment you were permitted to come into my life once more. The night isn't over, Fran, my night will never be over so long as I live, I know that; but the darkness is fading. I'm sitting now in your glorious light, but both in myself and outside myself there is something, maybe as the reward for those ten years of patiently being a cavedweller, something turning gray. I believe that if I were to cover my eyes with my hands now, I would be able to detour around all the dusk in my soul. Maybe that's the dawn of death trickling into me already, from the direction of your light, *your* light, Frannie, that shines through my whole being even if I close my eyes! In that case I must thank you for that, especially for that. Then you haven't only returned to me now—but you have simply come and at the same time have made this time propitious for me. How can I, out of my gray thoughts, make any sense to you or be able to ask you a great, decisive question? Listen, now, Fran, my beautiful, lustrously beautiful friend! What I mean to do is to make one idea out of the brilliance of heaven and the harmoniousness of my soul's planet. I believe I've seen a sample of it and heard an intimation of it. That was in those six months of school ten years ago, and—because of you, because of you alone, Fran! But then parting from you hurt so cruelly, at that terrible commencement, the most terrible I've ever seen. I certainly was indescribably foolish, because you begrudged me even one glance, even though I was behaving like a deplorable clown, because I hungered for that glance so passionately, and so futilely; and if I'd had it it would have made our parting so much easier, as well as my return to hard work and everyday life. But I hadn't come to the wisdom, then, that we shouldn't demand illumination from beauty, that it is a monstrous, Siamese-twin sister of charitableness. Oh, Fran, you don't know everything yet about my crazy actions that afternoon. When it was already late and you girls weren't doing anything but dancing with the boy scouts, I didn't know how to escape my lonesomeness any longer, the grief I'd been suppressing, my fear of the dreadful night that was about to come on; then—I'd fled from the room, upstairs, to our old classroom, just as Professor Unrath returned to his old empty school because of a blue, merciless angel of beauty. I stood up there in the hallway, looking in vain on the hatrack for the little ticket with your name that I had wanted to keep next to my heart as a souvenir, hidden in my wallet or the case of my watch—but it was gone, apparently it had fallen off, perhaps it had been loosened from the wood and curled up by the heat of the sun and fell to the floor, and perhaps at that very moment it was stuck fast to the sole of the shoe of some totally indifferent visitor and carried away God knows where. I'm not ashamed to tell you this now, Fran, I know that you won't do any more now than just think I'm ridiculous, and you won't misunderstand me—then I wept, Fran, there in that dark, lonely hallway, I cried out all my foolish grief; sobbing, I embraced your clothes hook, and witlessly I kissed the dark, empty spot, kissed it, where your name had shone in the pathetic loops of your schoolgirl penmanship. I wept, while downstairs the dance music thumped as if it was suffocating—it seemed to be playing that old tune from *The Blue Angel* that was running through my head: 'Ich bin von Kopf bis Fusz auf *Leiden* eingestellt!'—but I didn't sing that, I was singing, with my aching head pressed to the clean wood and the cool iron of the hatrack: 'Fran is leaving school! Frannie is leaving school forever now!' For those six months of happiness that I had known at our old school—only because of you, Fran, were they that; because of your enchanting presence you made them the one wonder of my whole life. That's the meaning you had for me these ten years; my worship is the miserable present that I want to give you now with trembling hands, in the twilight of death which is already trickling into my soul, and with eyes that are blinking in the light from your golden beauty: Fran, Frannie! that's what you've meant to me; that's what you have been to me throughout my whole night, though I haven't been able to find words for it; and that's what you will be to my last sob! Forgive me for this *de profundis,* this unasked-for confessional, this perhaps unwished-for adoration. I am not crying out to you, Fran, in the hope of moving you; of perhaps catching an echo from you; or even of persuading you to impute another significance to this foolishness and misery. You understand that, don't you? No, this is no declaration of love, let me swear that to you. My feelings toward you are too beautiful, too sad, and too difficult to deserve to be given a name, or to have to bear one, which is at the same time too large and too small—a name that offends me as much for its disrespectful narrowness as you must find it brutal in its shamelessness. So take my meaning, Fran, without being afraid of the question I've said I'll ask you. The word 'love,' that I've used only once, and then only to reject it, will never cross my lips again. Such a poor word for such an unfathomable concept, and often used for such a shameful referent! While I was once infinitely happy because of you, Fran, you have never once until today rewarded me with even a glance. At that commencement you didn't notice me once, and perhaps that was all right. For although we don't have to see any relation between the works of sisterly charity and beauty, with the physical basis of the one and the endless spiritual horizons of the other, surely both of them had their origins in God's warm bosom itself—and beauty itself certainly exists, it may even be *essential* to its full development that we should think of it only loosely in order to adore it in its solitary pride free from that the name of which I won't say again. That, that Beauty, is what you have given me, Fran, and it was unnecessary for me to think about it, wasn't it, although my all-too-human heart hungered for it so painfully then and later. But even in that hunger there was never any of the unnameable. No matter how much I was blinded by the glowing, bleeding, golden light of that commencement ceremony and later by the darkness of my night—at least I have always felt that. Now, thanks to the fact that I have begun to tremble, that feeling has grown to a timid knowledge. My hunger has grown somewhat clearer, enough so that I can say to you that what I have longed for from you so much is that it should be given me just once, with my own ears, to hear her speak to me, to be able to ask her with my own mouth and to be able to receive her answer from her own lips. Now that moment has come, like an unbelievable gift of fate; such an overwhelming gift has been given to me, the poorest tramp of all. I'll have to be careful not to be so overpowered by joy that the hard question I'm going to ask you now becomes unrecognizable in the noise of the storm inside me. Oh, Fran, *my* Frannie, let me call you that now just this once! I have already told you that that was *my* name for you. That's what I called you, in silence, to myself, during those six months, and by that name I treasured you so tenderly in my memory for ten years. In the meantime you have given yourself, as an artiste, the stage name Franny Veen—'Franny,' that is almost the same, Fran, you know! It gives me such a strange, such a sweet feeling, as if there were an understanding between us, when I think that we both, without knowing it, chose that particular, special name for you. Your little friends always called you 'Fra'; of course you remember that. But I thought that was too hard; that ended too brusquely on that open vowel sound. I wanted to give you a more finished name, a name from me alone, and that was it and still is, although now, by chance, you hear the same one publicly; but you gave yourself that one, no one but you, didn't you? If some indifferent third person had proposed that name for you, I would have felt betrayed, but now that you, who bear it, now that you have taken it for yourself, I don't feel that it is a betrayal of my innocent secret but on the contrary, it is like a consecration of it. The only second person who can hear the magic of a name without any outside influences, even better than the giver of the name, is the person who bears it, isn't that right? So now everybody can call you, Fran, by the name which we have both found for you and which you, on your side, can calmly lay bare in the public eye—and I am sitting on the other side of you, which no one shall ever know because I'll keep your secret in my mystery until Heaven. *My* Fran! Oh, let me say it once more! *Fran!* Do you hear how that syllable sings, vibrant and warm as your golden hair, chiming like the golden fringe on your forehead, and with the dear rustle of the name people gave that fringe in my youth? I can still hear the barber ask my mother whether he should cut my hair with a 'little frou-frou,' for once even this ugly head of mine, this callow, clammy clump, with its spotty nerves and its varicose veins and its eternal antics, Frannie, wore blond bangs. And that was called a 'frou-frou' then; I never understood why that was so popular; I suppose after the heroine of that sad play. But that name has always been dear to me, apparently because of the music I heard rustling in it, of silks and satins, supple and glossy as your hair, and, well, maybe a little because of the memory of that frivolous little heroine of long ago who, like me and my foolish head, never took any advice because of her turbulent heart and therefore died so deplorably. But I am wandering off the subject again. Fran! It must be so late now that day could come at any moment—I must hurry and get to my question, my great question. Forgive me, forgive me, that I have broken in here like a thief, to steal your night's rest! But I'll remain grateful to you to my last breath, un-speakably grateful, for the lighted window in the winter night at which you have appeared for this tramp and at which you have remained all the while, looking at him so beautifully and so gently, until he has told you all his happiness and grief. Just one night out of your rich life, but you can spare that for that poor devil, your old ex-teacher, can't you, Frannie? For you there are only a few hours of lost rest, that you can easily catch up on tomorrow, the day after tomorrow, on the glorious coast of a beneficent sea; but for me, for me, it is such a tremendous gift of God that it will last me to my grave, and even *into* my grave! Then listen, Frannie! I still have to tell you the last and most important reason why I called you 'Fran'; and then I'll get on to my question. You know now that on the one hand I didn't want to call you 'Fra' like everybody else. But on the other hand I also had something else, something intricate, in mind; yes, something in-tricate, or tricky: I wanted to save your real name, your beautiful, old-fashioned, wonderful real name—I wanted to save it from everyday use and in that way preserve its deep luster. 'Eufrazia!' How often, in those ten years we've been apart, I have thought of that, without ever letting it pass my lips! *Eufrazia!* That name is inevitable for you; or perhaps it isn't possible that anyone with that name could be any other way! You know Greek, don't you; and even if you didn't, you know what your name means, don't you? At least, to the extent that that beautiful meaning cen be understood and applied by human beings? *Euphrasia*, *εὐφρασία*, that is, the speaker of the good word, the happy messenger, or the celebrant of beautiful splendor which she gives bounteously, from her waist, that wonderful point of contact, for the ancients, between body and soul. *Euphrasia*—one of my dictionaries even translated it, with touching simplicity, as 'pleasure,' and in those learned works the expression does not, unfortunately, mean any more. It stands there in its classic purity, with its Greek harmony between the world and the senses. It means rest, just as beautiful music is tremulous rest, and happiness, but the happiness that we dream of finding in death, not that ordinary, noisy, deceptive happiness of life. 'Eufrazia'—it should be the name of my cool heavenly body, of that sweet planet of nocturnal brightness and lukewarm dew, that I keep telling myself might be my soul's real home. In the meantime, and I think it is a mixed, but inexhaustible, delight, I have learned, and you'll know it soon, that the name is also given to an insignificant little creature of this world, to a small, herbaceous, flowering plant which, except for a single, very rare variety, is somewhat more common in our northern clime. It has been known for a long time that bathing the eyes in the juice of that plant has been able to cure soreness caused by tears or other things, and for that reason scientists gave it your name, Fran, and now you can find yourself in any dictionary, defined not only as a Greek word of classical bliss, but also as the healer of sore, hurt, or blinded visions—as the silent, magical herb that in our region bears the modest but infinitely sweet name of 'Eyebright.' *Eyebright!* Oh, Fran, you can guess, can't you, that that last name is almost the dearest to me? *Almost,* because of all the poor wretches who have sat in your light, I am easily the most grateful, the most trustworthy, because you gave me your brightness ten whole years ago, even before you were fully aware of my shabbiness. You have continued shining in my life even when that life itself was unsteady in me; but alongside that grief which was still young but which already was weighing me down, I also cherished many youthful illusions. At that time you let your golden shadow pierce me—or at least so it seemed to me at that moment; but later, after those foolish dreams of confidence, after the last presumptuous sighs were wrenched out of me, I saw how, in anticipation, you had given me something of yourself, something of your refreshing light, like a healing salve for my wounds to come. That's why I would *almost* choose that dear herb *Eyebright,* but I've already told you that I try to guard against my human selfishness, my petty egocentricity. Maybe you think that name for you is too patronizing, and I can even see that myself. You are so beautiful that apparently you don't have to be 'good'; I want to protect myself against that monstrous desire to make beauty and goodness a child with two bodies and one head. No, Fran! I won't equate you with a jar of salve and a medicinal herb; that isn't what you are, and you can be that to me only by the other thing that's in your first name, by your perfect, proud, unapproachable beauty, by the only healing mystery of Beauty. Both your names are true, but the first has the most of *you* in it, and that's the most important and the truest. You *are* Beauty, Fran, while your last name—for *veen* means peat-bog in Dutch—your last name only expresses what—O costly outcome!—drips into our upturned faces from beauty, as a solace, but that demands none of your substance; it is like the golden shadow of your golden being. That's what you have meant to me, Fran, ten years ago and for the past ten years, and only because your face exists, and your hands and all of you, because of the sound of your voice, and it makes no difference what words you may have spoken to me. Your beauty has bathed my eyes even in the darkest night, Fran; it has laved the inflammations of my soul, and when everything in me had died, it became my only, but my greatest, illusion. I have received help from you because I didn't want to ask my scientist friends, like Professor Mato and his colleagues. That sound instinct, at least, has stayed with me unassailably, that we must not let science intervene in our souls. Everyone has his fate, which is written down, and he must take it as his test. We all of us never stop being children, students, to our last gasp, and we can't be promoted until we have gone through the whole dear and bitter schooling. We can't play hooky, not even a note from the doctor will save us from our difficult examinations, for one day death will close the doors of that pleasant building behind us forever, and only those who have actually worked their lessons will be able to elevate themselves by their own strength, while the cheaters, whose ponies will not have escaped notice, will flunk miserably, to put it mildly. But you, you weren't a science, were you, Fran, and you still aren't. I've never asked you for helpful hints, and as a matter of fact, such requests would never live to get through the glittering force field that continually shines around the cynosure of all eyes. I don't know whether beauty wears armor; it has always blinded me so much that my view of it has never been clear enough to make that out; but what I do know is that the beams it sends out surround it like a wreath of spears, and when some pure and obscure desires escape our human heart and try to creep near, with tightly shut eyes, that blind beggar wounds himself cruelly against them and scrambles, ashamed, back into his dark shell. And that's the reason why I have never been able to receive any unpermitted help from you, Fran; I have borne the trials given me alone, fearfully alone, with no help from anything or anybody. Still, having your distant reflection, perhaps, more than other people, who have to exist underground in total darkness forever, I'm conscious of the merciless size of the load I have to carry. And yet you have made my existence heavenly, Fran, without lightening it. Your light has not removed any weight; perhaps it has even added to it with all its golden weight, and yet that's been a relief to me; in that *light,* perhaps, I have fought more heroically—I look like a foolish clown, of course, and I don't even have a pitiful piece of a sword, but I fight with only a splinter from my soul, with torn nails, and with blunt, worn teeth like a decrepit deer, against all the wild beasts of this life—but still more bravely because of the light from the tragic stage, and from your divine presence, up there on that high, lustrous balcony. That was my *Blood and Sand,* Frannie; that was *my* stupid heroic movie, and now I am lying here under your eyes, ripped open and dying, with my wounds full of sand, and yet, still happy! I'm not angry with anyone; I understand the bravissimo that arises from the crowd for the strong, handsome bull, whom I myself look at admiringly, even with the dew of death in my eyes; and to you—no one shall ever know that I had chosen you queen of the *corrida*—to you I send my last respects in default of a blessing. Fran, that's how far I am now into the last mile between life and death, and I shall bear my trial to the end, without any scientific narcotics or . . . without even intervening. You know what I mean. I can't, not for my family, not for myself. That's the way I feel. I'm well aware that I'm only a stupid scholar; that's the reason I can't afford to take a vacation until class is over. I'll stick it out to the end, with the other boys, even though I know that I'll never walk off with a single prize and apparently won't ever deserve even an honorable mention. But you don't have to hope, to persevere. I shall persevere; I won't give up before the final test. Your image will always go with me, ever more beautiful, more lustrous, and more comforting than before. You are my St. Christopher's medal and my last sacrament, Fran. And here, concerning this, I must ask you my great question, I want to ask you a question of great weight to my soul. But—God, God!—the anxiety is making me perspire, Fran, I am floundering again in my hopeless tangle, I . . . I have forgotten my question! I can still hear it inside me, like a bar of fading music, but I can't follow the tune! Why did you listen to me so patiently? Why did you let me speak so long? Oh, Fran, Fran! Now you can see the whole extent of my trouble, my hard lot. I wanted to ask you something, only for my own information; something about beauty and its spiritual background. I wanted to ask you for something, something like a password, for later, in the Promised Land that you represent here on earth. But you've let me run on too long. I haven't even asked my question. This is just one more time that I've got everything so irretrievably tangled with my antic thoughts that I'm not able to put things back together again, even if it was only a question. Why, why did you let me say all those things, Fran, about the beautiful and the good, and about those monstrous or adorable twins? Before I could come to my question, I already answered it myself. I cut through all the threads of communication and acquaintanceship like a lunatic; I didn't untie the knot of the riddle, I hacked it away; I shaved my dizzy heart, my disordered brains, barer than my foolish head—and look at me sitting here now, with my trembling hands outstretched to receive one ray of your light, but with fingers too short even to hold my fragmented self together. I'll stop, Fran, I can't catch up any more, I have emptied myself in my unleveed flood of words, I have plucked myself bare and all that's left is a sea of flaky scum, a dancing firmament of fluff wheeling around me, as in *The Gold Rush,* when that poor fool of a Chaplin, mad with delight at being enchanted by the face he idolized, starts to tumble through his Christmas cabin, hauls the mattress off his bunk, and shakes it inside out until the

feathers that it was stuffed with, on which his poor head dreamed of such melancholy beauty night after night, begin a whirlwind between the wooden floor and the ceiling rafters, a whirlwind which it is impossible to calm, so that the happy idiot is finally covered with them. So I've told you everything, Fran; even that for years I've felt things growing darker, with handfuls of fluff and armfuls of shorn hair, like the great, the first and last, the highest question I wanted to ask you. But maybe you won't be confused about that clumsy clown; your bright eyes and your peaceful spirit will perhaps recognize and understand the soul in his whirling fog, which is made up of grindings and gratings—and so perhaps you can answer the threshed-out ravelings, the shorn stalks, of the question which, in the despairing, yet happy, hour of a single, late summer, flower-scented night, he has blown like pollen into your cool, deep blue, paradisical heaven and at the same time, like an insane child, into his own eyes! The question which I forgot, but which maybe you already know; the question which perhaps I never knew, but which maybe you'll be able to tell me, and the answer too, Fran—oh, Fran!—the question of all my grief, of my whole ineffectual life, and of your beauty, and, in spite of everything, of my impervious, but still unembezzled, luck! Thank you, Frannie, thank you so much, and forgive me."
—That is what I said to her then; as I have indicated, not all at once, but all those long hours, by halts and starts, which I have joined together here as *my* half of the unforgettable, lovely, and horrible dialogue of a night, with which my life also ended. I have repeated that half here in detail; perhaps the eventual editor of my story will find it too long and will prune it. He can do that without having to worry about it. But I am very happy that I succeeded in noting down just about all of my share in that last conversation with Fran. Perhaps I could have been briefer, but for once my weakness has not been an impoverishment! And now—oh oppressive, oh thrice painful end of my action!—I must transcribe Fran's words from my soul, where they are burned into the very fibers indelibly throughout my life, but perhaps, as I hope and pray now, in-

extinguishable by death. I do not know whether Fran spoke so long and so fully as I; in that night all the clocks in the world stood still until that irretrievable moment. Still her half, which I shall try to give here, will perhaps be shorter than mine. Oh, not from any lack of love for even the least of her words—do I have to confirm that? But just from a boundless respect. I intend to set her share down here as fully from her alone, besmirched by nothing that might have come from me. That is the last obeisance I can make her now. Her words, as I have said, are burned into me. I shall have to tear them from me in order to be able to repeat them, but I shall also have to tear myself from them in order to set them down here on paper clean and undefiled. At this time I shall not develop for the reader any sentence which was perhaps only half stated but which then took on importance only because of the presence of those concerned. I have had the floor long enough in this composition. Now come her pages. Stand by me, Lord, and let my stiff hand and my recently sharpened pencil call up once more the actual sound of her voice, her farewell, beautiful as death, melancholy and harmonious, in dear little sentences to which I was completely certain, at least then, that nothing of my own heavy, bloody clay could attach. Thus, then, she spoke, and then it was as if all the light of her lamp streamed from her to shine through me; it seemed a melodious cloud of the noblest metal; a cloud so clarifying as that had never stupefied me before. She herself became completely transparent, like golden gauze, like a veil that lies spread over a fearful secret, suddenly losing its opacity; but, no matter how pitiful the concealed object may appear, it did not affect her beauty—no, my God, my inconceivable Lord, it did not make the adorableness of her whole being, of her unearthly face, and of her abused body, too translucent, but *on the contrary,* if such a thing may be possible, merely strengthened it. Forgive me, God, forgive me the possible heresy which my ravaged senses may thirst to go in for here, but now I have experienced everything with such heartrending sincerity and sense-bewildering beauty and cruelty, and You know, compassionate Father, You must still be able to hear how even the wildest of my words, sounding in the malformed dome of my head, there, inside me, still has the relative excuse of the meager thing snatched from still poorer fortunes, and the fulfilled beauty of each paean sung You, by the hoarsest of animals as well as the poetic swan, in death. For with Fran's enduring voice, Lord, is preserved the great, wonderful riddle that I, like You on High, have sought behind, and which I hope and pray to be able to seek until my last sob. But I'll be silent, I'll be silent now for you, Frannie. "Govert, my poor, old Govert! I do believe I understand you. Yesterday afternoon, downstairs on the steps, I thought I felt it all. I'm sorry that I have never given you anything but sadness; but perhaps now you can have a last chance to find peace. I'm grateful for your love. Oh, let me call it love. Men have made me used to that by now. Even the best of those who come near me always seem at last to give that most elevated terminology to their unlimited desires. I don't believe the real thing has been offered to me very often, possibly because I carry it in my own blood. Instead, I think that that partial equivalence has helped me to see clearly. And what it should be! What does the word say, unfortunately, more than any other, no matter how holy or shameless? It's only the same old game of disillusionment played over again by spoiled children who have to have little stories from their daddy. The same ritual fussing about with inaccessible things, so as to hide even the least truth. Oh, well, even in the most extreme cases, the so-called scandalous and criminal ones, I still believe they always have a subconscious meaning, just as commonly as the miserable desire for holiness does. All of us are bastards of the spirit of beauty, as well as poor animals made out of clay, and that's the kind of paradox life is. You can call it terrible as long as you aren't involved in it, though you don't like it any better after you are. Anyway, I'm grateful to you for one thing and another, not only for what you've said, Govert, but also for ten years ago. I'll have to admit that I didn't understand you well then, not because I was too innocent, but I think really it was your own fault.

Why did you always make such a greenhorn fool of yourself? You must have been greener than the grass, greener than all those sawed-off, new-laid scouts and other bottle babies. To be honest, I saw you then as a kind of buddy of that puerile principal and that fine duck Klazina Klazinasdaughter Klaassen. I was badly mistaken, but why couldn't you understand then that it is precisely young hearts which can't be served by a romantic in a youthful mask? Then I would have picked a graying widow's peak over the most flourishing curls, and you had such a boyish head! At least that's the way it seems, and everything in life is the same, always too much and at the same time too little. If you had had your hair cut even shorter, almost bald, as now, perhaps I would have understood why your hair looked boyish and then would have sensed the lines and grooves in your prosperous face, where perhaps there was only one blemish then, but where so many may be seen now. For I am very bad for my sex, Govert, and that has a different concept of beauty from yours. Or rather I believe that our *fondness* for beauty is different. The beauty that men get excited about, whether frivolously or with your overwhelming seriousness, we recognize as much as you; as a matter of fact, no other exists. We are apparently in love with it, or have been, like you; but that is, or was, in the way we crave ornaments—we want to wear beauty on ourselves, for ourselves and for others, and the poorer the others, the men, are, the better, for then we can make them richer. That's why a real woman never loves handsome men, but 'character' types, to use a term from show business. That sounds a little fierce, doesn't it, but it doesn't have to be taken as merciless. We might even be able to say that it depends only on the union of souls, and that beauty only plays the rôle of a grateful means of recognition: the woman is looking for the negative sign, the scar, so as to find the soul that she can give herself to as a comforting caress; while the man needs the positive sign of beauty, as God's postmark, so as to recognize the feminine soul through which he can go from earth to the Lord. In that case we women play for once the beautiful rôle of being the only things able to give you men what you lack the capacity to receive. Or rather then your Siamese twin isn't such a monster but a Mardi Gras couple: the Good, with the mask of the fair sex, and the Beautiful, disguised as a boy who lives only in his highest dreams. The carnival ball is full of other couples, avoiding the lamps, in or out of costume; but that comes about only in the wonderful circumstance that, as science has demonstrated, man and woman are extreme cases—to which, undoubtedly, we may pay each other the left-handed compliment of belonging, Govert!—while, in between them, countless half-grown forms are hopping, forms of masculine women and feminine men. You can see, Govert, that even though I have made an antic out of my small share of everything, bear in mind that for ten years, in sad and happy plays, I used my memory, my voice, and my gestures, to silence my heart and my body against the vacant or genial antics of others, who when all is said and done always went over the same things. But now at least you know why I overlooked your scars ten years ago. It doesn't make any sense to ask your forgiveness for that now. Oh, well, if it will give you any pleasure: it was too bad, Govert, and I'm sorry. But why? It can't change things now, and if things had been different then it would have been bad for me or even worse for you. Because the worst thing about me, Govert, but the only thing that gives me peace, is that I don't believe any more. I don't mean in the Lord, though perhaps there are some of his commandments or prohibitions I haven't broken. The Lord may well exist, with all the beauty and goodness and wisdom that a person can dream of. That's no problem for me. Always, when I've had a good dream and it doesn't come true, then I was able to say that reality is a lie compared to my dream, but the fact that I've dreamed, and the things that I've dreamed, do not become any less true. And God is apparently nothing more nor less than something of that nature. But the reality of here and now, Govert, that's what I don't believe in. I don't believe in it any more, not because it is completely a lie compared to our dream; but because it is so incomprehensible, so incalculable and undependable, that you never know whether what you take as a lie today may not seem to exist tomorrow. I've been wrong so many times, I think every time, that I've given up. You get to the point where you can't keep tearing your soul up infinitely. It's like paper: the scissors are small, and the ream too thick, and your fingers too clumsy. And so you live on, out of habit, a little while longer, without soul. Oh, well, your question that you couldn't find any more words for, because you had already asked it in every word you spoke—your question has perplexed me, too. I'd really like to answer it, Govert, for you and for myself. Maybe I'm still confused, possibly as confused as you, for, who knows, maybe I also suffer from your 'something,' or at least a related form of it, although not even you have been able to recognize that in me. Your scar is now very clear to me, and I would rather not say that it awakened my pity, for you don't want that, but it is dear to me. I still have the impression, as I did ten years ago, unfortunately, that I'm farther gone than you, and that's why I think that the 'something' I suffered from then is now so much worse than your disease. Maybe you think it's bewitching, since you want to worship me as the living mystery of beauty, with nothing but a darkly lustrous, 'spiritual' background, as you call it. But now you have asked me a question, yes indeed, a question which may also weight down my soul, Govert, and unfortunately I can't answer you without disillusioning you; I can't spare you. You'll understand me better when I've synopsized my ten years for you, and even a little before those ten years. Oh, I can be very succinct and clear. I'm going to let you see four objects." Then she stood up and brought before me, who sat wiping the sweat off my forehead, the four objects out of her suitcases. One by one she laid them on the crocheted spread on her bed, with slow, dreamy motions. Then she sat by them, almost childishly, on the edge of the bed, inviting me with a scarcely noticeable gesture to take my place on the opposite edge. I am sure now that she smiled, tenderly and sadly, such as I had never been permitted to behold before this; and that I, as if to postpone the destined event which was going to follow closely, possibly to exorcise it, quickly and with a sudden, beautifully unreasoned audacity—thank you, thank you, good automaton, for that last of all your gestures in me!—understood her intention, poured our glasses full, picked up both goblets, carried them to her, gave her hers, toasted her one last, best time, which she received and even responded to. I knew already that she drank, and suddenly I could too. We didn't look at each other while we drank, but only after a horribly, beautifully long moment, of which I can give no complete description; it went so bottomlessly deep that it was completely inexpressible. I took the glasses back to the smoking table and offered her, just as instinctively, one of my bitter cigarettes. She accepted it, without hesitation, and we lit up from the same match. Then I sat on the bed, and she continued. "First, this pistol, a heavy-caliber service weapon, rusty, but loaded. Father gave it to me as a gift when I left home, when he threw me out. That was the Sunday after that commencement ceremony you attended. I had known it was coming for six months; Father had warned me, but the pistol still came as a surprise. *For six months*—haven't you guessed yet? That was about the time you spent at our school. And you know how you came to our school, I mean why, don't you? As a so-called acting instructor, because someone else had suddenly been too busy on account of the duties of his office; but you were surely given to understand that the position definitely would become permanent at the end of the year, weren't you? Well now, here's the second object which is going to make everything clear to you now. The whole fate of a person often takes no more space than such a little cardboard folder. Unfold it, and don't scream, and look at the picture in it. Do you recognize him? Yes, Brantink, naturally, Judge Brantink. I see from your expression that you really were ignorant, all that time. I must confess that the school, the City Hall, and the Palace kept the secret well. Apparently nothing trickled out later, either. But now you know, Govert. Yes, I loved Brantink, and he had me. You will disapprove of this, Govert, but don't judge him too harshly. Whatever guilt or crime there was, I'll take my share of it. There's no point talking about 'temptation'; nowadays girls aren't so foolish any longer—if they ever were! Or do you think perhaps that *I* tempted him? No, I won't make myself out any worse than I actually was. At the most, we were both tempted, by each other or by the devil, it doesn't matter, for perhaps I would be able to defend the position that an angel outwitted us. So much is clear, that I went precisely half way toward Brantink; no more, no less; and that I knew it and wanted to. That was a while before you came to our school. And if it hadn't been for the cock of virtue, that crows when he is offended, everything would have proceeded along its customary course, when unfortunately a spark from our fire flew into your eyes. Love, or adventure, walk just like all the other affairs of people, at least insofar as they have feet. And I was basically as sensible as Brantink was romantic. So everything could end as it had begun. I wouldn't have been any worse off than I am now, and you would never have come to the school, Govert, you would never have known your 'Eyebright,' perhaps never would have had to become emotional about that sorry herb. But now it has to bear fruit; from which this faithfulness can at least call up the edifying reflection that it was precisely in that that the punishment of my vice has lain. Moreover, through that I got to know you; that is to say that through it I met you, and now, after ten years, you have come back and I have gotten to know you at last, and in any case, with or without Brantink, this was just in time. My eyes ought to look sore, but it was all inside, in the flaming pool of my own heart; and since no herb, no matter how magically powerful you want to consider it, can cure itself, you're so welcome, Govert, after these ten years, because you may be able to do me a service, a service of love, of love of goodness or of beauty—one for you and the other for me, perhaps, as with our Mardi Gras couple. Come, put the portrait down; we ought to close up that folder again. The exposure of our love has already caused Brantink enough pain long ago. The cock that crowed then was only a cackling chicken. It had exactly the predestined name, too: Kay Kay Kay! Laugh with me once now, God-freed Antfield! Soon it will be dawn, and then laughter or other such antics won't be possible any longer. Yes, Klazina Klazinasdaughter Klaassen, with her heart of gold, her brains of tin, and her nose like a shrew-mouse—the useful night-prowler! I never bothered about her myself, certainly not where she lived, and naturally Brantink didn't either. Well, now suppose that that dear soul happened to live next to the empty house where Brantink and I met each other. She must have seen us vanish into it once; virtue purred, and naturally the master was told about the unheard-of scandal at once. What could she have got out of it, I wonder? I can still feel sympathetic with him, even though he finally, and just as timorously and precipitately as Miss Klaassen, wanted to call in outside assistance to fight off disgrace. I have never borne any malice toward either of them. They acted as they were created to act, with the innocent intention of doing what was best, and for my part they can both die in the sweetest self-assurance of 'mission accomplished,' about which, in fact, there's not the least doubt! The master then spoke to the alderman and my father. I didn't have a mother any more, and Father wasn't an easy man. A heavy, strong, quick-tempered fellow, who had had to work hard to get to be a supervisor in the Department of Roads and Waterways, and who still worked hard, perhaps because he enjoyed the company of rough workmen and their united struggle against dirt, water, and drilling machines; I know there was much that weighed on him ominously. Father didn't demand anything in particular of me, only that I should always be, and should always do, 'what was proper.' Whether or not that was really proper, I have certainly never known, perhaps because it mattered so little to me. But Father radiated a dark strength which oppressed me and which always warned me against whatever he found reprehensible. I learned that in all questions of conduct he alone could decide what was 'proper.' He nodded once, briefly, with a handsome smile, but handsome in the same way as the round opening of one of his heavy canal locks. The few times that he looked threatening, I had fallen out of my rôle; but only insignificant things were involved. Until the case of Brantink, when all those nineteen deceitful years were brought to light. It must have been an especially hard blow for Father, and therefore I can't bear *his* memory any malice either. I believe that we loved each other, each in his own strange way. With the passing of time I can't understand him any better, especially not his iron rule, 'what was proper,' that now seems even more uncalled-for than ever and leaves me more than ever cold. But in the last ten years I have gradually begun to feel that I am more—or just—his daughter. What he had of sheer physical strength, perhaps also as spiritual strength—these are the flames in my soul; and the ominous pressure which is now beginning, hand over hand, to oppress me, to stifle me—I know now that I inherited this, too, from him. Yes, Father, where are those many years we lived together, so little with each other and yet so involved with each other? Mornings I never saw him. He went to work early, on his bicycle, but when I got up, I always found the little table set for me, in our kitchenette, and the coffee ready, and, winters, the stove on. That never pleased me then, perhaps because Father did it in such a way that it was very clear to me that I should not consider it a mark of affection. But you can see now, by my foolish tears, that your glorious Fran is not a fool only about her body. Once I left home, I began to appreciate how nice my morning kitchenette was; sometimes I still return to it in thought, and when I die I would like the Lord to let my soul pause in that little room a while on its journey to Heaven or hell. I didn't see Father at noon, either, for he took his sandwiches and a thermos to work with him, while I ate with an aunt. Afternoons, after school, I lit the kitchen stove and cooked dinner for both of us. Father came home later than I, we ate together, and then he always read the paper and went to bed early. Sundays, and other free days, he still always went to his work, but then he came home at noon, and together we ate what I had prepared. After the meal he usually took a little nap, and after that he disappeared again to play cards with his friends among the workmen. He never once took me out anywhere. I could do anything I wanted to; he never asked what I had done. I only had to be back at the house on time and be careful that he didn't hear afterwards that I had done anything 'that wasn't proper.' You may ask, Govert, why I am sitting here telling you all this. Perhaps it interests you only faintly; but it seems to lie very near your question, and we will have to hurry on before our dawn comes. But look, I have brought this up because there is a dark secret, slumbering lightly, that possibly may belong to the same beautiful and turbid mystery which now I too, out of a foolish respect, won't call by name. As a child, though now I can scarcely remember this, Father must have shown me affection; but when I became a girl, he didn't do that any more. And the older I grew, the more he went out of my life. He never came in to wake me in the mornings; evenings, after his paper, he never stayed to sit up with me a little, and he never asked me to go anywhere with him nor wanted me along when *I* asked him to go. Sometimes, or even more often, he looked at me, or avoided looking at me, as if my beauty annoyed him. Do you understand, Govert, what I do not dare make clearer in words, notwithstanding all my fluency? I have told you already that he was overpowering and passionate, and, like me, with the nature that I inherited from him, he must have had deep within him heavy, opaque instincts; it is possible that *my* kind of instinct, my beauty, with all the miserable things that go with it, opened in him a secret power, against which he struggled grimly. That would explain much; among other things, his deep tenacity to what was in fact a very vague idea of 'what was proper,' and his terrified reaction to the case of Brantink: a girl who had done something indecent, wasn't she ready to do something even more scandalous, of which she had already planted the seed with her behavior? A similar challenge, a continuously similar deception—she must leave, and even— But that's enough, isn't it? We can let that secret rest again now, for it has never been waked out of its slumber and has died between loneliness and respectability.

But now you know, Govert, that though the case of Brantink was the first in deed, the spirit had already been prepared. And perhaps that will be counted as a mitigating circumstance in my favor, no matter how atrocious the laws of God or men may judge my crimes. I can follow it easily, for 'it' is always the same, no matter what beautiful or hideous form it may take; the same incomprehensible, glorious, but hopelessly unattainable, and only for that reason so miserable, thing. I might tell you about it; it belongs to the unfortunately dark answer to your dark question, which now is gasping for the light; and I, I wanted to tell someone about it, just once. Not even God can require any more of me than that I should *be* sincere, as I now am for once. Even if you ascribe everything I'm telling you to a depraved imagination—for myself, then, and I have finally realized that he who has given the most can at least not damage Father's memory. In fact, since I have understood him better, I have begun to revere him as a daughter. After I left home, out of that filial feeling I wrote him a few times, but no answer ever came to my letters. And a little while ago I received the news of his death belatedly from my aunt, for I was on tour in the North. He died at his work, without leaving behind a spoken or a written word, surly and violent as in life. When the principal had told him about my disgraceful affair, he waited for me at home, with an alarming expression. Brantink, who knew about it, went with me. Father met us in the kitchen, his hands in his jacket pockets, as if he had to restrain them from strangling me or striking my lover to the floor. Later I thought of something less violent: perhaps Father only held his poor, quivering fists so stiff out of the childish urge to hide his expression of shame and loss from our sight. However it was, he looked neither white nor red, but gray, and could not speak for a long time. At Brantink's request, I left him alone with him, and during the hours that they conversed with each other I was shivering in the front room, without even taking off my mittens or scarf, because I was sure that Father would forbid me to return to his house. Through the thin wall between the kitchen and the little front room I could hear both men speaking; but I wasn't able to understand their words. As a matter of fact, I felt no desire to listen more closely, or to press my ear against the wall—the sound of that conversation was expressive enough. First I could hear only Brantink; the monotonous pleading of a lawyer who is both accused and judge—cautiously persuasive and softly extenuating, and always reasonable, in his friendliest manner. Much later Father made a rejoinder, hoarse and heated, with jabs that pained me. It lasted so long that finally I was entirely deafened by the cold and my misery. My heart stopped beating again when I heard Brantink gradually raise his voice, entreating, vowing, threatening, while now Father apparently was the calm conversationalist, but I could imagine with what a throbbing forehead! His lips must have been as black as ink, and his glance charring. Finally Brantink came to call me back in. He gave me only a nod with his head, from which he was wiping off the cold sweat; I can still see him doing that, with the back of his hand, the fine, white fingers of which pressed against his pale, tired eyelids. Father stood in the kitchen, looking out the window; the curtain was up, but naturally he couldn't see our dark garden: it was a dark winter night, and the lamp was shining in the pane, which flickered like a black mirror. Father stood there, heavier than ever, still with his hands in his jacket pockets, staring not at anything outside but into the night of his own dark thoughts, into which no blonde reflection now fell. I couldn't help it; I began to cry, not to move him, for everything was now almost decided, but actually from pity, for him in the first place, but actually for myself, and for Brantink, who was already saddled with such a bad-tempered wife. She didn't want to consent to a divorce, she only wanted to plague him; and he could almost never entrap her into heated actions, because the shrew had as much sex as an icicle. And that was what was now pouring acid on the sweetness of our love! Brantink looked first at Father's back and then at my tearful face, and imparted to me in the manner of a respectable magistrate, which seemed to give me a painful blow, that I would be allowed to complete the school year; that Father would allow me to live with him until then; but as soon as that was over, he would give me my choice to go my own way. At that Brantink left. He bade farewell to Father courteously, expecting no answer and receiving none; he pressed my hand silently, hastily, and sorrowfully, but as sympathetically as before—a speechless squeeze of the fingers, expressing understanding and unaltered passion. Yes, he loved me with fateful beauty, the enviable sinner. I went at once to my room, upstairs, and didn't see or hear my father any more that evening. In the six months that we stayed together under one roof, I don't believe he directed a word to me more than a few times, when he absolutely couldn't avoid it. Household communications he left on a note in the kitchen, where my morning table was still always set and, just as before, the stove was lit and coffee ready. (Here Fran turned her head away, with a sob, before being able to continue.) On the evening after the commencement ceremony at school, when I got home again, Father wasn't downstairs. He had eaten alone and must have gone to bed already. I went to my room and packed my bag as quietly as I could, so as to leave early in the morning. Afterwards I sat for a while at the open window, which looked out on our meager garden, and looked at the silly glitter of the stars, and smoked a whole pack of cigarettes that Brantink had given me as a means of distracting my nerves. Then, in that armchair by the window, I had just fallen asleep when it began to grow light already over the rooftops. I waked with a start. It was a glorious Sunday morning; the sun was already high—it must surely have been noon. I let the water run in the sink; it was lukewarm. I examined my face in the basin as long as I could hold my breath. Then I walked slowly downstairs with my suitcase. I would never see Father again. I would still have been able to see him if I had been up before breakfast; maybe he had not got up so early, just this once, on this last morning. I couldn't expect him at noon; there would never be any more meals—I would never have to cook for him again. I would go eat one last time at my aunt's, and then I would 'go my own way.' I hesitated in front of the kitchen door. I wasn't hungry, but I wanted so much to know whether Father had set the little table for the last time that morning, for my last breakfast. Oh, well, that last breakfast was really yesterday's—all I owned now was what I had done. Yes, I knew how strict Father was. And that's why I didn't go in. But when I stood at the door, suddenly he came out into the front room. He hadn't been to work at all that morning! For several moments we couldn't say anything to each other. Again he had his fists in his pockets. He stood there heavily. I believe that he muttered something about 'Have you already eaten?' or 'You should have had breakfast first.' But I shook my head: 'I'd rather go.' Then suddenly he growled: 'Open your suitcase.' I felt a heavy resentment rise in me; he surely didn't think that I had taken anything with me besides my own personal things, and of those only what was strictly necessary? But yet, just the same, there must have been a darker feeling in me then: did I dare let him see my underclothing then for the first time? But I obeyed him, so strong was the strange power that he always exerted. But he scarcely glanced at the contents of my suitcase. Quickly he took his right hand out of his pocket and threw a gun, which I had never seen in his possession, on top of my stockings and blouses. I didn't know what to think; maybe I was wrong, but I thought his expression was even more fearful than on the evening Brantink came to him. He looked white and black at the same time and grinned pitiably. Then he closed the suitcase again himself. 'What does that mean?' I whispered foolishly. 'My curse and my blessing—they go with you!' he answered bitingly. I walked up the street, but I can still hear, Govert, how the door slammed shut behind me then, shut forever, hard, and yet, the more I think about it, softer than I had expected. Now you know the history of the service pistol, my father's curse and blessing. I have owned that old suitcase for a long time; but the gift of that violent man has never left me. In every suitcase, on every trip, it has accompanied me. And you also know what sort of man my father was. Six months ago, on a stormy winter evening, as I told you, he died violently. How it happened will never be made out with certainty. Something had gone wrong with one of the locks of a remote canal, after the working day was over. Father went up at once, with a few workers. It was pitch dark, and the wind and rain raged over the canal. The men had lanterns but could scarcely hold themselves upright. Did Father give them commands that they didn't want to obey, and did they have words over them? Or is it true, as they claimed, that he ordered them to remain on the shore; that he wanted to go on the canal alone, to look at the damage close up and to bear the brunt, as they swore to him, uselessly? But he would not listen to them. From the shore they saw his lantern go forth laboriously, struggling against the storm. And then suddenly that red light went out in the black depths. They didn't hear a cry or a splash; the roaring winds drowned everything out. The decision of the investigation held afterwards was that a decayed plank in a bridge must have given way under Father's foot. The two halves of the plank were found as driftwood in the canal, where they were held back by a projection in the bank. But no one was able to find Father's body. The current was so heavy because of the storm that it apparently was swept out to sea in a single night. If not, it is still in the mud and will rot there peacefully, unless it is ground to pieces by the propellor of some boat or other. However it may be, I have implored Aunt not to enter into details of Father's description. She had already filled out a questionnaire and sent it to me to see whether I could add anything; but Aunt seems to know more than I do myself. As anyone knows who knew him, Father had an obviously peculiar shape of skull, to judge by his round, bony, strong head; but I have destroyed that description, because it also mentioned four lead fillings and two broken teeth, and especially an old break in his left leg, from which almost no one who has seen Father has ever, to my knowledge, seen him limp. (At these words of Fran's I was scarcely able to suppress a cry of horror. How it happened that I didn't faint from the almost superhuman effort to hide my shuddering astonishment is still a mystery to me. I turned my head away with a jerk and rubbed my bald, clammy skull and along my face, grooved by nerves, like a drunk. Naturally that didn't escape Fran, but luckily she ascribed it to something else. She waited a moment, and then I felt her fingertips touching my arm softly.) Excuse me, Govert, I didn't have to tell you that; for a moment I had forgotten that you were working for the court. And you told me that you have just gone through an autopsy this afternoon that upset you. Swear to me, Govert, that you will never bring up what I've confided to you, for I don't want to have to remember my father as one or another hideously mutilated cadaver. That can't be necessary, and in fact it's impossible—Father doesn't exist any longer, and surely not in the lamentable remains that the dead leave us. Father's remains can only decay and scatter themselves anonymously, and so, undisturbed, return to earth, to water, and to air—to that beautiful, hard nature that he loved so savagely with his surly disposition. But let me be brief, Govert. The night may end at any moment. I have closed the curtains so as to keep it from us as long as possible; but the window is there, and we can't escape our dawn, Govert—*I* won't miss *mine!* Come, let's have another drink. Wait, here's a new bottle. Open it, while I rinse our glasses in the sink. And give me one of your bitter cigarettes. Your health! What am I saying? Oh, well, still to your health, Govert, power, and another dash of youth in expectation of your sweet, cool night planet, with my name if you desire—and wish me my dawn. Oh, how marvelously cool this wine tastes, and at the same time how fiery! So you know, Govert, that I like bitter cigarettes too? I think those sweet ones, with the golden mouthpiece, that Vaclav had made for me, are so abominable. I had always smoked your kind when you knew me before. I had almost no money before I went with Brantink and could afford only cheap cigarettes that I bought on the sly in the smallest stores, every time in a different section of the city, saying they were for my father. Do you see what a brother-and-sister pair we are fundamentally, Govert? And really, Brantink was only the first to help me in that work. His name will always stand at the head of the list of all those who gave me things and spoiled me and who by doing so took away all my illusions, one after the other, hand over hand. They fulfilled all my wishes and whims, and gave me, too, by and large, the most fearsome gift that a person can receive: the knowledge that our desires are only masks. Our desires can always be gratified, but afterwards we are still unfulfilled, for there is a hungering that remains always insatiable. That's why I feel no regret or shame over the way I have treated the men who have loved me. For I have not only, for a while, returned their love; I have also sent them away when, braver than they, I thought it was time, and therefore gave them something very rare: an undamaged appetite for their desires. No matter how frivolous and heartless I may have seemed, I really believe, Govert, that the 'vamp,' as that sad decoy animal is called in the virtuous world, is really an angel of mercy; for she does not slay with the soft wound of parting, which means only an absence and never really a loss. The lover rages with himself over the loss of a wench before he has had time to see that he never really possessed her or to realize that to do so does not lie in the power of a human embrace. So forget the streetwalker; she has at least left you her image, made out of light, as the dream-face of your desires, the dark mask of your existence. While it is just those men who have tried to give me everything who actually have left me lonely and passionless, full of insatiable darkness and surrounded by nothing but masks, ripped off and torn to shreds. Oh, well, their guilt was the least of all, and I can think of them all with friendly and grateful emotions. And at the head of the list certainly that good old Brantink. When the principal was told of our affair by K. K. K., not only did he speak with my father, as I told you, but also the alderman, and the alderman just the same raised his umbrella and crossed the street with me to the Palace. Thanks to Brantink's services as an official and his influential connections, the distasteful case could be covered up. Brantink naturally had to resign as a teacher, under the pretense that he was too busy with his duties. You could make a whole comedy out of all this. Brantink would at first request only a leave of absence, and you would replace him temporarily; at the end of the school year he would leave for good—and he had then just reached a good round number of years of service, twenty-five, I believe. You must still remember how pleasantly that farewell was concocted, just as with our commencement. Brantink was reluctant to attend it, because he wanted to save everyone's good manners to the end; but he never told me—he didn't have to—how painful it was to him. Perhaps the good intentions of the master weren't so good—that was Brantink's well deserved punishment for his unmentionable conduct. It couldn't make any difference to me any more; I was going to leave those people forever, and I wanted to be daring, even if only to tease everybody one more time. But the whole afternoon stuck in my craw; it all sounded so imperturbably false that I still can't understand how, apart from the people concerned, everybody there didn't laugh out loud. Naturally you were touched by your part in it, Govert, but that's why you were always you; and your disgraceful glance didn't get any wink from me. Now you know why I seemed to be so unapproachable then—I was in worse straits than you, brother! Once I had left home, I let Brantink help me a while; it was the surest way to reach, as fast as possible, a position in which I could do without any help. So, with a boost from him, I entered the theatrical world, and in that I found my 'own way' indeed, and pretty fast; Brantink kept reaching me his hand even long after my fingertips felt cool to him. Really, no matter what you may think of him now that you know everything, Govert, he *was* a nice fellow, as you must have learned to know at the Palace. He has always spoken to me very highly of you; I must say that he thought better of you than I did. But come, I won't speak of him officially; I understand well that that recollection must be annoying to you. I haven't seen Brantink for half a dozen years. He used to write me, and at first I used to answer; but then I was out of the country for a long time, and I neglected him entirely. He never writes me any more, and he has also given up trying to see me. Is he still in love with me? I think so. But he must be old now. No, don't tell me anything about him. It was all a long time ago, like Father, and I don't want my memories to be confronted with dead or living bodies. The conclusion then can't abuse me, and what I know is already depressing enough that I lack the courage to add to it unnecessarily. I stopped loving Brantink long ago. Maybe I had already stopped when the scandal broke. I don't remember—when our heart commits treason, the memory of it becomes unfaithful too. But this much is certain, that Bantink had the first *expression* of my love. Do you perhaps want to know, why he, exactly? I asked myself the same question later. Well, perhaps just because he was so much older and therefore, in my imagination, gave love a trace of darker maturity and criminal seriousness that made it just completely desirable to me. At that time I expected, no less than he, that he would be for me an instructor in its unbearably beautiful secrets. In fact, he taught me more, the poor man, than he himself knew: its unattainability and our inadequacy. When I wanted to bring him that in my turn, perhaps in the hope that he could still save me, he didn't understand me, luckily! And at that my sensual love for him was quickly extinguished. Oh, I won't pretend to be ashamed before you, Govert; we are to each other a little like a brother and sister in Dostoyevsky—you said that yourself, didn't you? Well, after Brantink I went looking for it with dozens of men. You might want to know why I needed to when I knew already its unattainability and our inadequacy. Yes, but the desire then wasn't dead enough yet. I had enough temperament not to give up so soon, the foolish power that my dark father gave me; enough fire and tears for always the same game of passion and despair. I must have used it all up; I had to wear out my life and my soul before I was able to know *quiet*, which I have known since Brantink. 'Quiet.' You see that I am not talking about 'quietude' yet; and if I still want to ask God for one thing, it is that I might die without losing my will. See, there's another trace that we have in common, brother, and the Dawn on which I count sustains me as your night planet does you. Yes, with almost everyone that I have been mixed up with, Govert, whether in the richest surroundings or in the cheapest dive; I have sought it in youth, from young men and even from boys—you can see that I am not hiding anything from you; and afterwards again from old men, from rough-and-ready guys and from almost impotent graybeards. I have loved them all, even if it was for only a moment; but every time the attempt to solve the problem must have seemed merely lamentable. I will confess even more to you: when I was looking for it from boys, in my indecent proposals, because I committed the sin of loneliness immeasurably more times than the other—Brantink had only half my virginity—I almost went with you, Govert, precisely because you seemed to me, in those six months ten years ago and—forgive me—especially then, at the commencement—you seemed such a kid. Do you remember this third piece among my souvenirs? It has remained in my suitcases for ten years already, and it has accompanied me everywhere. Do you still remember the colorful binding which then looked so brand-new and modern; the laughing young people, the sky-blue car, and the girl at the steering wheel, with her blonde hair waving and gallows-colored scarf? That is the book that you wanted to give me as a graduation present. Beps brought it to me in the dressing room, and it still has on it the stains of the beer that we spilled on it at an excited table in the dance salon, and that brown stain must have come from one of your chocolate drops. Doesn't it make you happy to see it once again? No, it is for me in any case a more refreshing object than the pistol; easily more so for you than Brantink's portrait. I didn't thank you for the book then, I believe, and now there wouldn't be much sense in it, would there? But as to the last, I can still tell you, Govert, that no matter how coolly and negligently I once seemed to accept it, later it became a favorite through blood-warm caresses by these same sinful fingers, and its binding, next to those visible beer stains and the chocolate spot, bore also the colorless watermark of the unmentionable desires and the speechless regret of your sister in shame, Govert. Now—here you have the fourth and last object, the label, the old school label with its blue printed border, and with the name of your Eyebright, in the curling hand of the child who was already so bitterly little a child. The label that once marked my hook in the school cloakroom. The paper, then so white, has lost its true color; just look how faded it has become, how the glue is gone from the back side because of the saliva used to moisten it. And the lovely blue ink has faded, too, although it has been in my suitcases all the time and has never seen sunlight. It's just like that amazing picture of Dorian Gray; that also was kept so safe in a dark attic, and yet every day it showed a little more horribly the vileness of its subject. Now, what does this label mean to me, that once you looked at with such loving eyes and that you couldn't find that evening at the commencement in the dark, empty hallway? Yes, Govert, it is the same that you kissed the empty space where it had been, and where the dark imprint of my own mouth still was. You embraced the hook with your sobbing body; you pressed your tear-stained face against the wood, you cradled your throbbing head in your arms, and perhaps thought of the mittens and the cloak that hung there so often, with all the lusts of my body and all the anguish of my head. So at least we were inseparably together once in space, Govert. And already time had separated us irretrievably, perhaps luckily for you and for me; in empty space there are close embraces, and in dreams there are long kisses, which can never again be unperformed. That's the last, brother, the rueful value that that little snip of paper has for me, since I know that once you too, notwithstanding your manly life, and at the risk of your social respectability, also wanted to steal it, like a childish thief in the night. *You too,* for the label hadn't come loose from the wood because of the sun's heat, you must know; it didn't fall to the floor, and it didn't walk off on some indifferent heel—Brantink had simply been there before you. When he told me, I was moved, and I asked him to give me the paper as a souvenir, with his photo. I did not really want it, so that later, when it was already no more than a dead thing to me, I regretted not having left it in its place: for Brantink it was more than a souvenir, and for him light would never dim it. But now, now I am happy with it again, Govert. May I confess that to you, and have I now answered your question with everything? Maybe I have and maybe I haven't. But apparently it's the same with my answer as it is with your question: you asked it in so many words that finally you couldn't formulate it any more. But that wasn't necessary any more—you had asked it. So I answered it in the same way, and the only thing I can say now is: Govert, Go for 't, stop looking for it, or keep looking for it, but believe your older sister, Fran, your fringe of Eyebright: *it* isn't there to be found; it may well *exist,* it almost must exist, but—it is unattainable, because we are now once and for all so lamentably incapable of attaining it. Possibly you can still hold fast to the illusion, because you haven't worn out as I have. For me it is threadbare, Govert, but if you can use it a little economically, the material will stretch from here to Golgotha, a journey each of us must take to reach his planet. Tie your dream to that, Go for 't, but never let it loose, and as long as you do your heart won't fall through the bandage. Live your life of seeking and doubting as long as you can stand it; it is moving enough, and then die suddenly, crushed by all the pain you've bottled up, beautiful and violent. You can see that I'm really my father's daughter. But your pain, Govert, will always be sweeter than mine, which knows all too hopelessly that 'it' is no longer here; that it can't be here; and which now can barely face it. Stay in your modest clerk's job, looking for what can't be found. It makes no difference where we look; or rather it does: you are safer at your desk, believe me, or at the most in the darkness of the theater seat when you want to go out of an evening. For idleness and irregularity at least always find their punishment, Govert, in that they bathe in the light of publicity, and for you the alcoholic glow seems to be wearing off as you quickly receive knowledge of the wretched emptiness backstage. While you, in the antic monotony of your existence, can perhaps still find at first a sort of confirmation of your illusion, to which you may drink a last warm draught before cold sleep overcomes you and the journey through your draughty space begins. *I* have only my weariness and an old service pistol. And I stand just as unprincipled about death, the death that a person gives himself, as about that other shame that I have laid to myself. Yes, Govert, that is my dawn: the hour that I feel near, at which Father's curse may indeed, and finally, become a blessing. But I am ungrateful, for I still always have you. The dark Lord has hesitated a long time and has strewn all kinds of obstacles on our path to each other. But if you haven't been the first, you can be the last, and you may not feel wounded at that, on the contrary; for perhaps you have noticed how the stars are listed in an American film—that is, in gigantic letters at the end of the cast, *under* the supporting cast. Yes, it is a wonderful ending, this meeting of ours. Unexpected and unhoped for, so old and so new, and extra special. It seems almost like a hint, for you don't still desire to go to bed with me, do you? You want our third meeting to be in Heaven, don't you? Well, Govert, at least don't begrudge me the means to get there. And that gift could be entirely wonderful, when you usher me out! Oh, Govert! The Lord can forgive you and even me. I have learned what I had to learn in this world, and I think I'm ready for the other. Really, I swear I'm telling the truth when I say that I see a sign of mercy. Listen! Do you hear the chimes of that clock from far away, early in the morning? Don't shudder, brother, but see how I am trembling for joy! Yes, truly, that must be the significance of your coming to me so late. In fact, today or tomorrow, it will all come to the same thing, and I have made up my mind for such a long time already. When Father threw his gift into my suitcase, he wanted this, or at least must have foreseen it. And are you afraid now? I'm not afraid any more; I was only tired and a little lazy. I waited until I heard it clearly. Oh, it would be an undreamed-of gift, Govert, for the chimes to come in person now and sit here across from me. I don't dare ask you; but look, then perhaps I could enter the mystery of death still with the living face of an undamaged illusion, with *your* lined but inextinguished features. Then that would really be a dawn! Oh, I'm not committing blackmail, Govert. I haven't asked for *anything*. To the end, I wouldn't be that bad. The consequences wouldn't be equal for us: so sweet for me, but so heavy for you. Even though we are each other's Dostoyevskyan brother and sister, it may not be, may it? It cannot be, can it?" No, it may not! No, it cannot! I shook my poor head, insofar as it still belonged to me, desperately from left to right. Tears of sweat or blood stood in the corners of my eyes. No, no, I jerked, imploring and doubting. Not out of cowardice, not because I feared the "heavy consequences" of which she had spoken. What could the roaring crowd matter to me, the slave galleys or the hangman, if I could give her hope and relief—if I could give her her dawn? If I could return her to Him who had created her, her beauty and her soul, delivered from a miserable body? And yet my whole reasoning, or unreasoning, being rose up against it. Not only my swinging head rejected it; my whole trembling and shivering body protested. I, *I* could not possibly be the executor of such a purifying murder! How could it be expected of me that my hand should be in a condition to strike down what my eye and soul had found so delightfully comforting? That I could destroy what I had worshiped as God Himself? But God, *God* must have willed it this way. Despite my protest, He must have willed it, just as He willed her rejection of me. She surely wished it for herself, but never shall I doubt for one moment the sincerity of her last words. No, my Frannie hadn't committed any blackmail! She knew of my miserable experience on the radio that time, and a power stronger than hers had taken the pistol out of the suitcase and laid it on the bed. That opaque power had moved her tongue when she invited me to sit on the other side of that bed, across from her. A wonderful power, stronger than the remaining power of both our lives together, had called to her lips, while she and I still honestly defended ourselves, the last, irresistible smile of being already Elsewhere, and drew down first her eyes and then, with them, my glance also to the weapon that lay between us, in the middle of the little distance which separated us from each other, there, on the white, crocheted bedspread. And that supernatural power, that divine Power, must have known the inescapable, the unavoidable, result of all that? That I then suddenly began to reason in my disorganized manner: God! *if* I now lost my control and, without wanting to, took up that lethal instrument and pointed it at her and cocked it—O God! stand by me, don't let the cock crow such a victory! I bit my fist then until I drew blood, at which Fran gave a last, plaintive shriek of sympathy. I seized the pistol and jumped up, just as she did, but only with the intention of drawing back the curtain and throwing the unholy thing into the canal—into the canal, from the other side of which music was still playing, and yet (O Lord! forgive me, forgive me the notions, perhaps sultry and depraved, that I have always had of Thy Kingdom!) at the same time a music overlaid with the dreaminess of the Hereafter. Then I let the curtain fall and turned around slowly. I saw Fran, smiling, unreally beautiful, and more mysterious than ever. And then I shot, just as I once screamed into the microphone. Fran spilled to her knees. For one moment I saw again the remarkable part that ran from left to right through the golden, dark-flaming hair of her head. Weeping, I had also fallen to my knees and grasped her arms, her hands, with the knotted vein and the bracelets, that suddenly did not seem golden any longer but shone like silver. Savagely I pressed her brown wrists, her white palms, her fingers, lacquered with coral red, to my lips and against my miserable skull. Then she whispered, "Godfried," *Godfried*, and not Govert any more as she had the whole evening. She sighed it gratefully: I dared not speak: gloriously, but surely also happily, in a soft hiccough, which made a spurt of her divine, beautiful, warm blood stream over her lips and sprinkled the housing of my always disturbed brains. Quickly then I whispered back to her: "Until we meet again, Frannie! Until we meet again, Fran?"—as she bestowed on me, on that evening of her last performance, a "See you later" full of sweet significance, and had kept her word. And then everything, everything was finished. My Fran, my little fringe of gold-blonde hair, was no more; my enchantment was worn off, and its Cause given back; my strange, dear schoolgirl had graduated from the whole school of anguish and pain—gone to heaven in search of her Dawn! Then, for a few moments, I felt for the first time in my life a great, strange peace in myself; the peace which I shall bear to my last days now, when this confession, which has now almost reached its end, is over. I clearly recalled a fragment from Fran's half of our unforgettable night's talk: *"you may be able to do me a service, a service of love, of love of goodness and of beauty—one for you and the other for me, perhaps, as with our Mardi Gras couple."* And then, with one finger of Love, and another of Goodness, I closed the night-beautiful, the dawn-beautiful, ivory lids of my Eyebright, in her still marble-like face, forever here on earth. After which, carefully and tenderly, I laid her, who—oh, most fearsomely beautiful of all God's gifts—had gone to soul in my arms, on the fleecy rug between our two armchairs, in front of the smoking table. At that her head nodded one last time, backwards and forwards; and I contend that it did did not do so lifelessly but that it was a highest sign of farewell, the most shredded and most beautiful "See you later" from the schoolgirl Fran, and from the woman of all women, who never was a gallows-pated beggar like me, a cripple with reaped and smashed braincage, who had to usher her out, to her old teacher and her youngest and dearest brother, in Dostoyevsky and in all painful sanctities. Then I turned back to the window, to the curtains again, and that time I stayed to draw them open. The music from across the canal had ceased, and the Dawn streamed in. I turned off the lamp on the smoking table and was ready. The pain, the trembling, the desperation could begin now; *my* show of blood and sand now must go on, as she had advised me, to the last rendition and with, perhaps, an insignificant chance of assisting science as a payment for, or at, that ending. Then the door flew open, and in the opening stood Professor Mato. I recognized him at once because of the full light of the dawn, which fell on him; but I could not make out the people who were behind him in the half darkness of the corridor. My eyes were, in fact, directed at the scholar alone and for a time saw nothing else clearly. During a breathless pause a heavy silence reigned; but then that was filled, resoundingly, by the soul-rending outcry of a hundred clocktowers in the distance. I wept; I felt so ashamed of myself, and Professor Mato cast such an inexpressibly depressing glance at me. Certainly the shot had wakened the scholar from his sleep. He stood there in his pajamas, white pajamas with blue stripes, like a convict's suit. But the miscreant, the criminal, the murderer, was *I*. Those nightclothes, in fact, didn't do a thing for Professor Mato; they were, in an incomprehensible manner, at the same time too long and too short for his very well proportioned, medium large, build. But they couldn't be *his* pajamas; the hotel must have lent them to him, since the professor had not been prepared to spend the night in a strange city. Then the pajamas in no way made him ridiculous, they did not completely suit him, thus his personality radiated a dignity of mind which dominated everything. Oh, that harmoniously beautiful seriousness of scholars, which nothing, nothing, can diminish! The clocks chimed, and Professor Mato looked at me with all the pitying heroism of the heroic world. And I wept, while the same gave way before the swelling tide of my burning loss. In my darkened eyes the blue stripes of Professor Mato's white pajamas melted together, and suddenly I saw him standing there in his white apron! Then I yielded, I collapsed, and on my knees I crawled to him to plead with him *not* to dissect her, *nothing* to investigate! It was a service pistol that I had shot with; I had aimed at her heart so that her desires should be stilled and in order to spare her gold and ivory head; but the caliber of the bullet was certainly great enough—there could not be the least doubt that she was dead, dead and released, beautifully and violently, like her father, and also as she had wished for herself; but she found autopsies horrible; I could, on the forfeit of my last honor, testify that she had assured me of that decidedly this very night; she had rejected the idea of looking back on anyone related to her by blood or spirit who was deceased; she found both unnecessary and repulsive that confrontation of a living memory with the lamentable clothing that the soul left behind after its departure—how she would have shuddered then at the prospect of intestines and all the other horrors with which an open body pollutes us further? That, *that,* is why, and it was undeniably the last desire of her dear heart which she was now speaking through my mouth, I cried out to Professor Mato that he and everyone should spare her lovely remains; that none of them would violate the peace of her body! I confessed everything: *I* had done it; I had given her, from guided ambush, her *coup de grâce;* I called on no single extenuating circumstance; I had in full knowledge and intent, disobeyed the commandments of the Lord and the laws of human society; I stood at the law's service and was fully prepared to plead "guilty," thrice guilty, and to take my punishment and to undergo the whole of it; yes, I even besought that someone might encircle my feet with fetters and take me away—I had sinned and now wanted to pay the penalty. And the wise and compassionate scholar softly nodded yes to my prayer. Then, peacefully, I turned for one last glance at Fran, who lay there on a white rug, haloed by the rosy light of a late summer morning, as if sanctified in her Dawn. Farewell, my little fringe of the noblest metal; farewell, my Eyebright; farewell, my night-beautiful Dostoyevskyan little sister! And perhaps, *perhaps,* O sweet and cruel, incomprehensible God —until we meet again, child, UNTIL WE MEET AGAIN! I had one last of all, sly and quick, endless moment of drowning, in which the dikes of the soul were broken through irretrievably, when she was being covered from my sight; a moment with which I have wrapped together more tightly than in an embrace all the shards and splinters of my life, of these ten years of sinking always lower, of my falling and of my going under, as well as of her marvels, which are beyond praise, and of God's dizzying gift—have wrapped all this together and pressed it to me, and have taken it with me to the prison, the courtroom, and to this last home, and to that kind-hearted hole which I have dug for myself, with a little mound of fresh-dug earth next to it, and into which I let down these final pages of my confessional, all of them, splinter by splinter, sliver by sliver, grateful and melancholy, composed and confident, and yet do not let them loose as, long ago, the Egyptian pyramids were equipped with fragments of their daily life so that when once they should step at last into those stone or earthen boats they were assured of a happy voyage to their far, merciful planet. At that I left the room for the last time. I knew already that it would be turned into a memorial room with lighted tapers, such as in French is called a *chapelle ardente;* but just since the day of Fran's death have I understood the full glory of this expression. Whoever coined it must have known everything of the consuming splendor of life and death. The unforgettable *chapelle ardente* of *my* soul, then, is in an international hotel along the banks of a still canal with the golden dawn above a rose and blue city in the window. It still smells of fern, the night-perfume of a woman beautiful as a painting, as well as of the dew of morning. The little breeze that played in the flame-colored drapes wafted the chilled after-fragrance of smoked cigarettes, of dark liqueur, and of burned gunpowder. But no matter how placid it might seem, it was in fact a glowing room, a blazing room, a chapel like the flame of a gigantic, distorted taper. The flame itself goes up peacefully, brightly, like a silent shout of joy; but it has wept fiery tears, all of which I have received on my bare skull like drops of molten metal, all, without losing one or wanting to. And with that, with the congealed sorrow over my face, tottering as if they were my own bursting brains, and with the glowing iron spikes nailed into my head like a crown of thorns, for all the rest of my days maimed and blissful, I went out the door and bowed my head to Professor Mato so deeply that I could not notice whether he, the handsome scholar, was willing to answer the greetings of his unworthy friend, of a pitiable destroyer of life, one last time. But I think, I believe, he would have; the high priests of science are always so magnanimous and understanding now. Some men went with me, downstairs, down the marble stairway with the wrought-iron railing. And everyone was silent and obliging; I want to note that here gratefully. I was taken to be questioned for a while in a little office, where I was considerately left alone. And then an automobile came for me. I will not now go into particulars about what happened then; my life's story was already over, in the same moment when I closed Fran's eyelids. Everything that I have written down here about myself, ever so many pages, belonged only insofar as it related to her, when her golden fringe of hair still jingled at her schoolgirl's nod; then the enchanted herb hadn't yet worn off; then my Fran, my Frannie, was still my omnipresent Eyebright. What followed that is the ailment of a completely isolated man; the forsaken evening tremors of a penitent; the pitching and tossing of a wreck. It deserves no development, and my last strength is now used up, expended for good. In my cell I received only the priest, the lawyer, and the doctor; the first from reverent love, the second only out of respect for his learning, and for the discipline of the law. I entreated the priest to speak with Corra and make her understand why it was my dearest wish that she and the family, and any friends or acquaintances also, should not visit me in the place of my shame. I also implored that they would not send me anything to soften my lot, which in fact was not hard enough. So no one came, and no packages were sent. The doctor and the lawyer asked me questions, and I answered them humbly and honestly. And then the trial began. It did not last long, but it was so confused for me that it isn't clear to me any more, in whole or in part. I saw too many faces out of my early professional career. The only thing I remember well is that Judge Brantink presided, and that everyone, magistrates and jurors, as well as clerks and policemen, as well as lesser people, were much too good-hearted and surely undeservedly compassionate toward the unworthy sinner. As through a haze I can still see Professor Mato, who spoke so long and quietly, with soft reasonableness and wise beneficence, and so mellifluously that it sounded through my soul like intellectual music, although very few of his words could pierce through to my shocked brain. I listened to him, especially, with my soul. Also I looked at Brantink often, who seemed suddenly much older to me then, but who still always appeared very neat and distinguished, still in the inscrutable manner of Francina vander Zwalm. His sparse, almost white hair was always parted correctly, and his facial color was paler than before. I turned my eyes on him whenever he let his own, which he tried to keep expressionless but in which I thought I could read a boundless, incurable melancholy, rest on me. Corra was not present in the room, for which I am grateful to God and Corra herself; once I had seen her, before the trial, for a split second, through a crack in the door of the anteroom; she stood, pale and in black clothes like a widow, as indeed she was, the poor thing, by one of the columns in the marble hallway, in conversation with Professor Mato, Brantink, the doctor, and the lawyer. Corra could not have noticed me, and immediately afterwards a policeman closed the door again. So Corra never saw me in return. Oh, good, good darling from long-ago days! Forgive me, forgive me, that I didn't foresee then to what a miserable man you were ready to reach your hand. I should have kissed it and blessed it—but I refused it! That little group by the pillar in the corridor flashed before my mind's eye again at the same moment that the sentence was read—the painfully magnanimous expression which reddened my unworthy head because in pronouncing me "not guilty by reason of insanity" they explained their conference to me. With soft hands they cut away the only remaining, clammy tangle of hair from this doomed head, and then the galley slave went to live in the oblivion of a quiet, affectionate institution, which is like an adult education school—too late though he was eternally youthful—and to have as his director a charming scholar who commands respect, a doctor with all the harmonious beauty and comforting brightness of science. Didn't the judges, the public and the private ministry, the jury and the citizens, understand me, then, or didn't they want to? I had told everything honestly and confessed convincingly, at least everything that was relevant to my unseemly behavior. But perhaps, moved by Corra's suffering and by the innocent faces of my children, of my healthy, vibrant Doos and San, they had wanted, with that pitiful fatherhood, to spare the honor of a name and the future of an innocent progeny. And what could I do but be grateful to them for it, and moreover for receiving lasting torment as my manner of penance for an unpunished crime. With these thoughts, with these feelings I crossed the doorstep of this institution, these stones of farewell to the life of the world. But now, now, O God, be thanked, be thanked, that now I know! I know now that I am indeed a poor innocent. O divine knowledge, glorious deliverance from myself and from my crime! Let me impart, as a conclusion to this dreary apology for my life, how that sweet secret was imparted to me. By a great chance, a few days ago I found in the garden a torn fragment of a newspaper. Newspapers are specifically forbidden here, so as not to disturb our rest with anything from outside; so that this clipping must have been sent to me by a merciful providence. There was no date on it, but I found information in it that has cut much joy and anguish out of my throat—*the announcement that Franny Veen,* FRANNY VEEN, *will appear in our city in a few weeks with her newest and greatest performance!* I hurried to the director at once to assure myself that there was no mistake; that everything was all right, that this wasn't an announcement out of an old paper from before the terrible occurrence that has brought me here. The director looked at me long and painfully, and then he carefully said, smiling, "It *isn't* a mistake." "Then I didn't murder her?" I asked, raving from joy, "or in any event, the shot didn't kill her and she is now recovered?" The director looked at me again, friendly and thoughtful; and then, after a pause, then he released the liberating word: "Indeed, Godfried," he said. One word, only one shamefully everyday word, that I had heard a thousand times and had even used, but then, how soft it came over the calm, finely chiseled lips, as if a toot from a golden trumpet had sounded in my dizzy ears!

One word, but through it the horrible burden of ten, of twenty years has fallen off like a nightmare from my suffocating soul; through it the misery, the anguish, the mistakes of a hopelessly unfortunate human existence were undone again, as a hateful page in a book is recalled by its creator, torn out, burned, and given as a prize to the whirling of the thirty-two points of the compass, in the form of a pinch of ashes and a curl of smoke; one word, by which the most persistent ghosts begin to shimmer, tumbling out through the rose windows of the Dawn, and lie resting in the refreshing water of the canals with which the silent sidewalks of beautiful hotels are washed, by the muddy dregs of nature and society, in the slimy deposits of all life, of stone, plants, or animals, under the rotting inflorescences of platanus occidentalis, little carrions of lost housepets, soiled shoes, and rusted service pistols! One supporting word, "indeed," by which, "in-deed," the glorious deed awakens the most beautiful of sleeping beauties, the most adorable of women, the most golden of all blonde heads, again to life. "Godfried," the director called me then; "Godfried," just as *she* had called me in her bloody farewell kiss! But then it wasn't a farewell; it really was an "Until we meet again," as I had hastily whispered to her, since that name, that last word of my earlier existence, now has become the first of my new life! *"Godfried"*—yes, Almighty, always surprising and noble Lord, since then I have begun to live in that freedom with Thee, from Thee. And already that beginning is an end, in the hours which still remain to me, of the disturbed maze, the gigantic despair, under which my best years lie buried and decayed; only an apron of grass and a little bed of flowers signify the sum of that existence—the infinite heaven still hangs above; I see it now continuously, and I shall never again lose it from my sight. Of the gardens of earth, I have known only this outer corner, and of the wall on which the dome of heaven rests only this little shameful bit of the end—but the little, forbidden gateway that stands in this silent section, overgrown with bindweed and wild roses, is dearer to me than the great, ornamented gate on the other side, that opens every morning and closes again every evening. The amnesties that come from that direction—and I wasn't under them, and Fran wasn't under them, and in fact was anybody under them?—God had to find them already in time; but I, the poorly endowed, could scarcely imagine myself then out of the soil of my misshapenness. It seems so painfully absurd to me, as the most foolish of all our illusions. No matter how fine that gate may have appeared, it is perhaps only appearance that it can open in the morning of life and stand while evening falls; which will hurt him inside, the arrow points of judgment fixed to the high trellis will indeed hurt him cruelly. And he will die of those wounds, early, as my Eyebright did, or somewhat later, like her poor, mad brother. Then when I straighten my little forbidden gateway, while the rain sprinkles my neat sandpapery head and a flaming chapel comes out to rest on my fingertips, and even if it is forbidden, with as much patience as confidence, that the smallest and most shameful of all garden gates should once open on Eternity in the night. "Indeed, Godfried"—I can still hear the director saying that! To my last breath I shall be grateful to him for his judicious confidence. I know that sick people of my type mostly may not receive any information about their circumstances; but our director is a scholar who understands humanity as deeply as he loves it—therefore he made an exception for me and spoke. I am thus senseless, *un fou raisonnant et imaginant*. The shot didn't kill Fran; perhaps it was never even fired except inside me, indeed in one of the many visions which make human existence so senselessly confused—and particularly toward Corra—apparently to dispel sinful shades. That will be my punishment and my penance, and now may I again, or at last, live in the shadow of God's mercy; that is, in the grateful knowledge of my imperfect state; in the happy awareness that I am not guilty by reason of insanity; and even innocent! The throbbings of my head, as polished as a billiard ball, the whirlings of the snarl of my nerve threads, the deadly shudder in the fibers of my soul—these are over now. Very, very slowly the good tiredness which precedes the merciful sleep of men descends over the edge of my brain. No more clouds waft by, neither of glowing gold nor of dead ashes, before my sore, inflamed eyes. Because of my daily work in spring and summer, because of my cordial intercourse with everything that flowers and perishes again in the always fresh and luxuriant earth, now I can even begin to think without screaming of that little churchyard at D—, and even, even, very carefully and gradually, of those mutilated remains of Fran's father, the man with the dark, beautiful soul—of the body to which there, in the little cemetery of D—, I may have brought, as the brother of his daughter, a last greeting. So now I remember that shocking afternoon, at least somewhat, with an effort. Step by step, the earlier grinning mask of death and transiency begins to take on a serious, soft, and almost smiling expression. From the dear, sorrowful beginning, I can now even see the process of decomposition and putrefaction psychically, as through the scholars' charming microscope. And thus a grain of Professor Mato's harmonious wisdom will become my own, if only in the twilight of my own death: that death is nothing else than the beginning of another existence, with all the many wonders of bacteriological life. That it does not mean the gradual return of a fleeting shape to a lasting formula; and thus also of a weary soul to the planet of its origin and promise. When I had thanked our director with respectful gladness, I asked him for the high favor of letting me go to the performance which Fran was going to give in our city, in one way or another. He replied that he regretted that that was really impossible; first on account of the regulations of our institution, which must be the same for everyone, and also because he believed very sincerely that it was better for me to suppress such a desire and make an effort to forget the past. I didn't even cry. Now I understood our director, and I told him that I believed him and that I would exert myself to follow his wise and benevolent advice. But that noble benefactor of all people with broken hearts and burst senses, that fine scholar, promised me something else as a substitute. We have here a little movie theater, in which sometimes educational or miscellaneous films are shown. And now the director is going to try to see whether he can get a film cutting from an old newsreel of Fran in one of her rôles, and he will show it to me for me alone. I believe that I gave a sob of gratitude and gladness. I wanted to press the director's beautiful, peaceful, bright, and beneficent hand to my blubbering mouth; but I mastered myself and only said that his kindness overwhelmed me and it would be for me an inexpressible happiness if Fran's vanished countenance, and what had once been the unforgettable music and movement of her living appearance was worthy of being seen in a safe, well-protected corner of our house, under the same roof with her surviving brother. I am convinced that the director will keep his word. Maybe the film is here already, but I will never ask. It is no longer necessary for me to see it. I know and am happy. And I am even happier now that I, in my turn, can fulfill my promise to the director. This history will be my last deviation from the laws of life and of human society. I have thus set down my confession, for myself and possibly for others; I can now vanish, as I once did into the army, orderly in the column of marchers, and with the anonymous company of my comrades in unworthiness. I shall not read over my pages again. There are too many of them, and I am too tired. Tomorrow I shall send the whole pack, anonymously, to a magazine, and information about my life may perish henceforth, like the bottle flung into the sea of which a French poet tells, and in which a shipwrecked sailor had stuffed, as a note, his last will and testament: *Dieu la prendra du doigt, et la mènera au port*—at least, *si bon Lui semble*. Afterwards I shall devote myself wholly to our garden. To the end of my days, the director has promised me, I may take care of it. For that clearsighted scholar has deduced that my earlier way of life was indeed a mistake. I should have been humble and tilled the beloved earth; helped soft, placid plants to live and die, and that is another privilege, for I have now seen, not only in flowers but in the simplest crops, the truth of the poet's words when he called them the ornaments of Heaven. I will aim first of all at the cultivation of the dear herb Eyebright. I shall bring all its beautiful varieties to bloom. I have not asked the director yet, but if I present him with my obedience to all his commands, which I shall attain with honesty and love, it is very possible that he will permit me to send, in each blossoming season, a little nosegay to Fran; to my Fran, my golden Frannie, who has now graduated from school and from life forever, for good, and so good, and whom I once ushered out, *into* her Dawn. As I said, that will be my work in the blossoming season. And in the others, I may work in the cabinet shop. I have already learned to saw and to plane with good results. As soon as my first small piece of furniture is finished, I shall ask the director to let me send it home; to Corra, as my last, silent contribution to the household; and to the children, to Doos and San, as my farewell gift, so that later, when they are grown up, and married, and happy, sitting on a chair or a bench which I have made with my own hands, they will remember their poor, benched father.

An Essay
on the Future of the Novel
BY JOHAN DAISNE

THE NOVEL: WHERE DO WE GO FROM HERE?

The future of literary creativity is no new problem. Even Chateaubriand, although the father of a new movement, Romanticism, believed that everything had already been said. Fortunately he repeated a little bit of that everything once again, but in his own way.

Nevertheless, the problem in literature today that is really international seems to be the current decomposition of the novel and its eventual recomposition in the future.

Since you have come to me to learn my opinion, I shall, to begin with, consult myself about my own crimes.

I have been an impassioned and eager reader, especially in my youth. Latterly my reading has gradually diminished, particularly since I myself have begun to write prose.

As a child, my favorite reading was Buffalo Bill and Nick Carter, and children's—especially girls'—books: *School Idylls* and Tine van Berken. Adventures and sociability, suspense and domestic smugness. At school I appeared to be a scholar who was not chained to his studies. Until my fifteenth year I played in the street, that is in the gardens of the Nieuwe Wandeling at Gent, on the fallow ground near the Leie, between the city and its suburbs, with the poor youngsters from the slums near the paper mills, now torn down. Winters I sat in the classroom reading Captain Mayne-Reid on my knees under my desk (I still remember that the black-haired heroine was named Isolina de Vargas); and in the fragrant summer grass of the Wandeling, Aimard's *Mexican Nights* lit a flame in my heart, with the corn-silk cigarettes of Juarez and the stars on the velvet heaven from the chapter "Amour."

My first French reading was at the age of twelve—the story of the film *The Mark of Zorro,* in the weekly paper *My Movie.* Two years earlier I had read with a glowing head *The Signalman,* by Conscience; that was my first acquaintance with the novel, and I still well know what captivated me: not the story, but the construction of the story; if I may put it in a scholarly way, the appearance of fiction as transposition of reality; or, in a word, the literary adventure. Halfway through the book I cried out to Father, "Dad, I know how it fits together, how it is going to go!" What I meant was that I knew how I should have solved the plot. And, as it happened, the plot was solved by the author as I had guessed. I was bursting with triumph.

A year later appeared the first instalment of the weekly children's serial by Abraham Hans, *Three Months in the Snow.* It was laid in the Alpine meadows; surprised by the first snow, a grandfather and his little grandson cannot move back to the valley. They endure the whole winter in a mountain hut. In the spring a solitary youth returns below; Grandad shall remain above forever. That was a shade too sad, but a following item, *Saint Gregory's Day at School,* made it all right again: a wholly pleasant, wholly amusing thing about a poor parish and an old custom, with the warm nostalgia of both. For a year I was writing their Flemish and French essays for a few classmates. Honorarium: a quarter, for a book by Hans.

Only one school-book poem—the others I naturally did not read—spoke to my mind at that time: a little verse by Virginie or Rosalie Loveling, about a foreign soldier, who in the early morning was dragged to his grave, alone, far from home.

I apologize for these naive digressions. But what determines our lives more than the experiences of our childhood years? All the man exists already in the child, and often the truth comes most easily from him. In my tender youth I sought from a book beatings and caresses, adventure and suspense, transposition and confirmation of my proper standing as a mischievous little rogue of a schoolboy; as a street urchin (Saturdays I stared at the vari-colored movie posters on the neighborhood bars, and for weeks at a stretch our gang played *Redgauntlet* near Einde Were Park); and as the child of a simple, clean home, with a sensitive scholar for a father and a wise and cheerful mother.

Later those innocent relationships became somewhat more complicated. Fired by the artistry of literature, I became a grind for "art for art's sake." Then and thereafter I read nearly all the classics and moderns, those one must have read. I absorbed them all. How different they were, too! Almost equally cherished—the impressionistic *Little Youth* by Borel as much as the romantic-naturalistic *Mother* by Anna van Gogh-Kaulbach, Dickens, E. T. A. Hoffman, Falkland, Conrad, Brontë, Louis Hémon, Carry van Bruggen, Turgenev, and Ehrenburg. For a long time Balzac and Couperus were not considered "serious" reading. But as early as a decade before they were at last generally accepted, my special affection went to Balzac (*Ferragus*) and Couperus (*Eline Vere*).

At present I no longer read very much. Sometimes a verse in a newspaper or magazine, seldom more than a few pages in an anthology. I find all the poems too unreal, even those which have been most truly called "pure," having lost so much essential ballast that they have become a wing-beat in the ether. I know only a dozen poets whom I retain; a few lines of Fritz Francken, some insights into life by Goethe. Experiments repel me. I'd rather write myself, and my manner is something between Francken and Goethe, I believe, which can be considered wholly natural.

The arrangement with regard to prose is more paradoxical. Here I have been called a modernist, and indeed the "magic realism" of *Stairway of Stone and Clouds* was something new in its time. And I myself readily say that my latest work, *Lago Maggiore,* while it is in the neoclassical spirit, is in its form very modern, for it meets all the requirements of the newest tendencies. In his introduction to the German public, my translator, Georg Hermanowski, declared, with singular German bombast, that my book is a "cosmos": all *genres* are cultivated in it, he says, but while organically connected still really disparate: the philosophical novel, the psychological novel, the adventurous novel, reportage, the essay, the aphorism, and (versified) poetry.

The paradoxical thing is—it is to this personal, yet politely restrained, statement that I have wished to come—that as reader I wholly disapprove of the kind of work I nevertheless cultivate as writer. As reader, my heart is warmed only by my old children's books (for which read "girls' books"), and my head is made to glow only by a Pierre Benoit. And there is but one Pierre Benoit, and I do not readily re-read a book (an undertaking as hopeless as drinking the same glass of water twice); so I don't read much and instead go week after week to see the successors of *Redgauntlet,* for the seventh Muse still continues to wink at me; while the novel in book form betrays itself, fortunately the movie theater remains the temple of the romantic, no matter how much the movie story, like the Western film, becomes "adult."

This paradox has often amazed me—and it is still somewhat annoying. Does my affection for a Pierre Benoit demonstrate that my taste is dubious? Or do I myself write in the "intellectual" modern line only because I am incompetent to perform in the proved conventional manner? For is the modern novel's diversity of spirit, its heterogeneous character, not a hodgepodge of the splinters and dust of our own personalities and existences, even the characters being drawn from our immediate surroundings—splinters and dust which we glue together in our mosaics because we do not possess the creative skill of our predecessors, who knew how to hew from a formless boulder monolithic figures of imagination?

Or am I, on the contrary, in a decline? Does my reason, drunk while writing, slacken off whenever I do not write? Does it, whenever the pen does not tickle it, sneak into childhood by the back door? I know that for many people, at least for certain ones, Pierre Benoit is not much better than Buffalo Bill. But to that I can answer that everything depends on how the reader behaves toward the book, and that for those who will contribute their share to the book even Buffalo Bill means a little more than Buffalo Bill.

And with your permission and in all objectivity: Pierre Benoit is decidedly far from the author of what a sourpuss has called "cette benoîte littérature" [that phony literature]. To begin with, Pierre Benoit's theme is the pure one of the human tragedy, as classic as the ancients; secondly, he is a poet just as affecting as the most masterful, a recreator of the eternal in its modern appearances; third, he is a magician of the montage: the tension of his books derives chiefly from the style, for the adventures are as simple as they are universal and timeless. And with that style he accomplishes the miracle of being exciting and unforgettable just with "conventional" novels.

For that matter, I am not alone with my paradox. Most authors put on a learned pair of spectacles whenever they are asked their favorite reading: never less than the Bible, Homer, Goethe, and other primaries of the catalogue. But how many do not eat sweets on the sly—the vicissitudes of the Saint, and even of Kuifje [a famous Belgian comic-strip hero]? Few are so honest as Hubert Lampo, who lets no occasion go by without proclaiming the praise of his Simenon. Perhaps Simenon deserves praise, but still to the "pure" belletrist he doesn't really count. Perhaps he possesses, as to method, everything that characterizes a great writer; still his aim is preponderantly suspense—another name for a separate category of the romantic *genre* of Benoit. Simenon writes traditional novels without becoming classic; while the work of Lampo himself must be called classical-romantic, poetically realistic (see his *Atlantis* and his *Alain-Fournier*), with the gradual beginnings of intellectualistic decomposition in the modernistic line.

My investigation of my own or related crimes will not be complete without the question: what would I read if I did not myself write? Naturally this is a rather unreal question: what would I be like if I were not myself? Now, I suppose that even then I should be a faithful customer of Benoit; but next to that I should harbor interest only for the modern *genre,* for the "novel which is not a novel any more."

And what have I learned from the librarian which I am in civilian life? That many people read nothing more than their newspapers and one or another weekly magazine; the others for the greater part read only the lightest of ordinary proper novels and wholly ignore the new *genre*.

And then finally there is literary history, the living and the recorded. How eagerly the old and learned Fausts of that discipline lech after the youngest Marguerite! Yet it is a fact that the survey and recognition of the new has involved no repudiation of the established. Also the modernists continue to respect the classics, as such. I do not believe that there is anywhere a serious new-fashioned writer who considers Stendhal worthless, even though he himself will do things differently, quite otherwise from the master.

And that must pain the thoughtful. It proves that we of the present moment do not stand for any first dawning, as Walravens believed, but simply for a new one that also will become noon and then evening. *Everything to Begin Anew,* Jan Schepens entitled one of his recent volumes of verse. Certainly each day begins anew, but there are 365 in a year, and one comes to nearly every year much as one did to the year before. The universe has now become round, like the earth and our hearts and the beautiful pupils of our eyes. And life forms a whole, in which today counts, but also yesterday. And the fact that yesterday still counts today, counts significantly for tomorrow.

So this factual inquiry has brought us of itself to a sample of the kind of philosophy which can be made up, and especially which can be made up to solve the stated paradox.

What, in essence, is the future of the novel? I believe it will always remain itself, particularly *the supplementing of life*—but, equivalent to the many forms life can take, the supplementing can occur on different levels. For example, we can distinguish a simple supplementation of life (in economics and sociology one would call it "horizontal"), as well as a higher or deeper ("vertical") supplementation.

The simple supplementation of life is practical, anecdotal; it enlarges the life of writer and reader in space and time, by holding fast to the memory and glorifying it, by joining others' lives to ours, by giving us the consolation of communion in our misery, by giving our wishes and dreams a start toward realization, by shattering everyday life with the unusual, in short by supplementing life to enrich and exalt it. That is now the synonym for composing, arranging, creating reality by the imagination—the formula of the traditional novel, to which a ballad like "The Two Kings' Children," an epic like the *Nibelung,* as well as *L'Atlantide* by Benoit and the Maigrets of Simenon, all belong.

The higher supplementation of life does essentially the same, but along the vertical level: the worldly adventure becomes a reconnaissance of heaven (or hell); here the life material is not arranged and recreated into experience by style and/or imagination—but is delivered in an apparently chaotic fashion, *apparently* (the art lies in giving this appearance) intentionally so, in order to approximate the chaos of reality and to bring actuality as close as possible to the truth that is hidden behind reality; for the area of difference here between a novel and a factual treatment is very narrow—a scientific or philosophical work should not have more truth than a work of art or literature.

Art can never cause more than the truth to be felt, suggested, or illustrated. The truth, genuinely investigated and demonstrated, comes properly under another domain of spiritual activity. That does not preclude the novel of ideas, but the ideas must be lived as ontological, eschatological, metaphysical adventure. And behold! Here is the modernistic novel—decomposed, disparate, but still entirely and actually a novel, of another sort, or on another level.

I see therefore no sharp break; the contradiction is only apparent. Instead there is growth and diversification, variation and compensation, by which it becomes even entirely logical and wholesome that a man who has his hair cut as short as a monk's goes sailing out with Benoit on adventures.

For the rest, all that is not at all surprising, for it is, as has been said, not entirely new. To go back to the beginning of time: what are the mythologies but novelized theologies? And doesn't even Jean Paul Richter, a complete romantic, write novels in which he suddenly breaks off poetic nature writing with a sober "and so forth," humorous sign of modern decomposition?

About which I repeat here what I set down at the beginning of my literary career: I believe and shall continue to believe in the permanence of creative art, as one of the cyclical variations of man and life. At the time I formulated a dialectic theory about it, with which my lamented teacher Dr. L. Brounts warmly concurred. I placed as thesis and antithesis, opposite each other, the poles to which people are called in art's supplementation of life: namely, reason and dream, actuality and poetry, or other synonyms for this dichotomy. Literary history, then, displays a vacillation between thesis and antithesis, always moving more closely toward a synthesis.

Thus pre-romanticism, based on the old heroic literature (dream), brought about bourgeois poetry (reason); classicism brought about romanticism; the last, realism; realism, the black romanticism of naturalism, the pink of symbolism and impressionism, the motley of expressionism and surrealism; whereupon a neo-realism and neo-romanticism have again resulted. The fluctuation continues between realism and romanticism, but in time the oscillations become continually shorter, quicker, more confused, always ever closer to the synthesis of all human powers which we have brought together under the antinomian categories of reason and dream. Actually the "decomposition" is then much more than dissolution; it is an *over*-composition, with the disparate character of all syntheses—an obstruction by over-satiation.

But that, likewise, forms a merely temporary condition. Life—as also in its prolonged form, art—is movement, an eternal search from earth to heaven. Whenever synthesis is reached, it will follow the law of life that is called dialectic; the red pendulum is repelled by anti-magnetism from the black center stripe on the dial, again to one of the farthest extremes of dream or reason, and everything can begin again to cut loose the same way. "I am going away," says Rilke's little marquis, "in order to return."

I am therefore easy about the future of the novel. It approaches today one synthesis, monstrous on the face of it, of dream and reason, but tomorrow it will be romantic adventure again, and the day after tomorrow a homecoming to realism. In none of these three phases has it actually ceased to be a novel. It merely conforms, in its diversity, to the demands for variation made upon it by generations and individuals; it strives for completeness.

Or does this artistic dialectic have any relationship with actual events in time? The correlation is too self-evident to require demonstration. However, I should only reluctantly draw up a law of causation. For the converse may well also be true, that it is not that the times determine our literature but that the times themselves are produced by the literature they produce. Let us admit that by its nature art is an expression of its times and its society. But it is also an expression of the timeless individual genius. And that consideration reminds us that it is not a goal of art to express one time or one society; the goal often lies in the opposite direction: literature must liberate us from time and from locality. Thus at least there is some sort of compensatory adjustment that must be made here.

The music of Mozart was written for a clavichord. One plays it on the piano nowadays. The clavichord was indeed already a piano, and as our piano becomes electronic tomorrow (or is it that already?), it still remains a piano. The novel will remain a novel. One can only write different novels, as one can play very different things on one piano. Every spring always brings again the same old-new sounds. And while these springs, similar from solar year to solar year, are perhaps very different from solar system to solar system, in the greater cycle of the universe they finally come back again.

Each "ism," in the arts as elsewhere, begins naively and egocentrically to explain that it alone is sanctified. Born from antithesis, it does not claim to usher in anything less than the millennium. A generation later it has become a *genre* much like its predecessors, a remedy for previous excesses, a new blot of paint on the palette as one continues to strive for the same goal. All "isms" die and leave behind them not programs but single masterpieces, a monster that outlives itself (as Dali outlived surrealism), and a key on our keyboard.

Concerning actual stagnation—to defend themselves against which charge they have thought to use the silly term "experimental," when on the contrary they point toward a final synthesis—we ought to stick to the facts. These are that at present the modern novel is the newest form of fiction and that one shape of fiction—the traditional—has for a time become exhausted. Perhaps—since the movie is such an inexhaustible supplier of the romantic (thanks—yes, thanks!—to the fact that it is a form bound to concrete reality)—literature can and will diversify itself in a more abstract-ontological direction. But the art of the word is also the art of the mind, and tomorrow the reader will undoubtedly ask again for literary fiction. That does not nullify today; for he will ask again day after tomorrow for the art of today. The greatest man, fortunately, remains a child who eagerly listens to a story. Now something about Kuifje, then something about his subconscious or superego. All that, the novel can do and does. Long live the novel, for it is life times life!

www.ingramcontent.com/pod-product-compliance
Lightning Source LLC
Chambersburg PA
CBHW070615310726
48982CB00001B/89

* 9 7 8 0 8 3 7 1 7 4 2 6 6 *